AIR BORN
GENERATION ICARUS - BOOK 1
J L PAWLEY

XIX
NINETEENTH HOUSE
PUBLISHING

Hi, good-looking! Do you comma here often? It's authorly good of you to stop by. Also, Falcon wants to know what kind of weirdo reads the copyright page. (Our kind, obviously. Welcome!)

Cover design by Damonza.com.

An earlier edition of *Air Born* was published by Steam Press, an imprint of Eunoia Publishing, Ltd.

This edition published by Nineteenth House Publishing

Auckland, New Zealand

Print ISBN-13: 978-1-7385994-3-1

1

TYLER

"Tyler, you are such a freak."

Grinning, I ignored Nico and checked my wrist altimeter. One thousand feet.

He rapped on my helmet with his knuckles, and his voice crackled in my headset again. "Earth to Tyler."

Finally, I pushed the mic closer to my mouth. "Yeah, I heard you, but it wasn't exactly breaking news."

"You're in a tiny metal tube hurtling through the air at a few hundred knots, wearing an ancient pair of overalls and a borrowed backpack, intending to jump out at fifteen thousand feet and literally hanging your life on a large piece of silk and a few ropes, and you look as bored as if you're on the school bus."

"And yet you're doing the exact same thing," I said, laughing. "Who's the freak now?"

He snorted. "Definitely you. Who the hell grows like a foot in a month?"

I leaned on the window to get a better look at the rapidly shrinking Californian landscape. 2000 feet. "Uh, most teenagers."

A new voice cut in. "Guys, can we keep this professional, please. No chatter on the radio."

Nico resettled on the bench seat and smiled sweetly at Hayley, across from us. "We're not on official CAP business now, *cadet* captain. This is strictly pleasure." He wiggled his eyebrows suggestively at the attractive blonde.

She kicked him. "You need to learn a bit of respect, or you're gonna get your ass handed to you at Officer School this summer."

As the two of them fell into the familiar banter that came from years of being in the same Civil Air Patrol cadet unit together, I checked the altimeter again.

3000 feet.

It was a climb we had made many times over the previous few months, but this was the first time we were jumping solo. At the rear of the little plane, the instructors were talking to the other trainees, all college students or older. Hayley and Nico were eighteen and nineteen and I had just turned seventeen. Nico liked to call me a freak whenever he got the chance.

I ignored Nico, knowing I'd have to survive a lot worse at basic training when I finally entered the real Air Force, hopefully in just a few months. But as I was barely old enough to apply, I had to make sure my résumé was the best in the pile, and that was where the skydiving came in. As soon as Nico and Hayley had heard I was going for my license, they signed up too. Competition between the three of us was genuinely friendly, but serious. We all liked to win.

4000 feet.

The plane tilted gently as it spiraled higher, the drone of the engine loud in my sensitive eardrums. I shifted in my seat, trying to get comfortable with the bulky parachute pack forcing me to sit upright. The familiar pain in my back flared as I moved.

I tried to hide it, but Nico saw the look on my face. He frowned, covered his mic with his hand, and leaned closer.

"Dude, I thought your back was better?"

I glanced at Hayley, but she didn't seem to be listening, distracted with her pre-jump checks.

"It's fine," I said, resisting the urge to reach over my shoulder. I knew that it was definitely *not* fine.

5000 feet.

"Ty, you shouldn't jump if you're not fit." Nico's thick black eyebrows met in the middle. I hoped I could rely on him not to tell the instructors.

"I'm fine, Nic, really. Do you think my mom would have let me on the plane if I wasn't?"

He grinned, his eyebrows relaxing. "What did the doctor say?"

I scrambled for something believable. "Uh ... she said it was just an inflammation thing. From when I skidded halfway across the gym on my back."

"Oh, when Hayley *literally* wiped the floor with you last week?" Nico started to laugh, letting go of his mic.

Feeling my face flush, I grinned, relieved that Nico was distracted by the memory.

"What's so funny?" Hayley demanded. As Nico gleefully reminded her about her decisive one-on-one combat victory over me during a martial arts workshop, I glanced out the window again. Now there were clouds appearing between us and the fields of the drop zone.

6000 feet.

Part of me wished I *had* told Mom earlier. I'd intended to. I had *tried* to. Several times. But each time I tensed my muscles and marched up to the kitchen or stood at her study door, something made me back away. I'd find myself curled up in bed, shaking with fear and pain. The instinct to *hide* was overpowering. Fighting it was like fighting the urge to breathe — I could control it for a few moments, but then natural reflexes took over. It was like my body didn't *want* me to tell anyone about the weird pain in my back, let alone the … other thing.

Nico knew. He'd busted me in the locker room after I thought everyone else had gone home. Luckily, though, that had been right at the beginning of the week, before the swelling had reached Quasimodo on the hunchback scale.

At first, I had thought the pain had been part of the growth spurt I'd been enjoying recently, which had made me feel almost permanently hungry to the point of nausea, and left me with a closet full of clothes that no longer fitted. Then I'd wondered if it was my body finally taking revenge on me for all the reckless stunts and accidents over the years, multiple falls off the garage roof included.

Just let me jump, I thought. I'd been dying for a solo freefall for *so* long. *Just let me jump, and then I'll tell Mom and go to the doctor.* I couldn't let anything affect my cadet reputation. If people thought I'd chickened out of the solo dive, the rumor would reach the unit's leaders and might even make it onto my record.

And, most importantly, my dad had been given special leave from the Air Force base to come and watch me jump on my own for the first time. I couldn't let him down.

7000 feet.

I had to pretend the weird lump did not exist. It now protruded several inches from my shoulder blades and tapered as far down as my waist. I'd woken up that morning to find the strange blistery whiteness had turned a brownish-gray, like a giant bruise, covering two thirds of my back. Weirdly, though, I wasn't scared. Not of the lump, anyway.

For some reason, the terrifying part was the thought of someone *finding out*.

But with Mom distracted by my little sister Cherie's upcoming ballet recital, and the aid of a super-baggy hoodie, I'd successfully hidden the swelling from my family.

8000 feet.

Nico's laugh became a little too loud and his leg bounced nervously as the altimeter ticked higher.

It felt like I had been waiting for this moment all my life. After all, flying was in my DNA. Sometimes it seemed that was most of what my African-American Air Force hero dad had given me, which my mom had then wrapped up in her lighter skin and mid-brown hair. Despite looking more like her on the outside, everyone said that I was a younger Colonel Robert Owen on the inside, and now was the time for me to prove it by jumping out of a perfectly good airplane. I'd tandem skydived nearly a dozen times before, but this first solo jump would take me closer to my ultimate dream of flying. My pulse had been elevated for days in anticipation, my eyes and ears aching from the stress of being on high alert.

Even the constant hunger from my month-long growth spurt was now overwhelmed by the flood of adrenaline surging through my body. I tried to take in a deep, slow breath but my heart was hammering so hard, I could feel the thud in my throat. As my chest inflated, the harness and overalls tightened uncomfortably. Under the rumble of the plane engine, I imagined I heard the fabric begin to rip. The nerves really were getting to me.

I'd been stupidly thrilled when I'd first seen the overalls that were the same olive green as a fighter pilot's flight suit. But when I'd looked closer, I realized they had once been much brighter and had simply faded from use. Unsurprisingly, this time when I'd put them on, I'd found they were a little tight around my ribs. Right now, I was worried the worn cloth might rip at the seams, and I consciously breathed out again, trying to deflate my chest. Unfortunately, the harness remained tight, and I had to loosen it slightly.

9000 feet.

The instructor, Franz, came to double check our gear and immediately told me to tighten my chinstrap. Then Franz started to run through everything one more time. I barely heard him, although I followed Nico and Hayley's lead and gave the 'okay' sign in all the right places.

Franz turned on the tiny sports camera attached to my helmet. There was another camera strapped to my forearm. The whole jump would be recorded for me to watch over and over in high definition. But I really wanted to focus on being in the moment. To live it, and remember how it *felt*.

The clouds were far below us now, and the earth was a distant map. As pumped as I was, and as much as I wanted to burn every second into my brain, I was getting a headache from the constant auditory assault of the engine. I was determined to ignore it. I *needed* the rush of that whole minute of freefall. It was so close.

I just wanted to jump!

10,000 feet.

The instructor gave the signal and we all reached up for our oxygen masks. As I pressed it over my face and breathed in the now-familiar metallic tang, my lungs cooled a few degrees.

Nico turned round to give me a thumbs-up. His eyes were a little wider and wilder than usual. I loosened the harness strap on my chest again, just a fraction of an inch. The weird itching in my back was almost unbearable, so I tried to focus on my breathing.

11,000 feet.

Suddenly the plane juddered. Our butts left the bench, then came down hard. We laughed our way through a few more tremors, and then the air smoothed out. I briefly flashed back to my first flight in a small plane, when I was a brand-new cadet. Turbulence had shaken us up and some of the kids had screamed or cried. A couple had made generous donations to their sick bags. But not me.

I'd laughed.

There was something about heights, about flying, that had always attracted me. Maybe it was because Dad was an Air Force pilot. As a kid, I was always looking up to see if I could find Dad's plane in the sky. Maybe it was the stories of the Wright Brothers, or Amelia Earhart, or Mae Jemison, that he'd read to me when he was home on leave.

Maybe it was just in my DNA.

Nico was right. I was a freak, had always been a freak.

And I loved it.

After what felt like hours since take-off, the plane seemed to lean forward as the pilot finally reached target altitude and leveled out. 15,000 feet. The engine's whine eased back into a happy hum.

Franz slid open the door. It was like someone had taken their hands off my ears as the harsh rush of the wind became a roar. In a second, all the warmth was sucked from the tiny cabin. Eagerly, but with shaking hands, I removed the oxygen mask and detached myself from the plane's radio comms. I didn't need them anymore. In just a few minutes I'd be racing back into thicker atmosphere, at terminal velocity.

Franz tugged on the harness around my body as he triple-checked the gear. My eyes didn't leave the door. Divers disappeared one by one. Hayley lined up, took a huge breath, and then she was gone. Nico threw me a massive grin, crossed himself, and stepped out.

Then, it was just me and Franz. I shuffled to the end of the bench seat. Suddenly, I was at the door, looking out of the hole into complete emptiness. A perfect sky fading to white at the edges of the world.

"Ready, rookie?" Franz shouted over the roar.

I gave him the thumbs up, with an idiotic grin carved into my face. I took a breath.

This was it.

"Three … two … one …"

I jumped.

2

TYLER

Freefall exploded in my gut, fizzing through my whole body. As I tumbled, I caught a glimpse of the tiny red plane soaring above before it was whipped away by the spinning horizon. I screamed pure adrenaline as a river of air battered my face.

The training kicked in and my limbs shot out. My fall stabilized. I looked down through ten thousand feet of nothing to the clouds below. Amazingly, I could pick out the still-falling dots of other skydivers just as easily as those whose parachutes had already opened. One canopy vanished into the white fluff of the cloud layer. The buzz of freefall faded as gravity pulled on my body, but adrenaline was sending me higher the faster I fell.

"WHOOOOOOOO!" I yelled. But the sound tore away before I could hear myself. Every cell in my body was buzzing. The air was freezing, but each breath made me feel incredibly *alive*.

As blood pounded through my arteries at full speed, I was hit by an insane urge to start flapping my arms. I laughed, then gasped in agony when my entire back suddenly spasmed.

Something inside me, something *inside the lump*, was trying to claw its way out! As the image flashed through my mind, I was gripped by pure terror. Pain blinded me.

I was falling through the sky, and yet the sudden sense of claustrophobia was overwhelming. My arms seemed straightjacketed to my body. I had to break free!

As my sight flickered back, I felt more than heard something tearing. Claws sank into my ribcage and tried to split me in two, lifting me skyward and flipping me sideways. Panicking, I ripped the drogue from the bottom of my pack and let it go. But the chute didn't engage. A hard yank on the reserve seemed to help as I was pulled up from the other side, but, instead of straightening and stabilizing, I began tumbling out of control.

The other skydivers yelled as I dropped past. Nico was bellowing my name, Hayley was shrieking. As the world flashed around me, I screamed in agony and fear.

In that instant, I knew I was going to die. The spinning sky was now more white than blue. The thing hauled on my body like it was trying to wrench my arm from its socket. I tried to turn and see what the hell had got me.

A dark shadow lunged, and then jerked away as I completed another turn. Weirdly, I could *feel* it moving, like a point of rotating pressure in my shoulder blade. As the air spun me and the shadow lunged again, I saw details. A spray of blood. A ragged fluttering edge. Dark mottled colors. A familiar shape.

A wing.

As if reading my thoughts, the wing jerked again.

Holy crap, a wing.

It's a WING.

And it's coming out of me!

Fighting the force of the tumble, I tried to look over my other shoulder, but it hurt too much to twist. I sobbed.

A thousand tiny specks began stinging my face and hands. Clouds.

I realized my family would watch me fall to my death in front of them.

No!

Panting, I screwed my eyes shut against the hypnotic spinning and *concentrated*.

There was something else. I could feel another wing curled up on the left side of my back. I imagined it moving, flexing — and it began to stir. The pain intensified, only now it was like the good pain of a hundredth push-up. But the wing was trapped by the harness straps which curled around it like a giant's fingers. I roared with pain and effort, and the wing-arm jerked. With every last atom of strength, I *pushed* sideways, the pressure making my eyes and eardrums bulge until I thought I would burst.

A sharp burn ripped down my left side. The giant's grip gave a little. I pushed again, and the left wing burst through the jumpsuit, out through the armhole in the harness.

An incredible sense of relief flooded through me. For the briefest moment, everything felt *right*. Then the wind caught the new wing, wrenching it backward. I cried in pain. But, somehow, that movement had slowed the spinning.

Holy crap. The tumbling had been caused by my right wing throwing me out of symmetry, ruining my aerodynamics. But now, with two wings, I had a chance.

I knew if I couldn't control them, I was dead. The parachute was wrapped around my legs, completely useless. Throwing out my hands, I imagined the fledgling wings copying my arm movements.

Somehow, they did.

About as long as my arms, and already aching with fatigue, the wings just weren't strong enough. My back and neck screamed in pain. It was not a graceful maiden flight. It was barely even gliding. Struggling just to keep the wings outstretched as I fell, I felt like I had a large wooden panel strapped to each arm and was trying to push both down into turbulent water.

I was simply an organic parachute, and not a very effective one. Still, I preferred to be a live parachute than a dead bird.

All of this was concentrated into a few seconds, and I had even fewer seconds left to live. Trees, buildings and the hard-baked ground were coming up fast. Abandoned parachutes lay across the grass. People were running, some away from me, some toward. I was falling slower, but not slowly enough.

In the last few hundred feet, the air warmed and thickened. I spotted a large tangle of bushes at the edge of the drop zone. Groaning with effort, I tried leaning toward it, lifting my left wing and arm, and dropping my right. It worked. My fall veered sideways.

My legs dragged through the leaves and branches, which snatched at the tangled parachute, slowing me a little more. A heartbeat later, I hit the ground. My legs folded, dumping me on my side. One wing bent painfully underneath me, and the other fell forward over my shoulder.

Everything hurt.

There was a moment of absolute stillness. Then, slowly and painfully, I rolled onto my stomach. The limp end of the wing — *my* wing — dragged across the grass. Vaguely, I noted the mid-brown of the feathers was the same color as my hair. The

muscles in my back trembled. I took a deep breath and got onto
my hands and knees. The ground swayed under me. My eyes
seemed to be on permanent zoom, focused on the thousand tiny
details of crushed grass blades and crumbs of dirt. Small insects
fled from my shadow. My mind felt too loose.

Slowly, I pushed myself along, still attached to the tangled
ropes and parachute fabric. My heart was sprinting, but I didn't
feel out of breath. The pain in my back was fading, leaving only
the aches from impact. I crawled out from the tangle of straps,
lines and chute fabric, and shakily stood up. I staggered forward.

"Tyler! Don't move!"

I fell into my father's arms.

"Son, thank God. Where do you hurt? What the hell…?"

He sat me down, all the time speaking in the same calm voice
that had always made me feel safe. Dad would know what to do.
Bewildered, I gazed helplessly at him. My throat closed. I had
tried to live up to his standards, to be as good as him, worthy of
being Colonel Robert Owen's son, but all I'd done was scare the
shit out of everyone by nearly killing myself and turning into a
freaking bird!

Dad helped me unbuckle the harness. Getting it off wasn't
easy.

"Let's have a look at you." There was a sharp intake of breath.
I could feel his hands separating the feathers as he examined my
back. "Oh my God, Tyler! What's happened to you?"

Then he gently lifted my goggles onto my helmet. The look
of shock on his face was undeniable. For the first time in my
life, I thought my father might cry.

"Tyler, your eyes! What's wrong with them?!"

Suddenly we were surrounded by people. Someone aimed a phone camera at me like a gun, and I automatically raised my hand in self-defense.

Dad jumped to his feet and began issuing commands in true military style. Struggling to my own feet, I unthinkingly tightened a few muscles and my wings folded behind me into their familiar hump position, snagging slightly in the ragged remains of the jumpsuit. The movement caught the attention of the small crowd. I shrank back at the gasps of horror.

The world began to spin once more. I tripped, collapsed. The last thing I saw was the sports camera hanging from my arm, staring accusingly into my face.

I blacked out.

3

MIGUEL

"Miguel! The volume, my boy, louder! *Rapido!*"

"Yes, Abuelita," I said, not taking my eyes from the TV screen.

A young reporter pressed on her earpiece and shouted over the apparent riot behind her. *"It's total mayhem here outside the hospital. Several hundred people have gathered in the hope of finding out more information about the mystery parachute boy at the center of the incident. Please be warned, some viewers may find the following eyewitness video disturbing."*

The news program began playing a shaky video of blue sky. A tangled parachute trailed behind a tumbling figure. The image blurred as it zoomed in.

My grandmother crossed herself, whispering in Spanish. *Angel.*

It did look like a dark-winged angel had gathered the boy up, but he continued falling. Abuelita mumbled again, but I wasn't listening. I was hypnotized.

The sudden appearance of trees gave the boy's fall a frame of reference. My heart thumped as he dropped out of sight.

The reporter's face flashed back on the screen.

"Earlier today I spoke to Reverend Carter, who believes that what you have just seen is a miracle. An intervention from the Hand of God that confirms the existence of angels. Others say the boy must be the product of genetic engineering, or, what they're calling 'deliberate

evolution'. Unsurprisingly, there's considerable tension between the two groups."

Suddenly, the camera swung around. A couple were storming out of the hospital. The woman was crying. The crowd rushed toward them.

The reporter forced her way to the front and shoved her microphone into the man's face. *"Sir, are you related to the boy from the skydiving incident? Can you tell us his name?"*

The tall, African-American man was an imposing figure in his military uniform. His arm tightened around the pale woman beside him.

"Tyler is our son—"

His wife interrupted. *"He's only seventeen. And the hospital won't let us see him!"*

The reporter pressed closer, eagerly. *"Do you know why that might be the case?"*

The man paused. I could see he was trying to keep his composure, but there was no mistaking his fury. *"I don't know who they think they are, but there will be serious consequences to this. Our lawyers will make damn sure of that."*

"Were the wings attached to the harness, or his clothes? Or to his body?"

The man's composure vanished. *"Damn it, let us through!"* He tried once more to steer his wife through the crowd.

But the reporter wasn't done yet. *"Some people here believe that your son somehow grew wings. Do you have any comment on that?"*

For the first time I saw vulnerability on the man's face. *"I have nothing further to say. Let us through."* His voice seemed dangerously close to breaking. His wife had tears streaming down her cheeks.

Abuelita murmured in sympathy.

The couple tried to make their escape, but the raucous crowd were blocking their path.

Then there was the sound of smashing glass in the background. People screamed and rushed away from the hospital, shoving past the camera and the reporter.

"Good Lord, someone has smashed a window! And … is climbing out onto the ledge!" the shocked reporter cried.

The camera zoomed in to the top floor of the hospital building.

"Tyler!" his mother shrieked.

The reporter strained to be heard. *"It appears that the mystery boy from the parachute incident, a 17-year-old called Tyler, has decided to leave the hospital the only way he can."*

There was a collective gasp as the boy lost his footing.

"Oh God, he's not going to make it!"

But he grabbed the window frame just in time.

Beside me, Abuelita wheezed.

Hospital staff gestured frantically to him through another window. The boy shook his head. It seemed he didn't like what they were saying, because he lifted one hand off the wall to extend his middle finger.

Several nervous laughs erupted from the crowd. A sudden breeze caught his hospital gown and he faltered again. More people screamed, then—

"Did you see that? Did you see it?" the reporter cried. *"Wings just burst out of his back! It seems the rumors are true! What we can't tell you yet, is whether this is due to a biological mutation, or whether it's a device of some kind, strapped to his body."*

Abuelita pressed her crucifix to her lips.

And then he jumped.

"Go on, fly, fly!" I begged him.

Twisting in mid-air, he made one partial flap, and landed on the roof of another wing of the hospital. Then he scrambled up and over the roof, towards the back of the building, disappearing from the camera's view.

"Well," the reporter began, as she dodged the people rushing past her, *"no one can see where the boy landed because there is no direct route to that side of the—"*

The news anchor's voice cut over the hysterics breaking out on the screen. *"Courtney, we're going to a commercial break now and we'll come back to you shortly. Hopefully you'll have some good news for us."*

The spell was broken by dancing toothpaste.

"Eat, Miguel."

"Only if you do, too, Abuelita. You need your strength."

"No strength needed for sitting in a chair all day, boy." But my frail grandmother made a visible effort to pick up one of the tamales I had made for her. Her mind was as sharp as ever but her body was increasingly failing. I ached to see the shell she had become, and did everything I could to help. But one day, I would not be enough.

After some minutes of silent chewing, my thoughts were interrupted by the reappearance of the TV anchor. *"Welcome back, viewers, and we are going straight to our correspondent in LA, who is on the ground for the unbelievable story of the boy with wings. Courtney, do we know the fate of the mysterious Tyler? Did he survive his second dramatic fall?"*

"I'm sorry to say that we have been unable to locate Tyler. As you can see," the TV replayed the footage of the fall, *"he was able to halt his descent and escaped over the roof of the outpatients wing to the other side of the building. Dozens of people are searching for him, including his parents, hospital staff, the police and many of those who were gathered here earlier."*

"So, evidence points to his survival?"

"It certainly seems that way, Chris, as there is no trace of him anywhere."

"Thank you, Courtney. We'll check back with you later. Now, we turn to a major accident in…"

I tuned out with relief. Tyler was alive, I just knew it.

"It is time for sleep," Abuelita said abruptly. I looked up at her, surprised. My grandmother hardly ever went to bed early.

Kneeling by her side, I took her hand. "Are you all right, Abuelita?"

"I am not feeling well." She was pale. "It is time for me to sleep."

I carried her to her tiny room where I helped her to wash, brushed her soft wispy hair and settled her into bed. It was hard, caring for a frail old woman on my own. But *mi abuela* had saved my life, and it was the least I could do in return.

Abuelita sighed as she sank back onto her pillows. "Ah, you are a good boy. A real angel to me."

I froze. Abuelita continued. "Just like that poor boy in America…" She trailed off. After a moment, I assumed she was asleep, and tiptoed out of her room.

In the bathroom, I stood in front of the mirror. I had changed so much in such a short time. Abuelita hadn't noticed, but she was rather blind and deaf, especially when it suited her. The irises of my eyes had grown dramatically. They had once been brown, and were now a much paler, almost metallic color. I took off my loose shirt and slowly spread my jet-black wings.

I'm not the only one.

It was a sign. I was sure of it.

My grandmother was a devout Catholic. When Mama and I first came to Mexico to live with Abuelita, I had said my prayers each night, because that was what she expected. Then Mama died and my life fell apart. I'm ashamed of what I became and the things that I did. But Abuelita had led me out of sin. She and God had saved me. My prayers became heartfelt; I prayed for forgiveness, for strength, and sometimes simply to survive the next day. But I knew how lucky I was compared to many others. Because I had Abuelita. Someone who loved me. I'd never prayed for a miracle, but now, perhaps, I could ask for a little one.

"Dear Lord," I whispered, eyes tightly shut. "If Tyler is the sign I have been waiting for, please help him escape and survive. Amen."

Before I went to bed, I scrolled through social media and flicked through all the TV channels once more, just in case there was any more news about Tyler. But all the TV had was a tacky news show with the same raw video playing over and over in slow motion, while the hosts analyzed every single frame, circling blurred limbs that might be wings, comparing them to known birds, hang-gliding equipment, even costume props. Social media was even worse, with any real new content impossible to find beneath the reaction videos and bad memes and attempts to guess what the 'viral advertising stunt' was for. I knew better than anyone the reality of Tyler's 'condition.' So, I switched off the TV, plugged the charger into the phone, re-checked that the door and windows were securely locked, and made up my bed on the sofa. My thoughts were whirling in circles, but I must have fallen asleep because I was suddenly woken by a loud crash.

Rushing to Abuelita's room, I found her on the floor.

"*Está bien, está bien*, I'm here," I cried, scooping her up like a child. I gently placed her back on the bed and tried to calm her.

"Miguel, Miguel." Her thin voice trembled and her shaking hands clutched at my shoulders. "I was praying to the Lord, and he has called me."

"You're fine, Abuelita. I'm here."

"At last, I will be with your *Abuelo* and your darling mother." She coughed. "I have been given a sign."

My heart tightened. "What sign?"

"The angel boy," she whispered, her milky eyes suddenly seeming very sharp as she stared at me.

I swallowed. "The one on the news?"

"I asked for an angel to come and take me home, and he is on the earth now. When he escaped … I knew it is also my turn to escape."

"He's just a scared guy." My voice shook. My wings arched in fright.

"Turn around," she said, her voice suddenly stronger. "Let me see before I go."

Reluctantly I turned, but spun back when she gasped. She couldn't catch her breath.

"Abuelita, don't go!" Through stinging eyes, I saw she was staring past me, her expression fearful, but exultant. Her arms and hands twitched, and she whispered three words:

"*Forgive.*

Lord.

Angel."

"Abuelita, can you hear me?" I took her worn hands in mine. "What can you see?"

She frowned, tilting her head, as if she was listening to something far away.

"Abuelita?"

"Miguel. My good boy." She gave a crackling sigh. "The Lord has ... chosen you."

"For what?"

"I will watch ... from Heaven." She heaved a breath. "Won't ... be easy."

"What am I meant to do?"

She shut her eyes. "Find him."

"I love you, Abuelita, don't go!" I begged.

"Find ... him..."

I heard her last, long, rattling breath leave her body.

Abuelita had gone.

4

MIGUEL

After the funeral, I sat alone outside the church, staring blankly, while the world carried on as if nothing had changed. I'd found it hard to accept that Abuelita had really gone until the little service had ended and she'd been taken away.

Find him.

The echo in my mind was just a whisper, yet it was louder than the entire crowded city around me.

Find him.

The padre walked out of the church and looked down at me. Instinctively I hunched my shoulders, although my thin wings were completely hidden by my best, only slightly faded shirt.

"This is yours now," he said softly, pressing Abuelita's crucifix on its black chain into my palm. My fingers curled tightly around the smooth wood.

"You have been a good boy," he said. "Always putting others before yourself. Now your future is in your own hands. God bless you, son." He patted my shoulder, and disappeared into the cool depths of the church.

Slowly, I dropped the chain of Abuelita's crucifix around my neck, and trudged back to the apartment, dodging cars and mopeds, street vendors and stray dogs, and other pedestrians, all on automatic.

Kicking aside trash in the stairwell, I ignored the shouting from the next door tenement, and let myself into Abuelita's apartment. My apartment, now, I guessed.

Abuelita's chair looked so empty. I couldn't stand the sight of it. On impulse, I grabbed the arms, intending to hide it away in Abuelita's room.

As I picked it up and took a step, my shoe hit something. A cardboard box, that had been wedged underneath, and hidden by the trailing edges of her blanket.

Placing the chair to one side, I opened the box, and found a carefully wrapped bundle. Inside was a photograph of my mother and me, taken when I was just a baby, when Mama was happily married and had everything she could ever ask for. Her dark eyes laughed as she cuddled me close, her wild, curly black hair cascading down her shoulders. There was a jagged edge where the image of my wealthy white father had been ripped away.

Beneath the faded photograph were our passports. Two American and two Mexican.

As I sat there, holding my American passport, my thoughts accelerated. I'd disowned my father for so long, I'd forgotten how useful being half-American could be. Would be.

Wrapping up my mother's passports, I put them to one side. Last in the box was a paper bag. When I saw what it contained, I almost swore.

"Where did this come from?" I whispered, although in my heart I knew that the seven hundred US dollars must have belonged to my mother. All these years, living at or below the poverty line, and Abuelita had been saving a small fortune for when I needed it most.

Now, I could find Tyler. There was just one more thing I needed to do.

I'd worked for Juan for several years, both at his timber yard and as his personal errand boy. But Juan knew that I knew the business was just a front for his shady dealings in far more lucrative hardware. I'd never been involved, operating a strict 'don't ask, don't know, can't tell' strategy. Still, I couldn't help but notice when heavily armed 'businessmen' paid regular visits, and unopened stock boxes appeared and disappeared overnight. It made me uncomfortable, and if there had been any other work available, I would have taken it. But I could always rely on Juan to pay my wages on time, which he did as a point of pride, unlike many other dealers. It was one of the ways he flaunted the fact that he always had cash to spare.

I needed all the money I could get, and I had two weeks' wages owing. But I didn't want them in pesos.

It was time to make a deal with him of my own.

I walked into Juan's warehouse with a single backpack containing everything I had in the world. Nervously, I adjusted the cartoonishly-large pair of cheap reading glasses which had no real magnifying ability, but explained away and disguised my dilated irises. Luckily, Juan was in a good mood, and listened to my rehearsed speech about being evicted from the tenement apartment and having to head back to the States.

"Ha!" Juan barked when I finished. "Our little Miguel has been getting up to something!"

I spread my hands and shrugged, admitting and denying nothing.

Chuckling, Juan nodded. "My boy, you have worked hard for me, for longer than many of these other hopeless *payasos*. We have a deal. And I'll even throw in a little farewell gift for you!"

He picked up the smartphone that he had given me for running his errands around the city, which I'd just returned to him. "You can keep this."

Blinking in surprise, I took it back. "*Gracias,* Boss."

Juan majestically waved a hand. "*De nada,* my boy. Just make sure you use the factory reset, *¿si?*"

Nodding, I followed Juan through to his office, closing the door behind me. I laid my mother's passports on the desk in front of him.

He touched them gently, almost caressing them. "They are the real thing?"

"*Si,* Boss," I said, quietly. I looked away as he opened each document and eyed my mother's photo. Again demonstrating that he had a little more class than most other men in his profession, Juan didn't comment.

Spinning his enormous leather chair towards the safe, Juan spun the dial and scanned his fingerprints with rapid ease. He counted out my final wages, plus a healthy bonus, in crisp American dollars. No doubt Mama's passports would be converted into forgeries before I'd even made it to the border. I prayed that Abuelita would smooth things over for me in Heaven.

Juan personally walked me to the side door through which I normally came and went on his errands.

"*Suerte con todo,* boy," he said, slapping my back as he wished me luck. Until recently, I had been barely as tall as his shoulder, but now we were the same height. I tried not to flinch as his hand connected with a bony wing elbow beneath my shirt. As Juan frowned, I hastily tugged on my pack.

"*Gracias*, Boss," I said. "*Adiós*." And I slipped away into the crowded street. One block later, I triggered the phone's factory reset. I didn't want any of Juan's men deciding they needed a final cut of my pay, and tracking me across the city to get it.

During a nerve-wracking series of bus rides, zig-zagging my way towards the nicer part of the city, I kept my backpack on my lap with my arms clenched tightly around it. Once I finally reached the highway, I started walking, with my thumb out.

The curve of my thin wings under my shirt gave me the appearance of bad posture and, when combined with the fake glasses, this made me seem more vulnerable than threatening. My first ride pulled over for me within half an hour. They took me nearly half the distance I needed to go, and it was only two other changeovers before I'd hitchhiked the whole way to the Mexico-Arizona border. Despite a tense moment when the border cop made some comment about my evident growth spurt, compared to my younger ID photo, the authorities didn't give my genuine American passport a second glance.

Before a rough night's sleep in the cheapest motel I could find, I treated myself to the biggest meal on the diner menu. Afterwards, for the first time in months, I didn't feel hungry. In the morning, with my determination only growing, I continued into California. I prayed that the relative ease of my journey meant I was, somehow, doing what I was supposed to be doing.

The hours spent in the back of pickups or walking along the highway, waiting for my next ride, were filled with my now-obsessive internet searches for any update, sighting, or hint of 'Tyler the mystery bird boy'. The phone was almost constantly in my hand, and I was among the first to view each new video as it was uploaded and then went viral.

First, there was a sighting from a group of students working on a nature reservation several hundred miles to the north of LA. They captured a few seconds of someone running away through the trees, brown wings folded against his back. The students pursued him for about half a minute, catching a few glimpses before they gave up and promptly posted the clip online.

Within an hour, new edits of the video were uploaded, freezing on the split second when his wings half-opened as he dodged around a tree in the distance. The still frame was displayed next to a picture of his hospital fall for comparison, while rapid, high-pitched commentary endlessly debated whether it was real.

Soon, the state police released an official statement, asking the public for information. *If anyone should make contact with Tyler Owen, encourage him to remain where he is and wait for help. He is believed to have sustained minor injuries which may be affecting his faculties. Tyler seems to believe that his strap-on wings are real, and his parents fear he may harm himself by trying to fly.*

That one made me chuckle, a little bitterly. *Strap-on wings? That's the story now?*

My own wings ached in sympathy. Since I'd left Mexico City, they were almost constantly tingling, with the occasional muscle spasm thrown in. Between going to sleep and waking up, my shirt seemed to shrink further. The now-steady intake of food was fuelling another surge in wing growth. I had to find Tyler quickly, before my wings were too big to hide.

The next day, as I was trying to hitch a ride north from LA, a private corporation offered a substantial reward for Tyler's return. Shortly after that, the internet went into another meltdown. The raw skydive footage from Tyler's sports cameras had been leaked online.

Watching the sickening spin of the image on the small screen, I had to stop and sit on the dusty verge for a minute. The screen was split into two, playing helmet cam and arm cam footage side-by-side.

The first few moments seemed normal for a skydive; the excited rookie at the door, the countdown, the jump.

Then, a few moments into the dive, Tyler stopped grinning.

No matter how many times I watched it, my heart accelerated. The arm camera tilted as Tyler yelled, clearly in pain. Something dark flicked into view behind him, then suddenly he was tumbling again, the helmet cam in a sickening whirl of cloud and sky.

Then something dark brown and wet slapped onto the arm camera lens and stuck there. I *knew* it was a feather, still sticky with Tyler's blood.

The sounds of breaking branches made me wince every time, and then the cameras jolted hard, the feather flicked free as Tyler hit the ground. The last image was of Tyler's face. His eyes were bloodshot. Just before his lids closed, I watched it happen. The color in his eyes stretched until there was almost no white left, the brown of his irises fading to a pale bronze.

I remembered the fear and pain of my own wing 'birth' several weeks before. My first instinct was to run to Abuelita's side and beg for her help to understand why God had done this to me. But she was so frail, I'd been terrified the shock would be too much for her heart. Instead, I'd hidden in the bathroom for several hours, slowly cleaning the blood and fluid from the room and then from myself.

The first time I touched my feathers, they were slimy and alien. But as I stood under the dripping shower head and the pink water slowly ran clear, I saw the subtle colors hidden in the black vanes, even in the dull glow of the overhead bulb.

As I dried myself, I'd pulled a wing forward for close inspection. I could feel the rounded head of my new wing bones grinding between my shoulder blades, and in the mirror, I saw the strange new muscles flexing in my chest. The remains of the skin cocoon dangled like a thin fringe down my sides, like a disgustingly enlarged peeling sunburn, too thin to be leaking blood. Tender new skin stretched across my back beneath my wings, all my childhood scars and freckles gone.

Then, when the feathers were finally dry, I'd hesitantly run my fingers through them for the first time. The sensation had been like I was playing with very long, thick hairs on my arm, and was a strangely intimate feeling. It had taken me many days to accept that these *things* had been grown inside my own body, and I continued to wait impatiently for God to send some sort of explanation.

My memories were interrupted by a loud honking and the crunching of tires. A truck had pulled up, the driver waving me over. I jumped to my feet, refocusing on the task at hand. There would be plenty of time to compare experiences with Tyler later, assuming I managed to find him before he fell off the radar altogether.

Following the trail of reported sightings like virtual breadcrumbs, I continued chasing Tyler north, hoping I was closing in on him. People who spotted him dumpster-diving, or jumping off the back of big rigs at truck stops, gleefully took to the internet to announce their encounter, joining in the mass manhunt that thousands, perhaps millions of people were following online. It was extremely helpful, but also terrifying. If someone noticed me, I knew I'd quickly become a target right alongside Tyler.

Shortly before I arrived in Sacramento, someone going by 'SophieReports' on social media claimed to have just seen him fleeing into the woods on the outskirts of a town only a few hours to the east.

So, as night fell, I found myself standing at the entrance to the trail that 'SophieReports' had named. I had no wilderness experience, no camping gear, and only enough food to last me twenty-four hours at most. I did have my phone and a paper map of the area that I'd picked up from a local visitor information display, as well as a cheap flashlight and packet of matches. My rational side was begging me to step back, find somewhere to sleep for the night and start my search methodically in the morning.

But every major social media platform was reporting the same thing. Hundreds of people planning, both jokingly and seriously, to zero in on the same place and begin hunting for the mysterious bird boy at dawn. I couldn't let them find him first.

Breathing deeply, resettling my backpack over my hidden wings, and trusting in God to guide my steps, I strode into the dark forest without looking back.

5

TYLER

Somehow, the day just kept getting worse. There I was, climbing onto a window ledge 10 floors high, in a hospital gown and my underwear. But with the only alternative being strapped down for scientific experimentation, I decided to take my chances. I knew I'd never get past the guards outside my door, especially as they'd stripped the room of potential weapons, so there was only one way to go. Calling on everything I remembered from years of martial arts training, I pulled off the greatest side snap kick of my life. The window cracked into a thousand tiny veins under my bare foot. Hissing in pain, I kicked again. The glass crumbled.

The guards shouted, rattling the door against the chair I'd shoved under the handle while praying that trick wasn't another movie myth. With my hand wrapped in a towel, I smashed out the remains of the glass, then nervously clambered out onto the narrow ledge. Struggling with my new center of gravity, I tried to sucker myself to the wall as I eased sideways. The breeze hummed with the sounds of the city, and played with the back of the damn gown. Once, not that long ago, I would have said I wouldn't be caught dead in nothing but underwear and a hospital dress.

But seeing as being caught dead was now actually an option, I didn't tempt fate by thinking it. Instead, I focused on what I was doing and ignored the shouting mass of people on the ground. After all, I did have a plan. Kind of.

No matter what, I was going home.

Clinging to the side of the building, my heart pounding on my eardrums at a dozen beats per second, I inched away from the broken window, my face sliding painfully over the rough concrete. After a sudden slip, I knew I couldn't go any further that way, and my fingers were too sweaty to cling on much longer. The pompous moron in the next room, trying to shoo me back through the other window, got a good look at my favorite finger as I tried to work up the courage to put the next part of my sort-of plan into action.

As the breeze tugged at me again, I felt my balance wobble, and this time my wings flared out. I knew I couldn't fly, not properly, but I could fall. After surviving fifteen thousand feet, the ten-foot drop to the roof of the neighboring hospital building was nothing.

Still, it took all my courage to let go of the wall and jump. Twisting in mid-air, I threw out my arms and my wings copied faithfully. With aching muscles, I half-glided, half-fell onto the roof. The shock shuddered through my bare feet and I yelped in pain, but staggered to the far side of the building before the pain subsided.

From there it was another ten-foot jump to a small substation built into the side of the hill. Then I scrambled up the slope and down to the road on the other side, and kept running.

In the shadows of an untamed back yard, I dumped the hospital gown and stole an oversized Hawaiian shirt and a pair of cargo pants from a washing line. Two doors down, I grabbed some flip-flops from an open car. So disguised, I walked and walked, until exhaustion overcame me.

In an empty park, I curled up under a bush and finally gave in to the tears. My feathers ruffled against my back as I shivered, and the freaky sensation was weirdly calming. Eventually the sobbing subsided, and I stayed curled up until the sun had properly set and it was as dark as it ever got in Los Angeles.

As the hours passed and the night deepened, I zigzagged my way back home, my newly-sharpened eyes and ears nearly overwhelming me with the amount of info they were sending to my brain. Without my phone, I had to trust I was moving in generally the right direction, until I finally spotted a large landmark I recognized, and was able to home in. Literally.

As I finally reached the end of my street, two police cars were cruising past. I hid in the darkness of the neighbor's garden until they'd gone, then ran across my own front lawn and round to the back door, grabbing the spare key from the birdhouse.

I listened at the door before quietly letting myself in. The clock in the kitchen showed it was after midnight. I put my mouth under the faucet to guzzle a gallon of water and, after a raid of the cookie jar, climbed the stairs toward my parents' voices.

My little sister Cherie's night-light shone onto the landing. All I could see was a tangle of dark curls on the pillow. By her deep, ragged breathing, I guessed she'd cried herself to sleep. I desperately wished I could crawl into my own room and do the same, and wake up the next morning to find it had all been a nightmare. But my new wings tucked underneath a stolen shirt were not a dream.

Dad's voice was loud, even without my newly tuned ears.

"I can't sit here doing nothing. I'm going out to look again."

"But the police said—"

"Julia, the cops don't know what they're doing either! He's our son. And I'm beginning to think we can't trust anyone else where he's concerned."

I heard the trembling clink of ice in a glass. "Why? Why us? Why is this happening?"

"I don't know, and I don't care, right now. All I know is that Tyler is out there. He's alone, and scared, and hurt. We have to *find him*!"

Taking a deep breath, I pushed open their bedroom door. "I'm here."

Mom dropped her glass. A moment later, I was squashed between my parents. For a few seconds, I felt safe again.

Then Mom drew back, a strange look on her face. "Do they hurt? Could we see?"

Wearily, I unbuttoned the shirt and dropped it on the bed. As I turned away from my parents, my wings relaxed from their tight fold and partly opened.

"Good God," Dad said.

"May I?" Tentatively, Mom reached out and touched the bruised place between spine and shoulder blade where my feathered bones emerged. She stepped backward as my muscles twitched.

Dad swore under his breath. "It's as if they've always been there." For the first time in my life, I heard nervousness in his voice. "How could something like this just *happen*?"

I bit my lip.

"Tyler!" Mom cried. "When did this start?"

"I don't know," I admitted. "My back started hurting last week, and then it went all gray and bumpy, and then when I jumped out of the plane, they just sort of … burst out."

"Why didn't you *tell me*?" Mom wailed.

"I don't know! I thought everything would be okay and I wanted to jump solo, and…" All the things I'd told myself now seemed ridiculous, pathetic. "And now I'm a freak!"

"Don't ever say that," Dad said, gripping my shoulders. "We've just got to figure out why this has happened to you." He took a deep breath. "And what we're going to do about it."

"I'll call the cops, they're still out there looking," Mom said, reaching for her phone.

"No!" Dad and I yelled. Mom flinched.

"You heard them," Dad said, pulling me close. "They were going on about *his own protection*. They won't let him stay home in his own bed, not when he's got *wings* growing out of his back! Not when they wouldn't even let us see him in the hospital. They'll take him away to God knows where. Believe me, Julia, I know what I'm talking about."

"You're right, you're right," Mom said, rubbing her face. "But what should we do?"

As relief made me dizzy, I sank onto the bed.

"There's no way those clowns who were outside the hospital will leave us alone once they find out he's here." Dad went to the closet and pulled out their suitcases. "We have to get away for a few days, somewhere we can think clearly and make a plan."

"But Cherie…" Mom began.

My gaze had been bouncing between them like I was watching a tennis match, hope slowly growing in my chest that they'd take control and sort it all out, like they always did. That I'd just have to follow orders, and everything would be okay.

But as soon as Mom said my little sister's name, I realized my family would never be okay again. Not while I was around.

I was dangerous. A threat to everyone I loved. Who knew what other weird mutations I would go through? And what if it was contagious? I couldn't let Cherie suffer. Her life was only just starting.

Dad's career in the Air Force Space Command. Mom's job at the university. The happy life and comfortable home they'd worked so hard to build. They were going to throw it all away, just for me.

I couldn't let that happen.

My heart ached as I realized what I had to do. It was worse than the physical pain of the Change. But before I broke it to them, there was one thing I had to know.

"Mom?" I said, my voice shaking. "Dad?"

They turned to me, despair in their eyes. I hated seeing what I had done to them, but I had to ask. "Was I ... am I really your son?"

There was a split second of soul-destroying silence and then they broke into violent exclamations. Somewhere in the middle of it all was the revelation that I had been artificially conceived. In vitro fertilization. IVF. A test tube baby.

It was then that all three of us began to comprehend that something had happened to my DNA during that process. Something had been *added* to the vulnerable embryo they'd entrusted to a doctor.

Whatever else happens in the rest of my life, whatever's left of it, I thought hysterically, *I will never be able to trust a doctor ever again.*

"Where did you have it done? Who was the doctor?" I asked. Furious that this had been done to me. To all of us.

Mom squeezed her eyes shut and rubbed her temples. "I can't think."

"It was a bit weird," Dad said. "The clinic was in Beijing, but the doctor was from somewhere in Europe."

I gaped. "What were you doing in—"

"Mommy?" Cherie appeared in the doorway, blinking in the light and trailing her teddy.

"Sweetie, look, Tyler's home!"

Cherie blinked sleepily at me. "There's a man outside. I think he's lost something."

I froze, and Mom gasped. Dad swung around and pointed at me. "Tyler, get under the bed. You're not here. Julia, take Cherie to her room and lock the door. Start packing. I'll get rid of him."

As Mom swooped over to pick up Cherie, I grabbed Dad's arm. "It's me they want, Dad. I have to get out of here."

"We're *all* getting out of here. As soon as I've—"

"You can't take a six-year-old on the run! I mean, she's just a normal kid! Right?"

Suddenly worried, I glanced at Mom, and she nodded. "She was conceived naturally. Our little miracle," she whispered, burying a kiss in Cherie's curls.

My heart cracked a little more. There was only one way I could protect them.

I waited till Dad had got rid of whoever was outside and Mom had finally decided I'd eaten enough. They were determined we would all stick together, but I knew they'd be safer without me. Clutching my hiking bag, I slipped out the back door while they were upstairs packing.

Of all the stuff I had to leave behind, abandoning my phone was the worst. The notifications had maxed out before I'd even got home, but all the hysterical messages from my friends (and the crazy notes from internet weirdos) had to remain unread. As desperately as I wanted to reach out to my friends, to reassure Nico and Hayley that I was still the same Tyler, I knew I had to cut myself off from them. It would be far too easy to track me by my phone signal.

At first, it was kind of exciting. Blame the adrenaline junkie in me, but I imagined I was in some sort of spy film or action flick, dodging bad guys and always one step ahead. That lasted for a few hours, until my final home-cooked meal wore off and total exhaustion set in.All thoughts of action heroes seemed idiotic and childish. It turned out that real truck drivers were usually much more responsible at locking up their trailers than in films, and that dumpsters very rarely hold the fresh half-eaten food that movie characters seem to find on their first try. And they smelled *so* bad.

Days passed, almost in a blur, in my weird new half-life. Sleeping for no more than a few hours at a time, stealing what food I could, and thinking only about survival, I sometimes forgot that I'd ever been a normal kid in a normal family.

Fear and exhaustion turned to anger. I wanted to kill that doctor. And what was it all for anyhow?

My wings were growing. Quickly. When I'd first had a decent look at them in the hospital room, they had been the same length as my outstretched arms. A few days later, each wing was nearly a foot longer on each side. I still hadn't changed my t-shirt, partly because I had a feeling that I wouldn't be able to get my wings through the new back slits I'd cut without ripping the whole thing apart, and partly because I couldn't see the point. But one day soon, I would have to figure out what the hell passed as practical fashion for a mutant bird kid. In the meantime, I kept my wings hidden by folding them tightly under my faithful no-longer-baggy sweatshirt.

One night, as I examined a loose feather in the flickering streetlights, it occurred to me that my wings were the *exact* same color as my hair, apart from some mottled lighter markings. I recalled from Advanced Biology class that hair, nails, feathers, and horns were all made of the same type of protein, keratin, so it made a sick kind of sense that my hair and wings would match.

I tried to remember everything I'd ever learned about birds. Their heart rates were typically fast, which might explain why my own resting pulse rate was now about a hundred per minute. I assumed that my amazing new vision and hearing was all part of the bird thing too — and maybe even the increased body temperature that had got the doctors so worked up during my short imprisonment in the hospital.

But none of that made me feel better, or helped me figure out why this had happened, let alone what I actually *was* now. It definitely didn't help my constant hunger. And nothing could take away the bitterness of knowing that I'd been so close to graduating high school a year early; all that hard work so that I could enter officer training with the Air Force. Now I would never have the only future I'd ever wanted.

Instead, I lived with the constant fear of discovery in a world where cameras were *everywhere*. And anyone who caught sight of me instantly reached for their phone. I'd never sprinted so much in my life. I was totally focused on getting away, but had no idea where I should go. Without ever making any definite escape plan, I found myself heading northeast, and just kept moving.

When I ended up in some small town near the California/Oregon border, I thought maybe my luck was starting to look up. I found a diner where the waitress looked old enough to have never heard of social media and she served me two helpings of waffles with everything, without giving me a second look. But, after loading up on food to go, and when I'd got as far as the parking lot, a girl my age squeaked with excitement and made the horribly familiar gesture of raising her phone.

As always, I ran. Which was not a great feeling, given the number of waffles I'd just put away.

And that was how I found myself on a hiking trail, heading deep into a national forest, still with no idea of what the hell I was going to do next.

I spent a couple of hours following the trail before I realized I needed somewhere to settle for the night, and decided to head off-track. The further I got from the trail, the more alien and threatening the forest became, even though my eyes rapidly adjusted and I could see quite well with the moon and starlight filtering through the forest canopy. I kept my hearing on high alert, until I was completely certain that I was alone. Still, I had to move quite a way, hiking uphill, before I felt safe enough to burrow into a pile of leaves beside a fallen log, using my wings as a blanket. I briefly hoped Dad would be proud of me for remembering all my cadet training, and the stuff he'd drilled into me on hunting trips in the good old days.

Despite my exhaustion, I could only drift into brief snatches of shallow sleep. So, I snapped wide awake as soon as the night sounds of the forest were disturbed by the gentle rhythmic crunch of footsteps in the leaf litter. The hairs on my arms and the feathers on my wings prickled as the nearby night creatures fell silent.

After concentrating for a few moments, I decided the footsteps were some distance away, but were heading in my general direction as the noise was growing steadily louder. The glowing numbers of my watch said 3:30 am. I doubted the sound was a ranger on their rounds. But the steady, regular steps suggested it wasn't someone trying to conceal their presence, so it was unlikely to be a hunter. And again, I thought, who would go hunting at 3:30 in the morning?

My curiosity now wide awake, I eased myself out of the pile of leaves and began creeping down the hill toward the footsteps, trying to keep my breathing and heartbeat under control. My wings twitched as if in anticipation. *Flight or fight*, I figured.

If only flight was actually an option…

Through the sparser trees along the edge of the trail below, I caught a glimpse of movement, and froze. The steps continued, and now I could also hear a low humming. I frowned, vaguely recognizing the melody. The shadow moved closer, and the humming grew clearer.

Who the hell hikes through the forest in the middle of the night, humming Amazing Grace??

Now I absolutely *had* to see.

Timing my own movements with the footsteps, I eased closer to the trail and climbed into a tree, the bark rough under my hands. I scrambled higher until I was half-lying on a limb about ten feet above the path, and hooked my backpack over a broken branch. There I waited, my eyes fixed on the corner of the trail. My wings continued to twitch, and my breath was rapid. I wondered if the person would be able to hear my thudding heartbeat, but it was too late to move.

He finally appeared in the gloom about fifty feet away. I choked, unable to believe what I was seeing.

Dark wings, roughly the same shape and size as my own, were open behind him. His pack was hanging off his chest, his hands gripping the straps by his shoulders. His steps were loud and shuffling as his feet dragged through the fallen leaves. I could see enough of his face to know he was about my own age. The poor guy looked exhausted, and I knew exactly how he felt. I wondered how long he'd been holding his wings half-open like that for. And why. It was hard enough holding out my arms for that long, and they weren't brand new limbs with poor motor control and limited muscle strength.

All of this I absorbed in a few seconds, and the sense of danger quickly faded. He looked like he was going to keep walking on automatic pilot all freaking night. As he shuffled past my tree, I took a good look at his wings, and knew that he was the real deal.

There were *two* of us.

Steeling myself, I rolled off the branch, landing on the trail with a light thud.

He stopped cold. Weirdly anxious, I waited.

It took him a few seconds to turn around. His pack dropped on the leaf litter. He looked me straight in the eye. I slowly opened my own wings.

"Hi," I said. "I'm Tyler."

A smile slowly spread across his face. "Thank God," he murmured, before taking a deep breath. "Hi, Tyler. I'm Miguel."

6

TYLER

The strangest part of the whole weird situation (which I had thought could *not* get any weirder) was the overwhelming sense of relief. I was not the only guy running around with wings growing out of his back.

Miguel and I found shelter in a hollow at the base of a steep rocky slope. It wasn't deep enough to be called a cave, but was far from the trail and seemed a safe place to build a fire. In the flickering light, we exchanged back stories, awkwardly at first, and then with increasing confidence, until the night sky lightened into dawn.

I cringed as Miguel described the sports camera footage of my accident.

"I can't believe the whole world has seen it. My friends … the other skydivers." I shuddered. "I can't imagine what it must have been like watching it happen in real time."

"And I thought *my* wingbirth was traumatic." Miguel grinned. "At least I only traumatised myself."

"Wingbirth?" I asked, tilting my head.

He shrugged, poking a stick into the fire. "It seemed to fit."

I had to agree. "Are you sure you want to keep hanging out with the most infamous face on social media?" I joked. Then I shook my head, imagining the insanity unfolding on the internet. "Actually, it makes me kind of glad I don't have my phone. I do *not* need to see the memes about my, uh, wingbirth. I guess being all alone in the woods isn't so bad, after all."

Miguel looked up. "That reminds me. Most of it was probably just messing around, but don't be surprised if we have to start dodging hunters soon. Like, today."

I stared at him. "Hunters?"

"Bounty hunters," Miguel said, calmly. "They've offered a pretty big reward for your return."

"Who? Not my parents!"

Miguel shook his head, his black wings rustling. "No, some big private company. Didn't say who. I guess because they're being charitable?"

"Doubt it," I said, darkly. "What about you?"

"What about me?" he asked, suddenly guarded.

"Is there anyone who might come looking for you?"

"There's nobody alive who knows about my wings. And nobody left who cares what happens to me," Miguel said, matter-of-factly.

Surprised, I spoke without thinking. "Not even your dad?"

Miguel's eyes dropped to the cooling ashes of the fire, and didn't answer. Absentmindedly, he pulled a black crucifix on a chain from under his shirt, his gaze still on the embers.

As the awkward silence stretched out, I tried to ease my numb butt by leaning backward, wondering what his deal was. Then it occurred to my tired brain that it was really none of my damn business, and I shouldn't have asked. At least, not like that, and not when I'd only just met the guy. "Sorry, Miguel, I—"

He glanced up, his voice cool. "My dad might be dead, for all I know. Although I doubt it. I haven't seen him in about five years."

I blinked. "Why?"

He shrugged, and his wings bobbed up and down with the movement like twin shadows in the dawn light. "He did something terrible, so Mom and I left and went to live in Mexico City. That's the last time I saw him."

"Where were you living before?"

"New York City. Manhattan." His lips briefly twisted into a smile that didn't reach his eyes. "The total opposite of what was waiting for me in Mexico."

It was obviously a no-go-zone, so things went quiet for a while. He went back to staring into the fire, and I experimented with propping myself up on my lower wing elbows, like I would with my arms. It was surprisingly comfortable, even with the feathers bending against the dirt.

Then I remembered something else and, again, my big mouth blurted it out before my brain could get involved.

"Do you know if your parents ever went to Beijing for fertility treatment?"

Startled, Miguel dropped the crucifix, and it bounced against his chest on its chain. "What?"

"I think that's where I … you know." Leaning sideways, I stretched out one wing. My control was improving, but I still had to consciously think: *Move, wing!* "I assume the same thing happened to you."

"No! I'm sure they didn't. And anyway," Miguel gripped his crucifix again, "don't you think there must be … a higher power behind this, Tyler?"

"Huh?"

"This could not have happened without God's will." His voice was soft, yet determined. "As for why … I'm hoping we'll find out soon."

"Really? I'm just hoping we'll be able to use these things for something other than decoration," I said, grinning weakly. Miguel was *way* more religious than anyone else I knew.

For a moment, I thought I'd offended him. But then a smile broke the frown, and he chuckled. "It does seem a little weird that we'd be given wings, but not the ability to fly." Tucking his crucifix back under his shirt, he stood up, using his wings as levers. "Have you tried?"

Stiffly, I copied him, trying to stamp the blood back into my feet as I did. "I managed to glide a couple of times. When the skydive went wrong and then at the hospital. But I had no real lift. Human muscles are not designed for that type of exercise. It's going to take some serious training before we'll be strong enough."

My stomach groaned. Miguel's rumbled in response, and we laughed.

"Food first, then?"

"Let's hope we've got enough."

Generously, Miguel shared some of his food with me, supplementing the granola bars which were all I had left. After we'd shoveled down our breakfast rations, we huddled over his phone, searching for anything that might help us crack the mechanics of flying.

As early morning brightened into full daylight, I saw the bags under his eyes, and the thinness of his neck, shoulders and arms. I felt like a fat, pampered turkey compared to this lean, determined guy who'd tracked me down like he was some sort of bird of prey.

But the last few days I'd spent scavenging on the run hadn't been kind to me either. I had superficial wounds — scrapes and bruises from rough-edged dumpsters and jumping from slow-moving trucks — but that was nothing compared to the crushing exhaustion in Miguel's face.

As he scanned diagrams showing how a hummingbird flaps, I discreetly tried to get a good view of his wings. Evidently, I wasn't as discreet as I thought.

"You can look as close as you want," Miguel said cheerfully, shuffling around and extending his wings while he continued reading on his phone. The page was struggling to load with the weak signal, appearing in bits and pieces. As he patiently scrolled through each new section, I peered at his new limbs. It felt awkward at first, but soon my curiosity overcame the weirdness.

Instead of two wing holes, he had a single slit from just below the collar to halfway down his back. However, the fabric was so tight I could see that it wasn't going to be a practical solution for long, assuming our wings would keep growing. His shirt would rip trying to take it on and off, just the same as with my own shirt with the two slits.

The more I examined his wings, the more I understood my own. They were like another set of arms. Each emerged from a thick shoulder just below the normal shoulder blade, and had three large bony sections connected by an elbow and wrist. These folded into an N or И shape, and the massive vanes growing from the wing tip formed a fourth segment that was all feathers.

As Miguel demonstrated his folding and unfolding movements, I saw he had another joint at the tip of his wing arm. He could bend this like a finger, and at full flexion this let him rotate the end section of longest, largest feathers a full 180 degrees so that they were pointing upwards, tucking underneath the bulk of the main wing. I was pretty sure no real bird had evolved to do *that*.

Then I realized that this meant his entire wing lump could remain hidden, instead of poking out the bottom of his jacket, like mine did. This was how he'd been able to move through major cities and hitchhike along highways without being caught out as ... someone like me.

I tried copying the finger movement. It looked and felt weird, and the movement was jerky, but I knew I'd only get better at it. Unfortunately, having a bunch of large feathers stuffed between my wing arms and back wasn't very comfortable, so I had a feeling that when there were no regular humans around, our normal relaxed position would likely be the 'full angel' fold with the ends trailing down the backs of our legs.

Miguel's feathers seemed to be a uniform black, but a closer look revealed flecks of brown and red. There didn't seem to be any underlying pattern. A slightly musty smell wafted up when he moved them.I brought my own wings forward for a sniff, and the scent was nearly identical. Frowning, I thought about how birds looked after themselves.

"How are we meant to clean our feathers?" I asked. "We can't exactly preen like birds do, with no beaks."

"Hmm." Miguel glanced at my wings, then over his own shoulder. "Can't we just wash them, like hair?"

"Let's find out," I said. After a quick online search, I found a very compelling reason to start grooming in a more birdlike way. "It says the way the feathers sit, and a bird's natural oils, make a big difference to how well it can fly. Something about interlocking vanes and barbs making an aerodynamic surface. So, no shampooing."

"It's not like we have a shower out here, anyway," Miguel said, smiling slightly.

I snorted. "We'll have to experiment." If cleaning myself up would help me fly, then I'd do it without complaint.

Miguel gestured to my wings. "Can I have a look?"

"Oh, right, sure." I took the phone and turned my back to him. As he peered closely at my feathers, I searched for a slow-motion video of birds flying so I could study their wing movements.

"You're going to have some great markings," he said, after a few minutes. "You've got darker stripes coming through already. They're more obvious in the lighter feathers underneath."

"Cool," I said, distractedly, waiting impatiently for the latest link to load. Then the signal disappeared. With a frustrated groan, I tossed the phone back to Miguel.

"Find anything?" he asked, calmly turning it off to save the battery.

"Our bodies are completely the wrong shape. We might never get in the air."

"Don't worry, Tyler," Miguel said quietly, as he started re-packing his gear. "We wouldn't have been given these wings unless there was a reason."

"How do you know?" I demanded, too tired to be diplomatic. "Just because we've got wings doesn't mean we'll be able to use them. What about ostriches, and emus? They're tall with feathers and wings, like us, and they can't fly either."

Miguel stood up and hesitantly put his hand on my shoulder. It was the first time either of us had made direct physical contact since we'd met. It was both reassuring and unsettling. "Have faith, Tyler."

"In what?" I snapped.

He tapped his crucifix. "This was my grandmother's," he said quietly. "She saw my wings just before she passed on, and she told me that we have a purpose. I have to believe it's true. I *know* it's true. It's not a coincidence that you and I are here together. We're meant to be like this." As he spoke, he spread his wings to their full width. "You've already saved your own life twice by flying."

I snorted, my grumpiness already draining away. "Flying? Hardly. More like, 'falling with style'. And not even much style, really."

"It's still a sign that these wings aren't simply decoration," Miguel said. "Maybe we just have to earn the right to fly by figuring out the last step. Or, two."

"Hopefully it's not our final step," I muttered, seeing again that fateful drop out of the plane door.

"Abuelita believed we have a purpose, and all those people outside the hospital did too. I believe we're being tested, and I pray we will not be found wanting." He sounded like a priest. Then he grinned and his voice slipped back to normal. "I'm sure we won't."

"What could our purpose *possibly* be?" As I threw up my arms, my wings shifted in a slow, copycat movement. "Do you seriously believe we're meant to be angels on Earth? Because I'd make a freakin' terrible angel. I can't sing for shit, to start with."

Miguel laughed. "I'm sure your singing won't have a major effect on it either way."

"You haven't heard me sing," I said, gloomily. "I can't carry a tune in a bucket."

He held up his hands, grinning. "Musical talent and ultimate purpose aside, what are we going to do now? We'll need supplies. How much money have we got?"

I didn't need to check the tiny wad I had left. "I've got a couple hundred bucks."

He nodded. "I've got about five hundred. That's enough to keep us fed for a while. Maybe even buy a tent."

"I don't think we'll get free delivery out here," I said, nodding at the rugged surroundings.

"You might be famous, but I'm a nobody," Miguel said, lightly. "We're not all that far from town, as the crow flies." He smiled. "So to speak."

"It'll take you all morning to get back to the trail and then walk out to the town, let alone buy food and haul it back up again," I objected, though I wasn't sure why.

"I'm fitter and stronger than I look. And I can move much quicker now that it's daylight, and I know where I'm going. You stay here and try to fix the place up a bit. Deal?"

We both laughed and shook on it.

"Just don't get caught," I said.

He smiled. "If I do, I won't give you away, promise."

"That's not reassuring."

He laughed again. "It won't come to that, I swear. See you soon. Ish."

I watched him go, with his fake glasses and big old jacket and all the money we'd put together, with a mixture of relief and dread. What if he didn't come back? Then I'd have no friends, no hope, no clue, *and* no money.

But Miguel was just like me. Whatever that meant. Plus, he'd hitchhiked all the way from Mexico City to find me. There was absolutely zero benefit to him in selling me out.

I put to good use all the great outdoors survival training that Dad and the Civil Aviation Patrol had drilled into me. In no time at all, we had a respectable, well-hidden base camp, with a bivouac for shelter and a fresh supply of firewood. I felt ridiculously proud of myself.

Still, Miguel would not be back for hours yet, so I decided to find a suitable training ground for flying. Somewhere that we'd have room to move, without bumping into a tree every time we flicked a wing. For a few hours, I hiked in expanding circles through the heavy undergrowth and rocky ground of the forest that surrounded our campsite, with no luck at all.

Then it started to rain. Hard. Lack of sleep made my movements slow and heavy, and almost as loud as Miguel's had been the night before. I was wet, cold, and miserable, and my doubts about him returned.

My last hope for the day was a clearing I'd spotted from on top of a ridge, but it was too small, and too close to a section of the trail while still at least an hour from camp. So, in the gloom of the endless rain, when I overheard distant voices, I was too fatalistic to bother running. Instead, I concealed myself high in a tree, and waited.

A group of six, three guys and three girls, were arguing as they tramped through the woods. While I listened to their bitching and snapping at each other, my blood pressure rose. They were intending to hunt me down and turn me in for the reward. And, I saw as they finally emerged into the clearing, they were all about my own age.

Although, they were so loud and incompetent, I soon realized they were actually the least intimidating hunters I could imagine. They argued about whether to continue looking or go back. About who had carried the heaviest pack, and therefore should not have to pitch a tent. Then they fought over how they would divide the reward. Finally, they had a heated debate on the proper protocol for taking a piss or a poop in the woods. The only thing they agreed on was to dump all their stuff in the middle of the little clearing, because no one could be bothered looking for a better one. Within minutes, they'd dispersed, still bickering, into the undergrowth. Leaving their equipment completely unsupervised.

The opportunity was too good to ignore.

Moments later, I was hightailing it with a tent, two sleeping bags, and a *really* nice hunting knife that had belonged to the most offensive guy of the whole group.

Re-energized, I made my way back to the campsite as swiftly and quietly as possible. The rain had finally stopped, just in time for me to add my new acquisitions to our base, setting up the tent on a patch of dry-ish ground I exposed by sweeping away the wet leaf litter. As I tucked away the sleeping bags to keep them dry, and despite being absolutely starving, I felt strangely optimistic about the near future.

Only then it occurred to me that, by stealing from the hunters, I had confirmed to the world that I was here. Damn.

All I could do was wait for Miguel to return. And hope that he was the only one on his way to find me.

7

MIGUEL

I took a few wrong turns on the way back but with the help of the map I finally made it to our much improved campsite. Tyler was nowhere to be seen, but I could hear the sound of gentle snoring from what looked like a brand new tent.

I had a feeling I knew where that had come from.

Crawling inside, I waved an open chocolate bar under Tyler's nose. I swear he grabbed it and shoved it in his mouth before he even opened his eyes.

"Thanks," he said between bites. "Any trouble?"

"Just had to dodge a grumpy and noisy hunting party on the way back," I said. "A hunchback teenager hiking through the woods with several bags of groceries is pretty suspicious." I glanced around at the tent. "Now I think I know why they were so angry."

"They deserved it," Tyler said, rustling around in another of the shopping bags.

"If you say so." I couldn't control the yawn.

With a granola bar gripped between his teeth, Tyler pulled on his sweater and squeezed out of the tent. "Your turn to catch up on sleep. I'll make sure the food is stashed safely for the night."

Wearily and with some difficulty, I stripped off my damp clothes, unrolled the second sleeping bag, and paused for a moment in silent prayer. When I finally climbed in, the bag was too tight for my folded wings, so I left them hanging out. With my head on my arm, I gave in to sleep.

The next morning, we set off in search of a good area for flight training. As we hiked up a hill that had been too steep and wet for him to climb the day before, Tyler discovered he could boost his progress by flapping, propelling himself forward much further with each step. It looked pretty cool. When I copied him, I had to stop and laugh.

"I feel like I'm moonwalking," I said. The surge of each flap pushing me up the slope did feel like walking with reduced gravity. Just for a few moments.

It made us even more impatient to start flying.

After a while, we reached the top of the hill, and partway down the other side we found a natural clearing. With the lower part of it flattened by the meandering stream that ran along its lower boundary, it was perfect.

"It's not *that* far to fall," Tyler said, a few minutes later.

Holding tightly to the branch above me, I leaned out. "Uh, yes, it is. It's at least twenty feet!"

Tyler laughed, and the tree bobbed slowly underneath us as he shifted. He was leaning back against the trunk with his arms folded, wings splayed to either side so his spine was flat against the bark, and his feet nonchalantly crossed at the ankle. "It is if you're normal. We're not normal."

"I guess so."

"I've fallen from much higher. Twice. And I survived."

My wings shivered. I hadn't tried to flap them properly yet. There had been nowhere private enough to try in Mexico City, and life had been too exhausting since.

"You have to do it sometime," Tyler said. "If you ever want to fly, that is."

My eyes flickered up to the blue vastness of Heaven curving over the forest. Our tree stood at the highest edge of the clearing, halfway up the hill. Although we'd listened as hard as we could, we couldn't detect the presence of another person anywhere within a few miles. The valley unrolled before me, green and lush, but it was the sky that drew my gaze every time.

Suddenly, the yearning to be up there, to feel the freedom, was as strong as the urge to breathe.

"Have faith in the Lord, and He will have faith in you," I muttered to myself, and I let go of the tree. In two running, staggering steps, I dashed to the end of the swaying branch and jumped.

My wings snapped open, wrenching on my ribs and forcing a gasp of air into my lungs. The air swirled around my feathers like water, and I could feel the current moving against the long feathers as their roots tugged against my skin. The air was welling up underneath me, trying to waft me higher. For a moment, I was weightless.

A second later, I remembered to breathe. Gravity reached for me, my body lurching downward with my own weight. But the ground wasn't just rushing *up* toward me, it was also rushing *past* — I was gliding!

Kind of.

Straining to keep my wings stretched out, the tingle in my tendons became an ache, my new chest and back muscles burning with the effort. As the ground approached, my legs swung forward, and I hit the grass heels-first. My wing muscles seemed to collapse a moment later, and I fell over.

I lay there, my wings flattening the grass on either side, staring up at the sky and trying to get my breathing and heart rate under control. But elation danced through my veins. I'd finally tasted it. That split second of freedom.

I had to have more.

"Incoming!"

Tyler's silhouette crossed above me, his roughly ten-foot wingspan briefly blocking my view until his feet thudded to the ground a few yards from my head. Even before he'd finished crashing, he was laughing.

"Let's go again!" he yelled, whooping, and jumping to his feet.

Grinning even as I shushed him, I rolled upright a little more carefully, rubbing my wrenched muscles. "We should probably keep our voices down, even here. But now I see what you mean about having to build up our flight strength."

"Yeah, guess so." He chuckled a little breathlessly, then his whole face brightened. "That's it!"

"What is?"

"We need an exercise routine," he announced, then dropped his voice as he glanced around. "We have to get stronger and fitter if we're ever going to fly." He seemed genuinely happy at the thought of working out. "It's not like we've got anything else to do."

"What exactly do you have in mind?" I asked warily, although his enthusiasm was contagious.

Tyler smirked. "Ever done a push-up, or a prone hold?"

A few days later, after a strict dawn-to-dusk routine of alternating who was exercising and who was on lookout, we'd already made massive progress. It was unnatural how quickly our bodies improved. Our feathers were longer, our muscles harder, and our stamina had doubled. Our wings were almost perfectly even in breadth and feather length, but there were subtle differences in the shape of our feathers, and in the shape of the wings themselves.

Unfortunately, none of that made any difference to our flying abilities. It didn't matter how many ab crunches, push-ups, chin-ups, or stretches we did, how hard we flapped or how high the trees we jumped from, we could not control our so-called flight.

"We're just too heavy," Tyler complained after an exhausting afternoon of trying to launch from the ground. "And we're not the right shape."

He threw himself into the grass in disgust, stretching out and apparently preparing to sunbathe.

I understood his frustration. My muscles had been aching constantly for two days. But I also knew we were on the right track. We just had to find the next piece of the puzzle.

I began playing with Abuelita's crucifix, making it appear and disappear as I flicked it in and out of my hand. The habitual movements were soothing and let me focus on a silent prayer, asking for guidance.

"How did you do that?"

Tyler's voice jerked me out of the semi-trance. Instinctively, I slipped the cross out of sight. "Do what?"

"What was that in your hand?"

A little sheepishly, I let Abuelita's crucifix drop a few inches on its chain, dangling from my loose fingers. I flicked it again and it vanished. "A trick I learned a few years ago. It kept my hands busy and entertained the street kids, with the added bonus of making them think twice about picking my pocket." Slipping the chain self-consciously around my neck, I tucked the cross back under my shirt.

Tyler blinked at me. "You're a master of sleight-of-hand tricks? Have you got any other hidden and potentially useful talents?"

"Nothing I can think of right now," I said, embarrassed. "What about you, any secret skills?"

He snorted. "Not unless you count being an expert at piloting simulated fighter jets on a state-of-the art game console."

"Interesting, but probably not particularly useful," I joked.

"Not really." He yawned. "Although, now that I think about it, five years of being a CAP cadet might be handy."

"You didn't mention that before!" I said, in disbelief.

Tyler shrugged, his feathers rustling in the grass. "That's how I know all this survival crap. Staying alive is a little more important than moping about my Air Force career going down the toilet before it had even started." He rolled away so I couldn't see his face. "I wish I'd gone to more martial arts classes, rather than extra flight experiences. Then maybe I'd feel more confident about protecting myself."

"Let's hope it never comes to that," I said, quietly. The pain in Tyler's voice was all too familiar.

Thanks to our extreme physical exertions during the day, we both slept heavily. The following morning, Tyler woke in a more cheerful frame of mind.

"It must be technique," he announced, reaching for my phone. "I need a proper look at that slow-mo. Hopefully it'll actually load this time."

Plugging it into the solar charger I'd picked up on my shopping trip, Tyler scrambled up one of the taller trees to locate a better signal. Every now and then he'd flap his wings as much as he could within the restriction of the branches, trying to boost his climb.

"Any luck?" I called, after a while.

I heard an exultant "*Uhuh!*" and then Tyler reappeared a few moments later, crashing down through the branches and thudding to the ground.

"It's not just thrashing up and down, or forward and back," he began, shaking out his wings and arms, a couple of small feathers coming loose. "Watch this…"

Talking me through each stage of the movement, he tried to imitate what he'd seen online. Holding his wings wide, he tilted his arms and swept them both forward in front of him. Then, instead of scooping down and back as if he was swimming, he rotated his wing arm *back* and *up*, letting his wing elbow loosen and his wing partly fold to reduce its surface area, before stretching wide and forward again.

"Look, our feathers have to be smooth and strong on the downstroke," Tyler said, talking too fast in his excitement, "and then when we twist and pull back on the upstroke, they all split up and let air *through* them. But it also pushes air *behind* us, like thrust!"

Stepping back to give us both room, I tried it. At first it felt horrendously unnatural and wrong, like I was twisting all the wrong way. *How could this possibly get us in the air, let alone keep us there?*

But as I watched Tyler's wings, and I adjusted each flap of my own, I felt my muscles easing into the new rhythms. I could *feel* the changing air pressure on either side of my feathers, like I was holding a large panel out in front of a gentle fan, the gentle breeze resisting and pushing on the new muscles in my chest. Was this the missing piece of the puzzle?

"Here goes," Tyler said, grinning nervously.

I stepped back as he bent his knees, held out his wings, and took a deep breath. I could almost hear him counting down in his head.

On the silent *three*, he jumped into the air and flapped his wings as hard as he could, the sound heavy and irregular, like a huge sail being shaken out. A choppy downdraft swirled in all directions, picking up a handful of fallen leaves and sending them skittering across the grass. I squinted against the wind.

For a heart-splitting moment, he seemed to sag downward. But the rhythm of his flapping smoothed out and his feet remained in the air, about level with my head. My gape began to spread into an ecstatic grin.

Even over the thumping of his wings, I could hear his ragged breathing. He was in the air, but he wasn't climbing, or moving forward. He hovered roughly in place, his feet bobbing slightly in between each flap.

It felt like minutes, but was probably only a few seconds later, when his flapping stuttered and he dropped roughly back to the grass. As soon as he landed, I ran forward and grabbed his shoulders.

"You did it! You did it!"

Tyler wheezed, struggling to breathe. He leaned forward, gripping his knees with trembling hands, but he was smiling around each painful inhalation.

"What did it feel like?" I asked, semi-patiently waiting for him to recover.

Finally, he straightened up, wincing and rubbing his chest. "Exciting — and frustrating," he said, still panting. "I could feel the lift pulling on my shoulders, but it was like the ground was sucking at my feet. Damn gravity!" He chuckled weakly. "Maybe I should chop off my legs. That should get rid of the deadweight."

"Might make take-off and landing difficult," I said.

"Yeah." Tyler tried to walk, but fell back on his butt instead, the fallen leaves and grass crackling underneath him. "It'd be better to have retractable gear."

The mental image made me laugh, until I thought about how birds tucked up their legs while flying.

"All right, my turn," I said, adrenaline already pumping in anticipation.

I imitated Tyler's initial take-off technique, bending my legs, opening my wings, and preparing to jump. On the first downstroke, as my feet left the ground, I felt the surge upward. But, just as Tyler had described, gravity quickly grabbed hold and pulled me back. After a few awkward flaps trying to find my rhythm, my chest was burning. My shoulders ached and begged to give up, but I pushed through.

Like Tyler, though, I still wasn't going anywhere. It was like fighting an invisible tether to the ground. I tried to pull my knees up to my stomach, but the effort put everything else out of rhythm. Crying out in pain, I dropped my legs, and sagged in mid-air.

With my last few drops of energy, I tried to lean my head and chest forward, to pull myself *through* the air instead of just pointing *up*. Tilting my downstroke so it reached forward, I felt the surge of air nudge me along, like a gentle beach wave, and I gasped.

But my core muscles failed and I bent in the middle. My legs slumped down and my flapping burned to a halt. I fell a few feet onto the grass, landing on my hands and knees. My shaking wings rustled as they hit the ground on either side of me.

I lay there for a while, trying not to puke from the acid overload in my chest.

Gradually, my muscles stopped screaming at me, and my lungs cooled. My heart rate returned to what was normal for me now, and the pounding blood drained out of my head.

Tyler sat beside me for a few minutes, letting me recover.

Eventually he said, "Guess the double amputation plan doesn't sound so dumb now, right?"

I half-groaned, half-laughed, and finally drew in my wings, the feathers rustling as they slid through the grass. Shakily, I levered myself onto my butt.

"I feel like we're missing something obvious," I said, trying not to let the frustration show.

"Let's check Google again," Tyler said.

As he reached for the phone, the crack of a breaking branch echoed across the clearing. We froze, scanning the edge of the trees around us. I suddenly felt exposed, as if I was in a zoo exhibit instead of in an isolated forest clearing.

"Movement, to your left," Tyler whispered. For a split second, I saw a flicker of something between the trees. I turned back to Tyler, fear radiating from both of us. In our excitement, we'd completely forgotten to keep watch. Silently, we slouched further down into the long grass.

"Was that a person or a deer?" Tyler whispered.

I concentrated, trying to listen for retreating footsteps. "I've never met a deer, I don't know what one sounds like," I muttered, and he smiled faintly.

"I'm sure we'd have heard a person coming," he said. "We heard that coyote the other night."

"But we were making a lot of noise." I fidgeted with the crucifix around my neck, anxiety eating away at my fading excitement.

"We're not now, and I still can't hear anything."

For long minutes, there was nothing other than the normal birdsong.

"I guess that was our cue to call it a day," Tyler said, at last. "We're starting to see and hear things from exhaustion."

I couldn't argue with that. Still, we took a very roundabout route back to our camp, constantly checking over our shoulders and listening for any potential stalkers.

But there was nothing.

8

MIGUEL

"Are you sure this will work?"

Tyler frowned, then shrugged. "No, but I'm not sure it won't work, either." He jumped off the tree branch.

Frantically flapping his wings in the technique from the day before, Tyler jerkily hovered in mid-air. I held my breath as he began to drift outward, but the visible effort he was making to move forward wasn't working.

Then he looked down.

"Oh, damn!"

He faltered and dropped, flaring his wings and gliding to the ground, landing roughly in a half-crouch.

I ran over. "You were so close that time!"

Tyler tried to stand up, his legs shaking, even though they'd been doing hardly any of the work. "The trick is to forget about gravity for long enough to let it forget about *you*." He grinned weakly. "I'm just not strong enough to fight it yet."

"I don't think it's weakness, not anymore," I said, reluctantly. "It might still be the lack of surface area."

"How big do you think they'll get?" Tyler spread out his wings and tried to look at them, but turned in a circle instead. He ran a still-trembling hand through his brown hair in bemusement. "They've got to be like fourteen feet now, tip to tip."

I opened my mouth to reply, but the words stuck to my throat as my ears went on high alert. Tyler saw my expression and froze.

"Can you hear that?" I hissed.

Tyler's wings sagged. "We have visitors." A large jumble of voices was rapidly approaching through the trees to the south.

"Run!" I said, grabbing my jacket.

We dashed for the trees, dodging through the undergrowth to take cover behind a couple of rocks and some thick bushes. Still panting from his attempt at flight, Tyler slumped to the ground while I peered anxiously through the leaves.

"How many?" he asked.

"Shh," I said, flapping my hand at him.

The voices became distinguishable as the group burst into the clearing.

The man at the front of the pack waved his hands in excitement. "This is where I saw them yesterday!"

Tyler and I winced, and I silently cursed myself, shrinking further back behind the bush as I eyed the dozen men and women of all ages. There were even a couple of teenagers, a blonde girl and an African American guy. The two of them were each nearly knocked over several times by the adults rushing about and shouting at each other.

"I definitely heard beating wings! They were too loud and heavy for birds."

"Where did they go?"

"How many?"

"Only two or three."

"Enough." An older, male voice cut through the babble. "You'll scare them away."

Immediately they all shut up, moving back to reveal the tall, gray haired and bearded speaker.

"Friends, let us pray," the man said, authority vibrating in every word.

I tensed. Tyler rolled onto his knees and peered through the vegetation beside me.

The group quickly gathered in a loose circle around the leader, kneeling one by one with heads bowed. He remained standing, arms outstretched and his chest rising. Judging only by the hair and beard, he seemed quite old, but my magnified sight scanned a lightly tanned, strong-featured and mostly smooth face, turned up toward Heaven.

"Dear Lord," he began, "please bring the angel boy to us so that we may guide him from the wilderness, so that he may, in turn, guide us from the wilderness in our hearts and minds. We know that You have sent him to us for this purpose, and for that, we are grateful."

I could hardly believe what I was hearing. I had been waiting for a sign, for anything that might hint at God's plan for us. But I hadn't expected it to be quite so … obvious.

If it were truly God's design that had brought the faithful there, then my whole life was about to change.

Again.

"Miguel?" Ty whispered, sounding worried.

My eyes never left the group of believers in the clearing.

The leader continued, appealing to the Lord in a way that suggested he had a lot of experience at it. I realized he must be a preacher or minister of some kind, and my heart filled with hope.

"We who have been struggling in the darkness saw the sign, and accept the trials that You have placed before us. We willingly sacrifice ourselves for Your purpose, to awaken the angels to their calling. Let them hear us, so that we may hear them. Let them approach us, so that we may approach them. Let them speak to us, so that we may speak to them. Let them learn of us, so that we may learn from them."

My hand crept to the cross around my throat.

I barely heard Tyler's urgent whisper. "Miguel? Miguel! Don't listen, they're religious nut jobs. It's probably a trick."

"They want to help us," I said faintly. "Perhaps they have been sent by God."

"Yeah, or maybe it's the marijuana talking. Don't they look like hippies to you?"

I glanced sideways at my friend. He was glaring furiously at the circle of faithful. Trying to understand what he was seeing, I did note that most of them were dressed in a rather mismatched selection of clothes. But, glancing down at myself, I knew I could hardly criticize. Some people just had to make do with what they had.

And if God had called them suddenly, who would stop to think about what they were wearing?

Some of them joined hands and began to sway.

Reminded forcefully of the Masses I had attended with Abuelita, I felt a yearning so strong that I started to stand up.

Tyler grabbed my wing shoulder. "What are you doing?" he hissed.

"I'm just going to talk to them," I said, gently nudging his hand off me.

"Don't be an idiot, Miguel!"

I squatted and glared at him. "I might not have been in school for as long as you, Mr. Advanced Placement Cadet, but I'm not stupid."

His face twisted. "I'm sorry, Miguel, that's not what I meant."

I took a deep breath. The prayer in the clearing was loud and fervent, and the rhythm called to me. "Look, Tyler, I get it. You're not religious." He opened his mouth but I forcefully carried on. "I am, and I need to hear what they have to say. At least *listen* to them before you judge them?"

Tyler's teeth ground together for a few moments as he chewed over his different responses. "I'll listen, but that doesn't mean I'll let them see me. It's too dangerous. And I have had *enough* of being stared at."

"Okay, I'll talk to them, and you can listen in."

I moved forward. After a moment, he followed, reluctantly creeping through the undergrowth. We were only a few feet from the open clearing when he grabbed my shoulder again and pointed.

"That bush. I'll keep an eye on things from there. I'll yell if I see anything dodgy going on, and you start running."

"All right, if that makes you feel better."

He let out a gusty breath. "Seriously, Miguel, be careful."

"I promise."

We crawled forward to the final few bushes between us and the prayer circle, only a few dozen yards away in the grass. They were beginning a hymn.

Just before I revealed myself, I leaned close to Tyler's ear.

"If it's any consolation," I murmured, "Spanish and sleight-of-hand tricks weren't the only things I learned while living in Mexico City."

I smiled at him, then stood up.

The crucifix bumped against my chest as I moved out of the shade of the trees and into the sunny clearing. The hymn disintegrated into gasps and exclamations of joy as the group saw me and my wings, half-open behind me.

The minister threw his head back and arms to the sky. "Thank you, O Lord, for hearing our voices this day, and sending us an Innocent. Grant us the strength to complete the tasks You have set for us."

I paused, suddenly feeling naked. Still, I knew I had to trust in God and face whatever challenge he sent to me.

"Greetings, O Angel," the minister said, dropping his arms and falling to his knees, exultation on his face. The rest of his congregation quickly copied him, some throwing themselves completely flat on the ground.

I felt awkward and my wings twitched, folding tightly to my back, like a pair of arms crossing defensively. I didn't think I was a real angel. There was too much sin in my soul.

But there had to be a reason why I was starting to look like one, and maybe this minister knew what it was.

Realizing I still hadn't said anything, I began to panic, trying to figure out what to say. But before I could put any words together, the leader rose and opened his hands wide, gesturing to the people gathered around him.

"O Angel, I am Reverend Carter, and this is just a small delegation from my church. We saw the signs in the sky, and came seeking your guidance and your heavenly message. With the arrival of the Lord's Angels on Earth, we have shunned all modern evils and have renamed our family of faithful in your honor."

A woman eagerly leaped up beside him. "The Angelists seek only to serve the Lord and his holy messengers!"

The rest of the Angelists added their fervent cries and nods.

The anxiety in my chest began to ease, and hope spread through my blood. My wings flexed in response, and the Angelists cried out in wonder as they saw my feathers move. None of them would look me in the eye, but they continually edged closer and closer.

Then, through the supplicating arms of the main group, I saw the girl my own age, hanging back. Her stillness marked her out, her blonde hair wafting slightly in the wind. With none of the group's enthusiasm, she watched almost warily, as if she was waiting for something.

Her resistance affected me, and I instinctively stepped back instead of forward as the Reverend approached.

"O Angel, are you all alone on the Earth?"

Refusing to lie, I gently shook my head, still wondering what to say. I half-feared that if I opened my mouth, I'd do or say something that was distinctly non-angelic, and I'd lose their respect as well as their help.

"Does the Brown Angel, Tyler, walk with you upon the Earth?"

I struggled to find an appropriate response. Behind me, Tyler hissed a warning only I could hear.

"I have walked with Tyler," I said, eventually.

The Reverend took another step forward. He was almost within handshaking distance. "And has the Lord appointed you with your heavenly mission?"

"The Lord has not yet told us what our spiritual mission is," I confessed. "I heard your prayers and hoped you might be able to guide me."

The crowding Angelists were still maintaining a respectful distance, but only just. As I spoke, they dissolved into excited whispers and longing sighs, crossing themselves and clasping their hands in prayer, even the other teenage guy. Only the girl remained still. Was she trying to catch my eye? But there were too many bodies, too many other gazes in the way.

"Of course, O Angel!" The Reverend raised his hands again, his voice rising in joy. "O Lord, I see now! You have sent us Your newly-fledged Angels so that we may protect them as they grow and learn! The honor and faith You have shown us will not be wasted, for we are Your most devoted and humble servants!"

The Angelists added their fervent thanks and pious cries as he held out his hand to me. "Come with us, O Angel, so that we may protect you in the sanctuary of our humble church."

Automatically, I felt myself stepping forward. I heard a muffled curse, and then rapid light footsteps in the grass behind me. The Angelists shrieked as they saw another 'angel' appear, apparently from nowhere, and grab my arm.

"That's a lovely offer, thanks, but we have our own sanctuary," Tyler said, his fingers digging into my bicep.

"O Angel, your concern is fair and warranted, but you *must* come with us," the Reverend pleaded, still holding out his hands. "It's not safe out here. We're not the only ones who have been searching for you."

"How do we know it isn't a trap?" Tyler demanded, pulling on my arm. "Anyone can say fancy words and pretend they're truly faithful."

I knew he was right, but I had a strong feeling that he was also wrong. The Angelists were not here to harm us. They genuinely wanted to help. I could learn so much about being faithful from them. Maybe this was God's will.

But if I went with them, I wasn't sure Tyler would come with me. And if there was one thing I was absolutely certain about, it was that Tyler and I had to stick together. It was Abuelita's dying wish, and something I knew deep in my gut to be true.

"You need to prove your devotion to God," I heard myself saying, and both the Reverend and Tyler looked at me, surprised. "We can only trust true servants of the Lord."

"You are indeed wise, O Angel," the Reverend said respectfully, clasping his hands in front of him and bowing slightly. "But how can we, humble men and women of the Earth, prove ourselves to you?"

"That's the first test," Tyler said, quickly. "If we told you how, it would be too easy."

The Reverend nodded. "We accept the test, and pray we will not be found wanting. We shall return ... say, tomorrow?"

"I will be..." I began, but Tyler quickly spoke over the top of me.

"We might not be here, but God will be watching and will let us know. Then we'll find *you* when ... uh ... the time is right."

"Of course, O Angels." The Reverend bowed again, then turned to his flock. "O devoted Angelists of the Lord, let us pray for the strength to complete our first task."

Eagerly, the Angelists huddled again and lifted their hands and voices in prayer.

"Come on, Miguel, before they change their minds and decide they really want two pet angels as guard dogs for their church," Tyler muttered, trying to force me to move.

But now I was equally as strong as him, and I resisted for just a few more seconds, gazing around at the worshippers. I hadn't seen such devotion even in Abuelita's church. Even the blonde girl was kneeling with the others, her loose hair now hiding her face. "What's the hurry, Tyler?"

"Miguel, if they're the real deal, they'll be back tomorrow, so you don't have to hang around now." Tyler let go of my arm and took a few steps toward the trees under the noise of the Angelists' new hymn. "Come on, last chance, or I'm leaving without you."

Sighing deeply, I turned away, and reluctantly followed him through the long grass.

"Wait!" said a new, British-sounding voice.

At the edge of the trees, Ty and I instinctively paused to look back.

The blonde girl stood up.

Holding our gaze, she took a deep breath and slipped off her zip-up hoodie.

Then she opened her golden wings.

9

VICTORIA

The boys with wings were leaving.

In the centre of the prayer circle, the Reverend was demonstrating his great love for the sound of his own voice. Oblivious to the so-called 'Angels' sneaking away from him, he conducted an invisible choir in the sky while belting out the bass line.

Having overheard every word of Tyler and Miguel's rapid, quiet conversation, I was certain they would not be returning the next day.

This was my last chance.

"Wait!"

They hesitated and then looked back. Shaking off the hands gripping mine, I jumped to my feet in the middle of the Angelists. My tentative plan of sneaking away had been smashed. I had one option left.

Slipping off my hoodie, my abnormally large grey eyes holding the boys' startled gazes, I let my wings unfold through the open buttons in the blouse I was wearing back to front.

The Angelists' hymn disintegrated into cries of shock and wonder.

"O Lord!" the Reverend exclaimed. "Another Angel has descended unto us!"

The Angelists closed in around me with cries of hysterical praise, reaching out to stroke my feathers.

Instinctively, my wings folded tight. I lifted a hand to protect my face, the other clutching my hoodie and backpack close to my chest.

"O Angels, you have raised another Angel from among our ranks!" the Reverend exulted. "We are truly blessed here in the sight of the Lord, on this day, in this holy place!"

Unfortunately, not all of the Reverend's followers seemed to agree.

"But she is not one of us, not truly!" a woman cried. "She is not of the church! She only heard the call this morning! Why is *she* the chosen one?"

"It is not our place to question His will," an older woman shouted.

The happy flock were turning on each other and I couldn't see a way out. My only chance was fading fast. Panic rose inside me as I tried to explain. "I'm really not—"

And then Chuck, the one who had grabbed my butt twice this morning, said, "Maybe this one is different from the other two, Reverend? She has lied to us. Could it be that we have found a fallen angel? I can talk to her alone if you want me to? I'm familiar with the ways of the—"

"Silence!" roared the Reverend. "Brothers! Sisters! The Angel is but newborn! A baby in the hands of the Lord!"

My whole body was shaking, my breath sharp and jagged. The Reverend pushed his way through the crowd. "You were sent to us today for a reason, child," he said. "Now you know your true calling. It is to walk with the Angels."

I couldn't speak, my eyes silently begging him to let me go.

"Our brothers and sisters are only human, and it takes time to comprehend the full majesty and righteousness of our Lord. His movements are mysterious, but always true. In time," he gave Chuck a stern look, "we pray we might find understanding and acceptance. Please, consider staying with us, so that we may learn from you, and in turn teach you what you need to know for your long and difficult journey ahead. The Angelists are devoted to serving the Lord and His Angels, in whatever way and however you wish."

"I wish..." I cleared my throat. "I wish to speak with the Angels."

The Reverend bowed and stepped aside, forcing some of the other Angelists to move out of his way. Reluctantly, the group parted, opening a narrow corridor between me and the stunned boys.

Trying to keep my head high, my wings shivering, I took a few steps towards freedom. Then a few more.

Until the first person broke.

"She can't *leave* us!"

My nerves snapped, catapulting me into a sprint.

Tyler shoved Miguel into the gloom of the trees, and then reached out for me. I took his hand, and we ran. Behind us, some of the Angelists gave chase, ignoring the pleading shouts of the Reverend to respect the innocent Angels and listen for the Lord in their hearts.

The forest floor began to slope steeply upward. Tyler didn't once let go of my hand as we dashed up the hill, dodging trees, bushes, and branches. His brown wings flexed and shifted beside me. His rustling feathers were so *alive*.

The thin soles of my shoes were sinking in the damp leaf litter, collecting a thick, slippery layer of mud and vegetation that slowed me down. The backpack swung awkwardly on my shoulder. My calves and thighs burned with the uphill sprint. But each time I stumbled, Tyler's hand tightened and pulled me upright.

Behind us, the distraught Angelists bumbled around in the trees, begging us to come back. But the hours I'd already spent tagging along on their expedition had been more than enough. Even as my breath rasped and my chest ached, I shuddered at the thought of returning to them.

As the slope became too steep for a headlong attack, Tyler turned and began climbing at an angle, his steps slowing on the loose surface. Massive rocks rose from the soil like mountain warts, some half-strangled by ancient trees. The cries of the Angelists were fading into the distance, replaced by a jumbled chorus of birdsong and insects. Taking advantage of the slower pace, I shoved my hoodie into my pack and settled it more securely on my shoulders, once again compressing my folded wings.

As we rounded a boulder, an old tree root broke under Tyler's foot. A small avalanche of loose leaves and soil cascaded down the slope. I grabbed a nearby branch, my other hand nearly yanking Tyler's arm out of his shoulder but arresting his tumble. His huge wings flapped, blasting more leaves everywhere, pushing his body back up.

"Thanks," he said, panting as he regained his footing. Only now did he drop my hand to brush himself off. His lopsided smile seemed a little embarrassed, but mostly amused.

"No, I should be thanking you," I said, as his well-developed chest muscles rose and fell right in front my face. Then, as he turned to resume picking a path along the slope, I wondered if his muscles were related to the size of his wings...

"Can you fly?" I blurted, then immediately blushed.

Tyler glanced over his shoulder. "Not yet, but we're working on it," he said. "You?"

"I don't think so," I said, trying to concentrate on where I was putting my feet and not on the twitching brown wings folded in front of me. My own wings seemed to move in response, which in turn threw me off balance with the unaccustomed shifts in my centre of gravity. That would have been disconcerting enough even if we hadn't been scrambling like awkward mountain goats along the hill.

"Haven't really had a chance to try," I added.

"So what were you doing with *them*?"

"Infiltrating for information," I tentatively joked. I was rewarded with a slight chuckle. "Mostly I was just lurking. And hitching a ride."

"I guess you came looking for me like Miguel did." Scrambling up the last stretch of slope, Tyler paused on top of the ridge, looking around. "Speaking of, where did he go?"

"I'm coming." A more tenor voice drifted through the trees, and we spotted the black-winged guy ducking branches on his way toward us.

"I'm Tyler, by the way." Suddenly awkward, he ran his hand through his brown hair with that lopsided grin, and my heart, which had begun to ease off its frantic pace, accelerated again.

His friend pushed past the last tree and stopped to catch his breath. "I'm Miguel."

I smiled, hoping I wasn't too flushed from the mad dash up the hill. "I'm Tori." I added, reluctantly, "It's short for Victoria."

"What's wrong with 'Victoria'?" Miguel asked.

"You sound English," Tyler said. "And Victoria is a very British name."

Feeling my wings twitching uncomfortably, I shrugged. "I am English, but ... it's a long story involving a bullying stepsister. Not important."

Tyler shot Miguel a warning look. "We don't have time anyhow. What are we going to do now that our training ground is compromised?"

"The Angelists aren't hunters," Miguel said, putting his hands on his hips. "They won't sell us out."

"I don't think he'd sell us out as much as brag about finding you ... us," I said, awkwardly. "The Reverend will do anything to get on TV so he can preach the Angelists' message to as many people as possible."

"How do you know?"

"Because that's what he was talking about this morning, when he was giving his church group a pep talk about the hike. Except he was calling it the 'First Pilgrimage to Angel's Meadow'." Raising my hands, I curved my fingers around the words in air quotes. Tyler smirked, but Miguel frowned.

"Angel's Meadow?"

"Where I ... uh ... we met. Just now."

"Our flight training field," Tyler said, annoyed. "Which we can't use anymore." His bronze-coloured eyes met and held mine. "Any ideas what to do next, Tori?"

Now I was definitely blushing. "Not really," I admitted. "I just didn't want to figure it out on my own. So ... do you mind if I tag along?"

"I'm starting to feel like Robin Hood, hiding out in the forest and acquiring a band of Merry Men," Tyler joked, then hastily added, "Merry People."

"Merry Misfits," I suggested, and they both laughed.

The sound eased the last of the tension in my muscles. Oddly, I was already feeling more comfortable with these half-bird, half-boy strangers than I had around my own family and friends for weeks.

"The Reverend is hardly the Sheriff of Nottingham," I said, "but I'll bet anything that as soon as they get back to civilisation and reliable cell phone signal, he'll be telling the whole world he's made contact with the Angels."

"Bringing more hunters down on us." Tyler groaned. "And I was just starting to get used to this place."

"We were running low on food anyway," Miguel said, lightly. "If we're going to relocate then we'd better do it soon, or there'll be no daylight left."

Tyler stretched his arms and wings, self-consciously glancing my way as his huge brown feathers flared out to either side. "Tori, you're allowed to keep your wings out now, you know."

Following their advice, I slipped my heavy backpack onto my chest and experimented with flexing my wings. At first, I felt uncomfortable with their eyes on me. But the relief of blood flowing freely through freshly decompressed veins, easing the hours-old muscle cramp, was overwhelming. "Oh, gosh, that feels so much better!"

"One of the few tricks we've discovered," Tyler said as Miguel set off down the other side of the hill, and we followed.

The curiosity, and longing to understand, was irrepressible. "What else have you found out?"

On the final leg of the trek to their camp, Tyler talked me through everything they'd learned and tried so far.

"...So, apart from strapping on a jet engine and keeping our wings static like an airplane's, I don't see how we will ever actually fly," Tyler said, only half-joking. I followed him as he stepped over the stream that carved through the bottom of the valley, and pushed through the last clump of trees that hid their camp.

"I guess that's why birds have tails," I said, dropping my pack to the ground and rolling my neck and shoulders. "Nice tent. Do you both fit in there with your wings?"

"We take turns," Tyler said, grinning, then his gaze flicked around the three of us. "Uh, I don't suppose you have a tent of your own in that backpack, do you?"

"A hunter's pup-tent, so I'll be okay. And enough food for a few days."

"Wait." Miguel was frowning. "What was that about tails?"

I paused in the act of unwrapping a cereal bar. "That I guess birds need them to fly?"

The look Tyler and Miguel gave each other nearly made me laugh out loud but I swallowed it in time.

"I can't believe we never thought of that," Tyler said at last, throwing his hands in the air.

Miguel was uncomfortably shifting from foot to foot. "I haven't been growing one, have you?"

Resisting the urge to check out their butts as they paced around the campsite, I tried to defuse their sudden agitation. "We might not need them. It could just be a matter of waiting for our wings to get big enough." I privately marvelled again at the size of theirs already.

Tyler groaned and began rummaging through the tent. "I'm so sick of waiting!"

Miguel chuckled. "You've had wings, what, two weeks?" Then he glanced at me. "How about you, Tori?"

"I was halfway through growing them when Tyler had his accident, but I didn't realise that at the time, obviously." The echoes of terror and agony made me shiver.

"So your wingbirth was a few days ago?"

"About four or five, yeah." I bit my lip. "It is *so* weird to hear you talk about it so … normally." Behind me, my wings twitched. I tried to move one, and it responded jerkily, like I was trying to move an arm while three-quarters asleep.

"That makes Miguel the big granddaddy bird," Tyler said, finally emerging with his hands full of packaged meals. "You came out, what, a week before me?"

"Give or take a few days," Miguel said, catching the packets Tyler tossed his way. "Strangest birthday present ever."

I hurried to swallow my mouthful. "You guys just turned seventeen, too?"

"Yeah, but he's from New York City, via Mexico City," Tyler said. "You already know I'm from Los Angeles. What about you?"

"I left North Carolina a few days ago," I said, "but I was born in England. London. I lived there till I was fifteen."

"Do you happen to know if your parents visited a fertility clinic in Beijing about eighteen years ago?"

I blinked at the sudden question, but figured Tyler had a good reason for asking. "I wouldn't have thought so, but then Mum refuses to talk to me about my dad. He's in England somewhere still, haven't heard from him in years."

"Join the club," Miguel murmured, and I smiled uncertainly.

Tyler was frowning. "But do you know if you were an IVF baby?"

I nodded. "I vaguely recall my parents talking about it when I was younger, but I thought that was how all babies were made. When I found out about the normal way, it seemed disgusting at the time." Blushing, I concentrated on picking imaginary specks off my third cereal bar to avoid his gaze.

Tyler chuckled. "I was IVF too. It'll be interesting to find out if we all were," he glanced at Miguel, "and if we all came from the same place. Or if there was a connection between the clinics."

I wrinkled my nose. It was weird to think of ourselves as tiny clumps of cells, unknowingly floating next to each other in test tubes or Agar plates, or however embryos were formed outside of the human womb. The thought that the three of us — maybe others? — might have all been together, so long ago, was bizarre.

Inexpertly, I resettled my wings, swaying as my balance wavered. "You think we were deliberately created as an experiment or something?"

Tyler shrugged. "Maybe. It's the only lead we've got so far."

Miguel looked increasingly uncomfortable with the direction of the conversation. His hand reached up to his shirt collar and pulled out a black wooden crucifix on a chain.

We've got a religious bird kid, I realised, and made a silent promise to be more careful about what I said. I didn't believe in God myself, but that didn't mean I wanted to offend him. I needed both Tyler and Miguel to like and trust me, just as I needed to be able to trust them.

Which, perhaps unsurprisingly, I already did.

I decided it was probably a good moment to change the subject. "Now we're refuelled, shall we do some research on tails?"

"Yeah!" they said in unison.

Tyler glanced at his watch and then up at the sky. The sun was behind the hill, but it would still be some hours before dusk. "As long as we don't get too noisy, we'll hear anyone coming from a mile off."

Miguel had already extracted his smartphone from the tent. "I don't have any bars down here, so we'll have to move higher."

"Let's get moving, then," Tyler said, flexing his brown wings and turning to the west.

"We should head that way." Miguel pointed to the more eastern side of the valley. "We got the strongest signal there the other day."

Tyler groaned. "That's going back toward the trail, and therefore the Angelists and the hunters. Let's go up there." He pointed west.

"But there's no guarantee there'll be any bars up there!" Miguel argued. "We'd be wasting time."

I waved at them. "Take it easy, guys, I have a smartphone that has satellite coverage."

They stared at me for a moment, slow grins spreading across their faces. "Anything else useful in that backpack?" Tyler asked hopefully.

"A solar charger, first aid kit, water purifying tablets, oh, and soap and toilet paper."

Tyler looked at Miguel. "I like her."

Miguel grinned. "You can *definitely* stay, Tori."

As I blushed for the hundredth time, the two of them huddled in on either side of me, leaning forward over the satphone in its sturdy case.

"I want one," Tyler said immediately. "Where did you get it?"

"I … uh … acquired it before I left home," I said, avoiding their gazes and quickly tapping in the passcode.

Miguel remained silent but Tyler chuckled. "Are you sure no one is looking for this? Won't they be able to track it?"

"Not anymore," I said confidently, and opened the internet browser before they could ask more questions. "What should I put into Google?"

An hour later, we weren't much more enlightened than when we'd started.

"How can four websites say four completely different things?" Tyler threw his hands up in the air and began to pace around the tiny campsite. "Yes, birds need tails to fly. No, they don't. Tails are only for steering, not lift—"

"It's the internet, anyone can post anything they want on there," I said, calmly clearing the results yet again. "There's no guarantee they aren't just typing up what they think is true, without any evidence. Or it's different for every bird."

Miguel leaned back on his wing elbows, his black feathers bending against the ground. "We'll just have to have faith that the right solution will present itself."

"Then I guess it's dinner time," Tyler said, grumpily.

As Miguel levered himself up to help, I absently tapped a few more random, vaguely flight-related words into the search engine, and scrolled through the results.

Several pages in, I finally tapped on something completely unexpected.

The Legend of Icarus

The architect Daedalus, designer of the legendary Minotaur's Labyrinth, was locked in a tower on the island of Crete with his son Icarus because his employer, King Minos, discovered he had given away the Labyrinth's secret. Daedalus used wax from their candles and the feathers of the tower's seabirds to make two sets of wings, which they used to escape. Icarus, overcome with the joy of flying, flew too high and too close to the sun. The wax in his wings melted, and the feathers fell out. He tumbled into the sea and drowned.

I stared at the black-and-white illustration of Daedalus and Icarus flying away from the tower.

"What have you found, Tori?"

Turning the phone so Miguel could see too, I read it out to Tyler.

"Depressing," Tyler said, and continued sorting through our pooled food supplies.

"Yeah." My gaze was drawn to the illustration at the bottom of the page. Curiously, I zoomed in on the screen, until all I could see was the wax-and-wood wing.

Something began to click over in my brain.

"Guys…" I said hesitantly. Tyler and Miguel paused, and looked at me. I took a deep breath. "What if we *made* ourselves some tails?"

10

VICTORIA

After a long night obsessively discussing possible tail designs, trawling the internet, and very little sleep, all three of us were shattered when the dawn chorus woke us the next morning.

But none of that dampened our enthusiasm for the experiment. Not if it meant we could, maybe, actually *fly*.

"Are we absolutely sure about this?" Tyler asked with his hunting knife poised.

Miguel and I nodded. "Do it," I said.

"Here goes, then," Tyler said, and sliced into the tent cloth.

Many hours later, we had some random leftover bits of tent, and three sets of kite-like tails. They were constructed from lightweight tent poles and fabric, and stitched with several layers of feathers we'd painfully plucked from our own wings. Using some inessential straps from the backpacks and tent bags, the barely adequate needles from my first aid kit, line from Tyler's survival gear, and as much information as the internet could provide on aerofoils, we had each constructed two right-angled triangles. Each attached to the backs of our lower leg, tightly strapped around our calves.

The top point of each triangle sat just below the knee, the right angle at each heel, and the hypotenuse reached out and down to the furthest corner, which flared about a step away from the ankle. We poked the ends of the metal struts into the tops of our shoes to anchor them. When we stood with our feet together, the two pieces met in the middle to form an arrowhead pointing straight up our spines. The hardest part was the stitching. We went over and over the seams to strengthen the weakest points as much as we could. Surprisingly, the poles were the easiest bit, as even the thickest ones snapped after some energetic bending. Miguel smoothed the burred ends by grinding them against a rock.

Now, it was time to test our mad, almost steampunk contraptions.

"Talk me through the flapping technique again," I said to Tyler, as we stared up at the chosen tree.

"You'll be fine," Tyler said. "You got the hang of it much quicker than Miguel did."

"I'm happy to go first instead," his friend — *our* friend — offered.

"No way," I said, more bravely than I felt, and walked toward the tree, my wings flexing. "If these things don't work, I should be the one to crash and find out."

"I'm sure that won't happen but, just in case, there's a handy bush over there that would break your fall." I could *hear* the smirk on Tyler's face. "Try to aim for that."

"Uhuh," I mumbled, concentrating on climbing. "Thanks. I think."

"We should just go back to Angel's Meadow," Miguel said, for about the third time.

"This tree will do," Ty said defiantly.

Miguel snorted. "This tree has been struck by lightning."

"And it's still standing! Therefore, practically indestructible."

"But it's *dead*."

"It feels solid enough," I called down. "And I can just see over the tops of the trees from here."

Standing at the base of the broken branch, about five metres from the ground, I held onto the trunk and gazed out across the forest. As the tallest tree at the summit of the ridge, it was obvious why it had been hit by a lightning bolt. Half of its trunk had shattered and crushed all the vegetation below, opening a big gap in the forest canopy. That, combined with the absence of smaller twigs and leaves on the lightning tree, meant there was nothing between me and the open air. Beneath me, the thick branch pierced outward for less than a metre before breaking off like a sharp-edged diving board. Assuming I didn't impale myself on it, it would be a terrific launch site.

Above was a clear, calm sky. Perfect flying weather.

I opened my wings. The long hours of repetition while we worked overnight had ingrained the movements into my muscles, and they spread almost as confidently as my arms. I knew I wasn't very strong yet, especially compared to Tyler and Miguel. But, even in the twenty-four hours I'd known them, I was sure my wings had already grown. All I had to do today was prove the tail concept would work.

"Ready?" Miguel asked.

Tyler grunted. "Just do it, Tori."

Ah, what the hell. Here goes...

I dived off the branch. As I launched, I remembered to swipe forward through the air, but the feeling of the wind gathering under my wings caught me completely by surprise.

"Keep flapping!" Tyler yelled. I gasped as my chest muscles moved in symphony with my wings.

Miguel shouted below me. "Legs together!"

Oh, right.

I straightened my loosely trailing legs, bringing my ankles and knees together with a snap. As the air swirled over and under my makeshift tail, my legs suddenly lifted of their own accord. Adrenaline surged into my arteries, filling my aching wings with light.

The trees ahead were rushing closer, but I kept scooping forward and sliding back with my wings, using the movements Tyler and Miguel had drilled into me. Streamlining my arms and legs, I wobbled only slightly as I kept moving forward.

I was *airborne.*

Then I made the mistake of looking down. I wobbled, forgot where my feet were, and began to drop.

Frantically, I thrashed in the air like a sinking swimmer. Pivoting sideways, I lost half my height. Just as the hard ground reached up for me, I realised my legs had parted in my panic. I locked my knees and pointed my toes, desperately trying to make myself straight and aerodynamic. The effect was immediate, but still too late. Landing roughly in a thick clump of coarse grass, I lay on the ground, winded and dizzy.

"Tori!"

I tried to sit up. It took considerable effort to move my wings out of the way, but eventually I was semi-upright and sucking in air.

"That was awesome!" Appearing on either side of me, Tyler and Miguel grabbed my shoulders and pulled me onto my feet. "It worked! I can't believe it! How do you feel? How was it?"

I groaned, their overlapping voices hurting my head. "I'm nowhere near fit enough for this."

"What happened?" Miguel asked, his hands tightening on my arm as I stumbled.

Self-consciously, I laughed. "I got distracted and broke the rhythm. As soon as my tail split, I was done for."

"We need something to lock them together, then," Tyler said. "But we also need to unlock them so we can land and walk."

"Some kind of hook?" Miguel suggested.

"Worth a try." I tried a step with shaky legs. "The straps hurt, though. Gonna have to work on that."

"But hey, guess what, Tori?"

Looking up at Tyler, I frowned. "What?"

"You *flew*!"

Turning, I saw how far I'd come from the lightning tree.

"Oh my God," I said as it slowly sank in. "I really flew?"

"You really did." Miguel grinned.

"Oh my God!"

Tyler was almost jumping up in down in his excitement. "My turn!"

As soon as he was on the right branch, he threw himself into the air. His extra days of training showed as he unfurled his wings. The spiralling downdraft ruffled our feathers and swirled the vegetation around us.

Miguel laughed as he watched his friend. Tyler's wings moved powerfully and evenly, and his tail clearly lifted his legs as he brought his ankles together. He whooped, the sound echoing. He flapped one, two, three, a dozen times, shooting right across the clearing. Almost gracefully, just in front of the wall of trees, he split his legs and lowered his hiking boots, his wings scooping down rather than forward. He dropped the last metre onto the rough ground. He fell into a half-crouch with one hand bracing himself on the earth, but otherwise he stayed completely in control.

As Miguel and I clapped and cheered, I lost my balance and sat down hard beneath the lightning tree.

"You okay?" Miguel asked, hunkering down next to me.

"Yeah. I'm just not used to the exercise." I tried to loosen the straps around my lower legs with trembling fingers.

"Allow me," Miguel said, reaching out to help.

"Oh, I got it. Thanks, though." Sliding the straps off my legs, I began rubbing life back into my indented calves.

Miguel picked up one of my tail pieces and turned it over in his hands. "They held up amazingly," he said.

"Yeah, they have," I said, examining the other. All the feathers had remained in place. One of the aluminium sticks in the 'bones' of the kite had bowed but nothing had broken.

Tyler thudded toward us, jumping over the ancient rotting branches in the grass. Realising he was out of breath too, I felt better about myself. My heart rate was almost back to normal already — that is, to what was normal now for us.

Tyler's bronze eyes met mine. "The tails work almost perfectly! Your idea was the key, Tori."

I smiled, thrilled that he was so pleased with my efforts.

Miguel put my tail down. "Almost?"

"Like she said, we need to work on the attachment to make it more comfortable, maybe pad it out so it doesn't dig in so much, but otherwise, we have lift off!"

"My turn!" Miguel said, finally betraying his excitement. And that was the beginning of the rest of our chaotic afternoon — although we did do our best to stay quiet and take turns keeping watch.

With the extreme exercise that Miguel and Tyler had been doing, they were soon able to fly around the clearing several times before stopping for a rest. I didn't think I'd be able to, especially after the late night, but even I completed one full circuit by the time the sun was setting.

"Now we just have to build up our stamina, and then we can fly for longer, and then actually start flying *up*," Tyler said, unstrapping his tail and preparing for the hike back to camp.

Miguel nodded. "It might have only been a few days, but the workouts have definitely helped already."

"I don't think it'll take me long to catch up," I said, hopefully.

He smiled. "I bet you'll be flying rings around us in no time."

"Speak for yourself," Tyler joked.

Laughing, I tucked my tail under my arm. "Oh, shots fired!"

While trooping down the hill to our new campsite, we animatedly discussed the possible alterations that we'd have to make to the tails to improve them, and speculating about what other sort of stuff we would need to somehow acquire.

On arrival at our temporary home, hidden behind the trees at the base of a small cliff, Tyler was reluctant to even put his tail down. Now he had actually flown, he didn't want to let it go.

I knew how he felt.

Later, while the three of us sat around the campfire, digesting dinner, Miguel was the one to raise the obvious problems.

"We'll run out of food tomorrow, and now we don't have any tents."

"It won't take long for people to track us here, either," I said, reluctantly. "Especially if we keep making as much noise as we did today."

Miguel stretched out his wings, his feathers shimmering as they caught the flickering firelight. "Definitely time to move on."

"But where will we go? And how will we get there?" Tyler demanded. "We can't fly far. Yet."

"I don't think I can hide my wings anymore," Miguel said, glancing over his shoulder. "So no more hitchhiking, I guess."

"Regular hiking, then?" Tyler suggested, unenthusiastically.

"Um," I said.

Their large eyes swung around to me.

"Yeah?" Tyler prompted, as I hesitated.

I half sighed, half blew my hair out of my face. "I have a vehicle," I confessed.

"Wait, you do?" He leaned forward. "What kind?"

"It's my stepdad's old pickup," I said. "He uses ... *used* it for hunting and fishing trips. That sort of thing."

"Where is it?" Miguel asked, eagerly.

Checking the map on the smartphone, I pointed to the southeast corner. "Back there. There's a parking lot at that end of the trail. That was where the Angelists congregated before starting their pilgrimage thingy to find you. So, if it's still there, then we could use it to go ... wherever we're going. We can take turns driving."

Miguel waved a hand quickly. "I can't drive. Sorry."

"I can," Tyler said. "I mean, I don't actually have my license yet, but I know how."

"If a cop pulls us over, driving without a license will be the least of our problems," I said, smiling weakly.

"But where will we drive *to*?" Miguel asked.

"Now we're off the ground, we need wide open spaces to practise flying properly." Tyler poked the fire, speaking slowly as he thought out loud. "Birds use thermals to help them save energy, right? What about ... the desert? That would be where the biggest thermals are."

"And the fewest people," I added, turning the idea over in my mind.

"You want us to go and camp out in the desert?" Miguel said, aghast. "Have you ever *been* to the desert?"

"I'm not saying in the middle of the desert," Tyler said, sounding increasingly enthusiastic, "but somewhere near the edges where it's not so intense."

"We don't have any other ideas or options, so we could at least visit and check it out," I suggested. "We can always change our minds and go somewhere else."

"True, I guess," Miguel said. "But don't expect me to be any use. I've lived in cities all my life."

Tyler slouched against his log, stretching out in front of the fire. "I've done a few survival courses and camped in the desert before." Miguel rolled his eyes, and Tyler chucked a twig at him. Miguel batted it away with a grin, and Tyler settled his hands behind his head. "If there's anything we don't know, we'll make it up as we go along. It's worked all right so far."

"We can't move without any plan," Miguel pointed out. "And don't forget, there's the problem of food."

"And I think we'll need fuel for the truck, too," I said.

"What about that little town we came through to get here?" Tyler waved in its general direction. "Miguel, you could go into the supermarket for another supply run, couldn't you?"

"That place is crawling with Angelists and hunters and nosy people," I said, shaking my head. "They'll spot us a mile off, especially you, Tyler." I shuddered. "They know what we *all* look like, now."

Tyler tossed a branch on the campfire. The flickering light deepened his frown. "Sometimes I wish..."

After a moment, I guessed. "That this had never happened?"

He sighed, ran his hand through his already-tousled brown hair, and nodded. "I'd still be at home, I'd still have a life. I just wish I knew *why*."

Miguel was running some dry leaves through his fingers, making them appear and disappear again. "I think there is a bigger purpose," he said, quietly. "This can't be coincidence."

There was silence for a while, broken only when a burning log collapsed.

"While I was running," Ty said, eventually, "at first, anyway, it seemed kind of exciting. Like a movie."

"What kind of movie?" I asked, lightly.

His mouth twisted into the ghost of a smirk. "At first, I was imagining a spy or action flick. But then I started thinking about superhero movies."

I shifted into a cross-legged position, my wings relaxing behind me in a gentle droop, stretching across the leaf litter. "If you're going to be a superhero, you'll need a secret identity, or a code name."

"Bird Boy?" Miguel suggested, and this time Tyler threw a handful of leaves at him. Miguel chuckled, brushing them away.

"I'd be so much more awesome than *Bird Boy*," Tyler said, snorting.

"All right then," Miguel said. "Bird Man?"

"Birdman and Robin," I added, starting to laugh. "Weren't you talking about being Robin Hood, before?"

Tyler groaned. "No thanks. External underwear and leggings aren't really my style."

I narrowed my eyes at him. "I'm getting the feeling you've already picked out your name."

He avoided my gaze. "Well, I had a few ideas…"

"You can't bring it up and then not tell us," I said, after his silence trickled on too long.

"Nah, now I know you'll just laugh at me." Tyler slid down until he was lying flat on his partly-unfolded wings, which formed N shapes on either side of his shoulders. He crossed his legs and arms and shut his eyes.

"Hey," I said, poking his leg with a stick. "No sleeping until after confession."

Tyler calmly brushed the stick away and resumed his sleeping-cowboy position.

Miguel grinned at me, shrugging helplessly. But my curiosity, having been awakened, would not back down.

"What about you, Miguel? What name would you take?"

He huffed out a breath. "I have no idea."

"Not necessarily a superhero name…" My imagination was tumbling along at full speed now. "Just something to reflect the fact you've changed. We've changed. Seems weird for such a major thing to happen, and then we just keep waddling along, pretending to be the same people."

"I don't waddle," Tyler objected, without opening his eyes.

"No," I agreed. "You fly."

He couldn't control the smug look. "And it's fan-freaking-tastic." Finally, he levered himself upright and met my gaze across the fire.

I nodded, my wings flexing with my gesturing arms. "It's brilliant! I think we should celebrate it, somehow. Looking ahead to the future, instead of mourning for the past. We need to mark the occasion."

"Uh, how, exactly?" Miguel said, but Tyler was looking more animated by the second.

"I like the new names idea," I said, trying not to let awkwardness creep into my voice. "In recognition of our new identities." When I saw the black-winged boy looking doubtful, I quickly added, "Not necessarily to replace your actual name, I mean, but as like a … a … spiritual title?" I sent a pleading glance to Tyler. *Help me out, here!*

"Like your favourite bird," he blurted. It might have been the glow from the fire, but I thought he might have blushed slightly. He began twisting a twig between his fingers. "Mine would be the hawk … that's what the alternate identity I was making up earlier was called. The Hawk."

"You look like a hawk," I offered shyly, and the colour in his face deepened.

"What about you, Victoria?" he asked, obviously trying to shift the attention away from himself.

I screwed up my nose when I heard my name. "Ugh, don't call me that. Only my stepsister calls me that, or other people if I'm in trouble."

"Exactly, you don't like your name. So why don't you take a new one?"

"Do you have a favourite bird?" Miguel asked.

Scratching around on the ground, I let my mind drift to see what floated to the surface. "I did a school project on the kestrel once, years ago," I said, eventually. "We were using birds as a focus topic, and I liked the sound of it best."

"Kestrel," Tyler said, slowly, and a shiver ran through my skin, my hair and feathers rising slightly. "Kestrel. Hawk." His gaze flicked to Miguel. "What about you?"

"I can't say I've ever felt a particular attachment to birds before now," Miguel said, neutrally, "so I don't have a favourite. I'd have to think about it."

Watching his large black feathers resettling behind him, I ran through a mental list of large birds with dark plumage. "What about condors?" I suggested after a while. "They're amazing birds."

He shrugged. "Sounds okay, but I'm in no hurry." He smiled at me. "If you want to take on a new name though, I promise I'll try to use it instead of Tori."

"I think Kestrel is the perfect name for you," Tyler said cheerfully, but with an odd note in his voice. If it wasn't for the confidence oozing from every pore, I'd have thought he was feeling shy. "Assuming you still like it."

Biting my lip, I sounded it out in my head. *Hi, I'm Kestrel.* Every part of me hummed with excitement as I tried on the name. "You think it works?"

"Definitely," Tyler said, nodding. Miguel agreed.

I hesitated just a moment longer. "Okay. Hi, guys. I'm Kestrel. Nice to meet you." As my mouth formed the words, they felt familiar. Right.

Both boys laughed, Miguel clapping his hands a couple of times. "It definitely suits you," he said.

"Cool," I said, my heart feeling lighter and warmer in my chest. "I was worried you'd think I was weird."

Tyler shrugged all four of his shoulders, his brown wings rising and falling as they flexed slightly in emphasis. "When we all have wings growing out of our backs? What's weirder than that?"

"Good point." I laughed, my shyness easing. "What about you then, Tyler? Do you want to be Hawk as an everyday thing, or just on special occasions?" I teased.

He hesitated, scraping at the embers of the fire with a discarded bit of tent pole. "I think you're right, about what you said before. We're new people now. And it was completely out of our control. I want to take back control. Changing my name is … important. Symbolic. You know?"

"Yeah," I said encouragingly, as he hesitated again.

"So … yes." Tyler awkwardly put the pole down. "I think I do want to change my name."

"Hawk?"

He finally looked up. I don't know if it was the flickering of the fire or the darkness around him, but he looked vulnerable and uncertain for the first time since I'd met him. His bronze eyes seemed golden in the firelight. "What do you think?"

"I think it's perfect."

Tyler grinned. "Hi, Kestrel. I'm Hawk."

11

HAWK

That night, after we'd built a rough shelter of hacked branches and leaves, I lay awake for a long time. Miguel and Tori — no, Kestrel — gradually fell asleep, their breathing softening and slowing. Gazing up past the edge of the lean-to, I waited for the moments when the gentle breeze brushed the forest canopy aside and allowed me to catch a glimpse of the stars.

I am Hawk.

I turned the name over and over, trying it out in my head in a hundred different contexts. Serious, silly, happy, excited, angry, sad. No matter how I said it to myself, it seemed to fit *right*, like a favorite sweater and jeans. I imagined my parents and sister calling me Hawk, and that was exciting enough to block out the pain that always came with thinking about my family.

But hearing Kestrel say it out loud had been more than exciting. It had felt ... momentous. Meaningful.

Meant to be?

Smiling, I shifted onto my side, burrowed deeper into the sleeping bag, and closed my eyes. Exhaustion and delirium would not help me fly any faster or higher.

As I drifted into sleep, my last thought was how I'd caught Miguel looking at Kestrel as she flew above us for the very first time, with the sunlight filtering through and around her golden feathers.

"I'm already starving again," I moaned, only half-joking, and whacked a branch out of my way.

Miguel chuckled. "I told you not to eat everything you had left for breakfast."

"What's the point in saving lunch if you die of hunger before you make it that far?"

"We've been hiking for less than an hour, Ty — Hawk." Miguel, in the lead, didn't turn around as he zig-zagged down the hill. "We haven't even made it to Angel's Meadow yet, and then we still have to find the trail that Kestrel took to get there."

"I know, I know."

As I swigged from my already half-empty water bottle, Kestrel appeared in my peripheral vision. When something touched my fingers, I was astonished by the thought that she was putting her hand in mine. Then she squeezed my fingers closed around an object, and I realized it was a chocolate bar.

Choking on my mouthful of water, I tried to say thanks, but she put her finger to her lips and winked. Then she cheerfully skipped ahead in line and began following in Miguel's footsteps instead of mine, starting a conversation about how far it was to the clearing, and which way to the trail.

Soon, we began hiking much more carefully and quietly, keeping our eyes and ears wide for hunters, or even other innocent hikers. When we did reach the clearing, we walked around it, rather than cut through the exposed empty space. However, it wasn't until we came to a low gully which Miguel's map suggested was the halfway point between the clearing and the trail, that I heard anything other than wind, leaves, bugs, and birds.

Voices.

"Guys," I hissed. Miguel and Kestrel instantly lifted their heads from the map, straining their sensitive hearing, their black and gold wings shifting uncomfortably. The anonymous voices were still distant, but definitely coming closer.

"That way," Kestrel suggested, pointing up the rock wall. With her heavy pack strapped to her chest, she began to climb, flapping her wings as quietly as she could to boost her ascent.

Miguel and I scrambled up after her, imitating her technique. Within moments, we were retreating from the lip of the gully, trying to step on the softest parts of the forest floor.

As the group of hikers emerged from the forest below and entered the gully, I dropped to the ground. Urgently, I motioned for Kestrel and Miguel to do the same. Silently, we waited for them to pass.

"Are you sure those idiot Angelists can even read a map?" a man said, his voice sounding tired and grumpy.

"Any idiot can follow a GPS," a woman said. "Even hippy dippy cultists."

"Not far now, anyway," another man said cheerfully.

The first man muttered. "I still don't see why we couldn't chopper in."

"And scare off every living thing in the area, especially the ones we want?" the woman snapped. "We're close now. Final weapons check."

My skin seemed to shrink, my hair and feathers instantly rising and prickling my flesh. Glancing at my friends, I saw the anger on Miguel's face, and the fear on Kestrel's.

Slowly, I pointed to my eyes and then to the gully. They nodded.

Easing out of my backpack straps, I belly-crawled toward the edge.

Through the sparse branches of a small bush, I spied on the three hunters. They were dressed in full camo gear, with compact but heavy-duty supply packs and long, weirdly-shaped air rifles.

I'd never had any issue with guns before, but these weapons, which were intended for *me*, made me want to puke.

A crackle, then a tiny, disembodied voice spoke. I couldn't make out the words.

The woman lifted a hand to her ear and touched a communications device. "Roger that. Team four, checking in." A pause. "Affirmative." She made a few hand gestures at the two men.

The high-tech hunters immediately dropped their casual attitude and fell into a clearly professional formation. I didn't dare move as they crept beyond the gully, their odd weapons held high.

Holy crap.

As soon as they were out of sight, I eased backward, re-joining Kestrel and Miguel. Their eyes were as wide as mine, having heard everything.

"If we don't get out of this forest in the next few hours, we're screwed," I whispered.

Urgently, Kestrel pushed my backpack toward me, climbed to her feet, and beckoned us to follow her.

As stealthily as we could, Miguel and I followed Kestrel through the forest as she headed not-quite-directly for the trail. Using the GPS on her satphone, as well as her experience hiking in with the Angelists, we soon converged with and began to parallel the main hiking track, keeping it just within our earshot.

After several drawn-out hours and three emergency dives for cover, Kestrel held up her hand, pausing behind a particularly thick clump of bushes.

I moved up on her right and Miguel huddled in on her left.

"The carpark is just through there," she whispered. "But I can see movement."

"How do we know the pickup is still there?" Miguel asked.

Kestrel leaned past me, and I blew her hair out of my face. She didn't seem to notice as she straightened up. "Oh, it's there."

"How do you know?"

She pointed. "The unnatural mustard color."

"Not exactly subtle," I murmured, grinning.

"At least I have a car," she retorted. "I didn't pick it for its style."

"Why did you, then?"

"It was the least expensive, oldest vehicle in the garage. No GPS tracker, not worth much, but full of useful equipment."

I brightened. "More tents? Food?"

"Possibly." Her grin turned wicked. "I didn't do a full inventory before I, y'know, stole it."

Miguel frowned. "You stole it?"

"From my stepdad. He has two other sports cars, and I bet he's bought a new truck already. Also, he's a dick."

I had to grab my own face to contain the laugh. Even Miguel looked vaguely amused.

"It's on the far side, nearest the road access, in case I needed to make a quick getaway." Kestrel held up the car keys.

I pointed to my wings. They nodded. As planned, we twisted our wing tips into the full hump fold, then pulled on our hoodies and jackets, which were much tighter than they'd been even a few days ago. After the freedom we'd enjoyed in the forest, it was time to resume covering up and pretending to be something we were not.

I crept to the edge of the trees and squinted. There was definitely someone in the parking lot, but it was impossible to see any details. They weren't making any noise, just listening to a radio on low volume. The staticky voices rose and fell without becoming clear.

"Right behind you," Kestrel whispered in my ear.

My rapid heartbeat accelerated, and I began the painfully slow, silent stalk around the lot. As we moved, stealing glances through the trees, I counted ten large black vehicles of slightly different models. All but one were empty and silent; the other was a large utility van with its back doors wide open to the marked entrance of the trail. Inside, a man in black fatigues was listening intently to a set of headphones, staring at a computer screen, surrounded by a large array of technology, including a mumbling radio. I wondered briefly why he had the door wide open on what was obviously a highly professional mission, but saw him pause to wipe sweat off his face. If it hadn't been for his obvious association with the armed personnel currently hunting for us in the forest, I might have felt sorry for him. Soon we moved beyond his angle of sight, and I picked up the pace.

We were a few yards from the closest point of concealment to the mustard-colored pickup, when the man started talking, rapidly and loudly. I jumped, but he didn't appear outside the van.

"Go, go, go!" Miguel hissed. "While he's making noise!"

The three of us broke cover and dashed across the gravel. Kestrel ran straight for the driver's door, sliding in the key and popping the locks with a soft clunk.

I yanked open the passenger door and slid onto the bench seat, Miguel right behind me. He and Kestrel closed the doors as quietly as they could, and then she turned the key in the ignition.

"Give me your pack," I said, as she tried to shove it further down her chest so she could see over it.

Kestrel slipped her arm from the strap and crunched the car into gear, then released the other side. Her foot pressed the accelerator even as I pulled her pack away and shoved it down by my knees.

"Did he see us?" She glared at the rutted track in front of the pickup, her hands white with tension, but keeping the truck to a slower, quieter pace, the powerful engine purring.

Trying to extract myself from my own pack, I twisted to glance through the back window, my folded wings pressing uncomfortably into Miguel's shoulder. "I can't see him. Doesn't mean he isn't calling in reinforcements though."

In answer, Kestrel shifted up another gear.

"Bad news, boys," she said, a moment later. "The warning light just came up for the gas tank." She pulled the satphone from her sweater pocket and tossed it at Miguel. "See if there are any other stations nearby apart from the one in that little town. Tyl— Hawk, keep an eye out the back, will you? This so-called road is crap."

"There aren't any," Miguel said, shortly. "Just the one in town."

Kestrel cursed as we reached the main road that cut through the forest.

"I guess we're going into the vipers' nest, then," she said, and turned right.

"It might actually help us," I suggested, trying to keep one eye on the road behind us without jamming my knees into Kestrel, or my wings into Miguel. "They'll be expecting us to run *away* from all those people, not toward them."

"If there are enough people, then we can blend in with the crowd," Miguel added.

"Hmm. Maybe." Kestrel flinched as a truck passed us in the opposite direction.

I eyed the hardtop of the pickup's tray behind me. "We might find something useful in the mystery closet. How big is your stepdad?"

Kestrel glanced at me. "As much as I'd love to say he's a fat slob, he keeps himself in good shape. Mum wouldn't have hooked up with him otherwise, money or not."

"How about height?"

"Maybe about the same as Miguel? Slightly taller, even."

"Let's hope he has some nice big hunting coats or something in the back, then."

Kestrel gave me a wicked grin. "I hope his old bomber jacket's in there. He loved that thing. That would do the trick nicely."

"Whatever he did, he must have been a real asshole," I said, wondering if it was okay to laugh.

"That's an understatement, but we can do more backstory later. Any sign of pursuit?"

"Nothing."

"Good." She took in a deep breath. "Only a few more minutes and we'll be there. There's a rest stop up ahead. Shall we pull over and see what goodies he's left for us?"

To Kestrel's delight, the bomber jacket was there. She insisted that I wear it.

"But I feel weird with it on," I said, resettling it over the curve of my folded wings.

"It looks good on you," she said.

"Don't you care that it was your stepdad's?"

Kestrel waved a hand. "Gavin might have loved it, but that doesn't mean he looked good in it. Mum only let him wear it on his hunting trips, when she didn't have to see it."

"What about this one?" Miguel asked, pulling out a brand-new coat. It still had the price tag attached. I whistled when I saw the amount.

"That's definitely for you," Kestrel said, laughing. "And Gavin was so looking forward to wearing that as soon as it got cold enough."

"Speaking of, I'm starting to sweat in here," I said, realizing I should have taken my other hoodie off first.

As I sorted out my layers, Kestrel frowned at Miguel. "That looks *too* good on you."

"Uh, thanks?" Miguel said, grinning.

She laughed. "I think the problem is it's too new. It'll stand out."

Sighing, Miguel took the coat off. Kestrel then startled us by throwing it on the ground, kicking it a few times.

"There," she said, shaking off the worst of the dust. "No longer brand new."

"Story of my life," Miguel joked, and slid it back on.

With Kestrel's smaller wings hidden by her own jacket, we resumed our cautious reconnaissance mission into the little town.

When we turned the final corner and left the forest behind, we all inhaled sharply.

The little town was seething with vehicles and people.

And we were heading straight for it.

12

HAWK

"Don't panic," Miguel said. "The more people there are, the less obvious we'll be."

"There are definitely a few weirdos mixed in there," Kestrel said, eyeing a few people in long white robes waving a sign. *Welcome Angels!!!!!* "Multiple exclamation marks are the first sign of madness."

I smiled tightly. "So, if we stand behind the crazies, we'll be fine?"

"Worth a try," Kestrel said, and prepared to pull into the gas station.

Apart from the Angel-lovers, there were also teenagers clutching smartphones, serious-faced hard-core hunters, and a few sharply dressed reporters rushing around with camera crews in tow. The occasional normal-looking person seemed either bemused or pissed off. Presumably they were the locals whose sleepy little town had been overwhelmed by this flood of strangers.

Keeping my hat pulled low, I filled the tank as soon as Kestrel had used her credit card to pre-pay at the pump. We couldn't help checking out the other customers and their strange mix of cars. Ours looked positively low-key next to the airbrushed mural on the Kombi van, or the bright pink truck passing by on the street.

"Seems like our hiding-in-plain-sight strategy is working," she murmured.

I nodded."Next stop, the supermarket."

Traffic was moving at a crawl. I couldn't figure out what was going on, or why everyone seemed to have lost their minds.

I couldn't believe it was over me. Over us.

"Imagine if they realized we're right here," Kestrel murmured in awe. "What would they do?"

"Surround us and drag us from the car?" I suggested sourly. Even jumping out of a tree twenty feet off the ground, with no tail, didn't scare me as much as these people.

"They're more like the paparazzi chasing a celebrity," Miguel said, evenly. "Although that doesn't sound like much fun either."

"I'll take anonymity any day," said Kestrel. "Especially today."

Although the parking lot was almost full, the supermarket was surprisingly empty. The few locals inside the store avoided making eye contact, which suited us just fine. Even the staff were too busy bitching about the crazy people outside to take much notice of us as we quietly took a self-service checkout each, scanning our overloaded trolleys as quickly as we could, and fed dollar bills into the slots.

As we loaded the groceries into the pickup, there was a surge of voices from the town center. And the noise kept growing louder.

Around us, people turned toward it. Some ran off straight away, while others checked their phones first and *then* ran.

"What do we do?" Kestrel asked.

Miguel glanced around. The few people resisting the tide were starting to give way, joining in the flow of people heading toward the riot which was apparently developing a street or two over. A loud regular beat, like the bass of a distant dance track, began to thud. "Take advantage of the distraction and get out?"

"*Oh my God, Raz!*" someone bellowed down the street. "*They found the angels! Move your ass, quick!*"

Someone yelled in reply. Kestrel, Miguel, and I stared at each other.

"But we're not—?" I said, as Kestrel said, "Are there others?"

"Can we risk going to find out?"

Kestrel's face betrayed her distress. "Sounds like they've already been caught."

Miguel swung around to stare toward the invisible commotion, his eyes wide. "We have to help them."

"How can we help them?!" I ran my hand through my hair, the panic surging through me. My wings twitched under the thick jacket.

Then, several familiar black vehicles slowly rolled past, the occupants clearly scoping the street. One pulled into the supermarket parking lot, and began to cruise the aisles of cars.

"We have to go with everyone else or they'll notice us," Kestrel hissed, shoving on our hidden, folded wings.

"Will they recognize the pickup?"

"Better they see the truck than us! Move!"

Joining the scatter of people, we hurried down the street, turning several corners and losing sight of the black cars. But I could feel them behind us, slowly closing in.

"I think we just walked into a net," I whispered.

Kestrel's face was pale and tight. "They can't trap this many people."

"What if they're the military? The government could arrest every single person just to find us!"

It was getting hard to hear each other over the noise. Kestrel squeezed my hand, and we followed Miguel to the end of the street.

Carefully, the three of us peered around the corner at the back of a massive crowd. I climbed onto a nearby trash can to see over everyone, steadying myself on the edge of the storefront awning by my head.

In the center of the noisy horde was a large group of people in those weird white robes, waving signs and placards in time with the drum someone was banging, chanting and enthusiastically praising God. Occasionally a sign would rotate as it was waved around, and I caught glimpses of more 'Welcome Angels!' and something about God's messengers I couldn't quite make out.

"It's the Angelists," I said to the others. Kestrel's jaw tightened and Miguel's eyes widened in hope as I continued reporting what I could see.

It looked like the local sheriff and his team had blockaded the Angelists from moving any further down the street. Flashing red and blue lights bounced off the street's windows, and cops were trying to move the people from the road onto the sidewalks. But no one moved far. They were too busy aiming their smartphones at the scene to take much notice of the bewildered local police.

Then a deep truck horn blasted from the other end of the street. The Angelists' chanting faltered, and the mob finally parted, allowing several big black vans to reach the police cordon. People in black combat gear jumped out. They were armed, dangerous, and definitely not amused.

The local sheriff sagged in relief, and tried to hurry toward the guy who was obviously in charge of the new arrivals, but armed men blocked his way.

As I described the scene, Kestrel cursed and Miguel fingered his cross, muttering a prayer.

"Seems extreme to call out the SWAT team," Kestrel said, her hands strangling each other.

"I don't think they're cops," I said slowly.

Then the Angelists' songs and drum faded completely. Instead, they were yelling angrily, pointing at the new arrivals. Specifically, at the vehicles.

I focused on the company name and logo printed in silver on the vans.

Evolutionary Corporation.

The hundreds of shouting voices seemed to jump up several notches in volume, and my head pounded.

"That doesn't sound good," I muttered.

Kestrel and Miguel couldn't hear me. "What?"

The Angelists pushed forward until they occupied the no-man's land right in front of the police cordon. Most of them promptly sat down, held hands, and started having a sing-along. As they sat, they revealed the Reverend, who remained standing and appeared to be haughtily lecturing the cops, gesturing angrily at the windows of the nearest store.

Through my rapidly-developing headache, I began to pick out words from the crowd in front of us. Something about bird kids and a bookstore.

Realizing that was the store in front of which the Angelists had just formed a human shield, I relayed the revelation to Miguel and Kestrel. They leaned further around the corner to see.

"Look!" Kestrel gasped. Half the crowd did the same, hands and phones shooting into the air to point at the bookstore's upper windows. A head jerked back into the depths of the dark room.

My wild gaze met Kestrel and Miguel's. With our magnified sight, we'd easily seen the face of the person inside.

He had eyes with huge mutant irises.

"There are more of us," Kestrel said, dazed.

The brief glimpse of the 'angel' inside the bookstore had energised both sides of the stand-off, while the delighted and slightly crazed crowd looked on with phone cameras held high. The Evolutionaries began advancing on the sit-in. The Angelists jumped up, waving their signs and fists in the Evolutionaries' faces. The sheriff, who apparently had a death wish, dashed between them with a bullhorn and some regulation tape, which didn't seem enough but made both groups pause for a few more minutes.

Then, from one of the black vehicles, an athletic blond man in an expensive black suit appeared. He looked around disdainfully. The noise and heat didn't seem to bother him in the slightest.

When I described him to Kestrel, she frowned. "He sounds familiar."

I let her up on the trash can in my place, and she eyed him over the heads of the crowd. "Uh oh ... guys, that's the CEO of the Evolutionary Corporation. I recognize him from the TV interviews. I think that's the company that announced the reward for Tyler, although they tried to keep their name quiet."

"He's the guy who's been sending all those hunters after … uh … the angels?" Miguel said, having to raise his voice.

"That makes him Numero Uno Bad Guy," I said, climbing up on the trash can again and trying to somehow tune in on what the man was saying to his attending minions, while the sheriff tried to get control of the crowd. There was a lull in the babble just long enough for me to hear, "…Goldberg's ick-are-eye don't have any options and so…"

"What's a Goldberg ick-are-eye?" I asked the other two.

Kestrel frowned, mouthing the word as she thought. "What would be the plural of Icarus? Icari? That can't be right…"

"Goldberg sounds like a name," Miguel said.

"Goldberg's Icari." I screwed up my nose. "I guess it's better than 'angels'."

Miguel looked upset but Kestrel's frown deepened. "Who's Goldberg then?"

"It doesn't matter right now," Miguel said. "The point is that there are at *least* two more people like us currently trapped inside that bookstore, and we don't have a plan."

My hand touched the tail pieces I had hidden in my jacket, gripped under my wings.

"I do," I said.

13

TUI

"How the bloody hell did my life come to this?"

I put my hands over my eyes — not that they looked like my eyes anymore — and took a long, deep breath. I was not going to cry. *Jeez. Pull yourself together, girl.*

The African American guy from New York, who I knew as H, started getting all literal on me.

"First, you grew wings. Then you saw some guy on the news who's got wings too, so you came to find him. And, damn, girl, making it all the way from New Zealand to the States, by yourself, while hiding said wings, is freaking impressive. Just saying."

Despite everything, I almost smiled. It was hard to believe I'd only known H a few days, because he'd turned out to be the most reliable friend I'd ever made.

He carried on as if the whole armed siege drama wasn't actually happening. "You got to the hospital where the mysterious bird boy, Tyler, was last seen. Then, in a shocking turn of events, you met the equally brave and winged, much more sexy and intelligent guy of your dreams." He flashed that H-bomb smile and leaned in toward me.

"Of *your* dreams, maybe," I said, shoving his shoulder. His dark wings rustled. "Get to the good part."

"I am the good part!"

"Keep dreaming, bro! Get to the part where it all went wrong, and I ended up trapped in here with you and two other random bird kids."

On the other side of the room, the blond guy and the Chinese girl didn't even look up at us. They were as close to a fetal position as was possible while crouched on the floor. Forehead to forehead. It looked like they were whispering to each other, except their mouths weren't moving. Yeah, nah. Nothing out of the ordinary there. Just another freaky thing in the life of Tui Mahuta.

H was still on a roll. "Then, proving that this Polynesian princess is also one smart cookie, you joined forces with the handsome hero and—"

"Save me," I said, groaning and rolling my eyes.

"I'm working on that part! And continued travelling north in his shiny pickup yoot truck—"

"It's just 'ute', I told you, as in *utility* vehicle."

"—continued travelling north with the handsome hero in his shiny ute, following the sightings of the aforementioned mysterious Tyler bird."

"Ooh, long word," I teased.

"I can be a badass *and* read books," he said with dignity.

"Comics are not books."

"Yes, they are, and so are graphic novels, which require much more interpretive ability and artistic awareness than a book where everything is written out for you, thank you very much."

"Uhuh. You still haven't explained where I went wrong."

"Then some wacko cult announced they had found not one but *three* so-called angels in the forest. We, being intrepid adventurers prepared to do whatever it takes to solve the mystery, immediately came straight here, where, in a shock plot twist, we met yet another mysterious winged couple—"

"We're not a couple," I said, wincing as the riot outside got even louder and scarier.

"If you keep interrupting, I'll never finish my fascinating story before the freak police smash their way in here."

"Enough, H." I knew the bullshit comedy routine was just his way of making me feel better, but the entire bloody world was downstairs trying to get in.

I shuddered at the memory of the crazy religious guy accidentally ripping my jacket and the storm that kicked up when my wings burst out. We'd run for cover into a bookshop and then for some stupid reason kept running up the stairs to this little flat. And now there was nowhere left to run.

The blond South African-sounding guy, Marcus, stood up and moved over to the window. He was so tall he had to bend down to peer out. He was only there for a few seconds, but it was long enough for him to be seen. The screams were instantaneous. Marcus quickly jumped back, out of view.

He glanced at the tiny Chinese girl and, with barely a flicker of emotion, nodded. She shuddered and buried her face in her knees.

Not for the first time, I wondered what the hell was going on between those two. They'd hardly spoken in the few hours we'd known them. In fact, the girl, Raven, hadn't said a word. Marcus had done all the talking in his weirdly deep voice. And no way was she seventeen. She looked about twelve, max. But whatever I was now, whatever H was, they were too. So, we trusted them. We had to.

My throat ached. "What the hell are we gonna do, H?"

His face had lost all the laughter. "I dunno, Tui," he said, drawling out the 'Too' and the 'ee' sounds of my name. "I really don't, but damn, we gotta do something."

Outside, a man shouted into a loudhailer, but his words were impossible to understand over the noise of the crowd.

H and I began prowling the apartment, trying to find something, anything, that might help. There wasn't much to see, the all-in-one-room flat was tiny. The windows at the back looked down onto a two-story drop to the street below.

"If only these things worked," I muttered to H, twitching my wings under his borrowed hoodie.

"Uhuh."

And then, suddenly, everything outside went quiet.

I bolted to the front window, and gasped. "No way!"

It was Tyler. The boy we'd all come looking for. He was standing on the roof across the road, big brown wings held wide. He stared down at the shocked crowd and they stared back. Hundreds of phone cameras swung up in his direction, and then, the shit didn't just hit the fan — it set it on fire.

The weirdos in the long white robes went crazy. On the other side of the police line, all the guys in black uniforms raised long, thin guns and started firing at Tyler. But instead of gunshots, they made a hard popping noise.

Putting my hands over my ears, I backed away from the window, hyperventilating. "I can't handle this," I said to H. He reached out to me, his hands shaking. On the other side of the room, Marcus and Raven stood wide-eyed and silent.

Then we heard something else. And it was bloody close.

Tap tap tap.

We all spun round like idiots.

I gasped.

A girl was hanging upside down outside the back window.

Even Marcus looked shocked. I ran to the window and threw it open, narrowly missing her head.

"Who the hell are you?" I demanded. Then I saw her golden wings flexing behind her.

"I'm Kestrel. My friend up here is Miguel. We're like you. Do you want to get out of here?"

"Well, duh."

On the street out front, a couple of real gunshots cracked and echoed, followed by genuine screams of terror.

I turned back to Kestrel. "What's the plan?"

"Hawk's distracting the—"

"Who?"

"It's Tyler, he's Hawk now and — you know what, I'll explain later. Just get your wings out and use them to push yourself up." Kestrel reached down, and I heard a male voice from above her. She twisted to look up. "Just a bit more, Miguel, hold on!"

"Wasn't planning to let go!" the voice replied.

Kestrel held her arms out. "Come on!"

"Go, Tui." H pushed me towards her. "I'm right behind you."

Sliding H's hoodie off my folded wings, I tied the arms around my waist. Then I backed onto the windowsill, awkwardly flexing my wings. While H held one of my arms, I reached out with the other for Kestrel. Her hand locked onto my elbow, and I grabbed her arm. There was a whole lot of nothing between me and the hard ground. Two storeys of emptiness yawned beneath me.

"And the other one." Kestrel gestured.

H nodded to me, and let go.

I grabbed Kestrel's other arm, and she yelled. "Now, Miguel!"

Kicking off the windowsill, I swung out past the gutter, flapping my wings as hard as I could, my breath scraping in and out. Kestrel's arms hauled on mine, and I shot up and over the edge of the roof.

Kestrel fell backwards. I crashed onto the tiles next to her. My dark brown hair fell loose from the knot on top of my head, and I flicked the plait out of the way.

"How many still inside?" a black-winged guy demanded.

"Three," I gasped, staggering to my feet on the shallow slope of the roof.

"Going down," Kestrel said, and dropped her head over the side.

The Miguel guy and I grabbed her legs. When she yelled, we pulled, and Raven appeared over the side of the roof. Then Miguel pushed forward to take his turn at being a human rope, and all three of us girls hauled on his legs. First we hauled up H, and then Marcus. Kestrel's eyes flickered between all four of us like she was having a hard time believing we were real. I knew how she felt.

"C'mon!" She waved for us to follow her, turning to dash along the flattened roof of the shop row. But before we could move, someone looked up and saw us. They shouted, pointed, and a whole platoon of black uniforms took aim. At us.

"Run!" Kestrel screamed, grabbing Raven's arm.

Marcus seized her other arm, and the three of them ran ahead. Two gunshots split the air, and I broke into a sprint, fighting to stay upright on the uneven surface.

"Not far, keep going!" Miguel shouted, running next to me and H.

Something whistled by my head and cracked into the roof in front of me. I shrieked, but kept running.

I thought we were going to make it. I could see a safe place to drop off the roof into another street, away from the chaos.

And then a guy climbed up in front of us. He had a gun, and he was pointing it at me.

Suddenly, Tyler or Hawk or whoever, dropped out of the sky like a freakin' guardian angel. He landed right on the gunman. The guy crumpled, smacking his head on the roof. His gun dropped to the street below.

"Shot, bro!" I yelled, ecstatic.

Tyler/Hawk grinned. But just when things were looking up, I stumbled and started heading down. As I slid towards the gutter, H's hand grabbed my wing and yanked me backwards. It hurt like hell, but only until I imagined how bad I'd be feeling if he hadn't got me in time. I crashed into him, and we hit the roof on our sides.

In a scared huddle, the seven of us watched the SWAT guys surround the building, blocking all our exits. But, amazingly, they were outnumbered by the Angelists, who swarmed them. And the TV crews were right in the thick of it, getting every word on camera.

"Go! Go, Angels!" a woman screamed. "We will hold them!"

"Who the hell is that?" I demanded.

Kestrel took Miguel's hand and scrambled to her feet. "Reverend Carter's deputy, I think. She's nuts."

"Who cares? They're keeping the Evolutionaries busy. Let's go!" said the Hawk/Tyler guy.

One by one we jumped, climbed and glided off the roof, then staggered through the no-man's land that the Angelists had created for us.

We had just reached the edge of the riot, when three people moved into our path.A tall, grey-haired, bearded man, a woman, and a boy about our age. They were all dressed in white.

I saw fear in Kestrel's face, and my own heart rate accelerated. But then the tall man bowed, his hands clasped in front of his chest.

"We will stop them, O Angels. We will wait for you. We will be ready."

He stepped out of the way, and they lowered their heads, though the younger guy kept gawking at us from the corner of his eye.

"Thank you, Reverend," Miguel said, and we ran like hell.

"So where are we going?" I asked, panting. "I'm Tui, by the way."

Kestrel frowned. "Too-ee?"

"It's Māori. I'm from New Zealand."

"Are you serious?"

"Do we have time for this?" the Tyler/Hawk guy demanded.

I turned to him, my long braid swinging behind me. "Prob'ly not, but you still haven't told me exactly where we're going, bro!"

"We have a pickup, but we won't all fit in it," Miguel said.

H jogged to a halt at the next intersection, peering carefully around the corner. "I have a truck too. It's parked that way."

"I have a car," Marcus said. Hawk, Kestrel and Miguel were all visibly surprised at the sound of his deep accent.

"Okay," Hawk said. "So, you and…" He stared down at Raven, possibly noticing the tiny Chinese girl for the first time. She was a full third shorter than him.

"Raven," the guy rumbled. "I am Marcus."

"Great." Hawk snapped himself out of it. "You and Raven and Tui—"

H interrupted. "Tui's coming with me."

"It's okay, H," I said but Hawk interrupted.

"No, it's fine, Tui, you go with … H?"

H glared at him, daring him to comment. "Yep."

"Okay." Hawk shrugged. "Tui goes with H. Having three vehicles will make us harder to follow anyway. We can split up if we have to."

H nodded sharply. "What about a rendezvous?"

Hawk pointed. "That road. We'll have to cut through the forest and hope like hell the Evos haven't thought about blocking it off. We'll meet by the town sign."

I grabbed H's hand. "See you there in five."

We dashed through the streets, H threatening extreme bodily harm on anyone who had touched his truck. But the ute was exactly where we'd left it on the edge of town, with all our stuff inside.

As H put the proverbial pedal to the metal, I wound down the window and listened.

"I can't hear much," I said, still nervous.

"Those freaky soldier guys were shooting tranquiliser darts," H said darkly. "They've probably put the whole town to sleep to get them out of the way."

"Drive faster, bro," I said, and H gunned the engine.

Soon we'd left the town behind and were speeding up the hill toward the sprawling forest. I peered anxiously through the front window as we passed the town's sign.

"Where are the others?"

"That's Marcus and Raven," H said, pointing ahead to a battered white sedan disappearing around the corner.

"What about the new guys? Kestrel and Miguel, and Tyler. Hawk. Whatever."

"Right behind us," H said, glancing in the rear-view mirror. "And they're not alone."

14

TUI

Twisting in my seat, I could see Hawk at the wheel of a mustard-yellow pickup truck, with Kestrel and Miguel beside him. But fast on their tail was a mean-looking black SUV.

The road took us into the forest, leaving the open fields behind. As we began winding uphill, the SUV dropped back. I slid sideways as H took yet another tight corner at high speed. As I steadied myself against the door, there was a *bang!*

Shrieking, I snatched my hand back. "They're shooting at us!"

"No, they're shooting at the others," H said grimly, his brown knuckles whitening as he gripped the wheel.

The mustard ute was practically on our tailgate with the SUV right behind them. A man in black was leaning out the SUV's window and aiming low.

"I think they're trying to blow the tyres," I shouted to H over the roar of the engines and wind.

A couple more cracks, and *ptangs!* of projectiles hitting metal.

H had the accelerator flat on the floor, the automatic transmission whining. "Come on, baby, you can do it!"

Ahead, Marcus and Raven's sedan disappeared around the distant corner. It seemed ages before we were doing the same.

For many long minutes, there was no sound but the roar of the engine and the swish of trees flashing past. The SUV stayed a steady distance behind, but the road was never straight enough for them to get off any more shots.

Then we reached the highest point of the road. The forest fell away in front of us, rolling down to meet a small town on the edge of the plains. It looked very close but very far at the same time.

Another *bang*. We both swore.

"Come on, baby," H urged his ute. "Downhill now."

Another few minutes passed with no gunshots, but we couldn't shake the brand-new SUV, which stayed a steady distance behind the mustard pickup truck.

"We're coming out of the forest," H said, his voice tight.

A sudden rush of wind made me jump. An oncoming car roared past us, driving into the forest. The SUV was gaining again, but the gun had disappeared.

Then, without warning, the SUV backed off. They just pulled over to the side of the road, and stopped.

Our utes whipped around a corner, and the SUV vanished from view.

"Maybe they're scared of witnesses?" H said, as we passed the final bend and warily slowed down for a residential speed zone. Marcus and Raven's car was a few blocks ahead. The road was a broad, straight line for several kilometres, slicing straight through the sprawling mass of buildings that made up the town. Rows of faded, enormous signs on tall poles loomed overhead. It appeared that some parts of America really did have fast food and car dealerships on every corner, like the movies suggested.

I was just thankful our own car chase experience *hadn't* turned out like the movies, with the bad guys firing randomly at the good guys without regard for civilian life.

It only took us a few minutes to get through the town and back onto open road. After a few corners and hills, and a complete lack of bullets and SUVs, I started breathing properly again.

Shortly after that, Marcus indicated he was turning right, and we followed him down a narrow gravelled side road, the mustard ute keeping close on our tail.

After snaking along for a few minutes and seeing no other cars, driveways, or any other sign of activity, Marcus went off-road through the trees, rolling along a thick carpet of pine needles. After all that drama, when we finally stopped and emerged from our cars, it seemed kind of awkward.

"So ... uh ... hi," H said. "Thanks for the rescue."

"You're very welcome." Miguel smiled. Hawk and Kestrel were still checking out the surroundings like they didn't quite trust we were safe.

"Um, we're hoping you guys have some kind of master plan," I said.

"Obviously, you're free to do whatever you want. You don't have to go along with our plan just because we yanked you out of a building," Hawk said, smirking.

Kestrel nudged him with her wing. "*We* yanked them out, Hawk, you showed off for the cameras."

His grin only widened. "Oh, come on, Kestrel, I did all the hard—"

"Okay, I have to ask," H interrupted. "What's with the bird names?"

"Uh ... it's kind of new," Hawk said, his confidence slipping slightly. "We just decided last night. In recognition of our new lives, and ... stuff."

"And some of us didn't like our human names much," Kestrel added.

H's wings fluttered in excitement. "Oh, man, that's awesome. Can we choose names too?"

The three of them laughed. "Of course!" Kestrel said. "Is H actually your name, or—?"

"It's just a nickname," H said quickly. "But a bird name would be so much better!"

"What would you choose?" Miguel asked.

He didn't hesitate. "Falcon," he said.

"You're sure?" Kestrel raised an eyebrow. "You don't want to think about it first?"

"I'm still thinking about mine," Miguel added.

H crossed his arms. "It's the only one I want."

"Works for me," I said, grinning. "Falcon."

"How about you … uh … Tui?" Hawk asked.

"My name is a bird name already, bro," I said. "Coincidentally, I swear. It's a native New Zealand songbird."

What I didn't say was that Tui had also been my grandmother's name, and so I would never give it up. It was part of me, my *whakapapa*, my lineage. It was one of the very few things I had left to connect me to my home. The other was the *pounamu* jade pendant that I wore around my neck. I touched it briefly. That wasn't going anywhere either. "So, while the idea's sweet as, I don't need a new name."

"You beat us all to it," Falcon said. I smiled back. 'Falcon' suited him, and he knew it. He was already standing taller and generally less aggro, as no one hassled him to find out what the H stood for.

Feeling everyone's eyes on me, I looked at Raven. "I wasn't the only one."

They followed my gaze. Raven's cheeks went pink, and she ducked her head.

"She chose Raven," Marcus said after an awkward silence.

"Before or after your wingbirth?" Miguel asked, kindly.

Raven fidgeted but didn't look up.

"After," Marcus said.

"Okay, so Raven's a bit shy, no problem," Hawk said. "Don't worry, we don't bite, Rave."

Raven glanced up when Hawk shortened her name, as if confused. Marcus's forehead wrinkled slightly, but otherwise they didn't react.

"And you, Marcus?" Kestrel said, patiently. "Do you think you'd like to take a bird name?"

The forehead wrinkles deepened, but it took him a while to reply. "I will think."

As the rest of us stared, not exactly sure how to talk to this tall, reserved, and awkward guy, he looked like he suddenly remembered something.

"English is hard to me," he said, almost sounding hopeful.

"Oh!" Everyone relaxed. Suddenly, Marcus and Raven's behaviour made a lot more sense.

"No worries, bro, it's hard for us sometimes too," I said, reassuringly as I could. Although now I was wondering whether Raven understood even that much.

"So, just to recap for the folks at home," Hawk joked, "we have Hawk, Kestrel and Miguel," he pointed at himself and his friends in turn, "Falcon, Tui, Marcus, and Raven. Did I get it right?"

"Yep." Falcon scratched his dark crew cut. "I can't believe there are seven of us."

"Are we sticking together?" Kestrel asked. "At least for a little while, as we figure things out?"

"Sounds like a plan," said Falcon.

"It is logic," Marcus added in his odd way.

"But is there an actual plan?" I asked. "Apart from hanging out like one big happy *whanau* of course. We gotta suss out our next moves."

The others, except Marcus and Raven, cracked up. I rolled my eyes.

"I'm looking forward to picking up a little conversational Māori with you around, Tui," Kestrel said, through her giggles.

"Sweet as, Kess. We'll probably start with your pronunciation. But, yeah, back to business. Is there a plan?"

Miguel's feathers rustled. "When we left camp this morning, we were thinking about heading into the desert."

"What the hell do you want to do that for?" Falcon demanded, as I frowned.

Hawk flicked a wing. "To take advantage of the massive thermals to improve our flying, obviously."

Falcon's aggression dropped away. "You can fly? Properly?" he asked. I felt the same burst of envy I could hear in his voice. We'd seen Hawk drop from the sky when we were on the roof, of course, but then the whole world had already seen Hawk falling from a plane and jumping from a hospital. As my stomach flipped in hope, I glanced at Marcus and Raven, and saw the longing on their normally blank faces too.

"We only figured it out yesterday," Kestrel said. "Long story short, you will be able to fly too, but you'll need to make yourselves some tails first."

Reaching into the cab of the mustard ute, Miguel retrieved a black feathery kite. "It helps reduce the deadweight of your legs."

We crowded close to have a look. Kestrel explained how they'd ripped apart their tents for the raw materials.

"You don't happen to have any more tents lying around, do you?" I asked, semi-joking.

"Let me check the truck." Kestrel walked to the back of the ute. She suddenly gasped.

"What?!"

Bullet holes had punctured the tailgate, and water was dripping from underneath the truck. Heaving up the hardtop lid, we assessed the damage. Multiple bullets had punched straight through the tailgate into the cargo bed, puncturing several big water containers and a small tank of kerosene for a camp cooker. Other bags of shopping had been shredded. Exploded food stuck to everything. A shallow oil slick began to drain over the opened tailgate, carrying all the smashed-up bits of whatever overboard.

"I didn't realise a tiny bullet could do this much damage to something that wasn't alive," I said, poking at the remains of a bag of fruit.

Hawk's face was tight. "It's a lot of kinetic energy packed into a very tiny point. When it stops, that energy has to go somewhere."

Together, we sieved through the debris, wiping the muck off the items that were whole, setting aside things that could be fixed, and tossing all the destroyed stuff into a pile. Marcus and Raven kept to the side, but helped by cleaning the items the rest of us picked out. To our relief, it gradually became clear that a decent amount of stuff could be salvaged.

When all the large items had been removed, Hawk scanned through the remains for anything useful.

"Anyone know what this is?" he said, frowning. He rolled a small green plastic thing in his hand.

"Trash?" Falcon suggested, impatiently.

Marcus peered at the object. Suddenly, his pale blond wings flicked, and he took it from Hawk's hand. Placing it on the ground and picking up a nearby stone, he smashed the green thing as hard as he could.

As the rest of us stared, he showed us the result.

Small bits of electronics spilled from the green casing like guts from a bug.

"GPS tracker," he said, simply, and tipped it back into Hawk's hand.

I moved closer to Falcon. He looked as sick as I felt.

"Now we know why they stopped following us," Kestrel said, trembling.

"But they can't track us anymore, right?" Miguel was stroking a black wooden cross hanging around his neck.

Hawk and Falcon walked around the mustard ute, peering into every bullet hole. "There might be more than one," Hawk said. "There's no way of telling how many were bullets, and how many were trackers, and if they're still embedded in the car." He slammed the tailgate shut in frustration.

"We have to ditch the yellow beast," Falcon said bluntly. "And quickly. We can't risk it."

"Oh, no," Kestrel said, dryly. "I will miss it so much."

"Will we all squash into the other cars, though?" I asked, waving at Falcon's dark red ute and the old white sedan.

"Three in mine, four in the other. It'll be cosy," Falcon said. He flicked the cover off the bed of his pickup truck. "We should be able to pack the extra gear in here."

"I'm still not sure we have enough stuff to survive the desert, though," I said, kicking a ruined water container. "And what about making four new tails?"

"We don't have much money left," Miguel said apologetically.

"Almost all my savings went on my plane ticket across the Pacific," I said, helping the others transfer the pile of salvaged gear into the back of the red ute. "And H ... I mean, Falcon's nearly spent all his, too."

"Don't worry, babe, we'll do what we have to do," Falcon said, confidently.

"Don't call me 'babe'," I said, and as he opened his mouth, I added, "or 'bae'."

I shoved an armful of equipment into his chest. He just grinned as he took it.

There was a loud clunk and a clang, and Kestrel emerged from the mustard ute with a satisfied smile and grease on her nose.

"Let's take this, too," she said. "Just in case." She dropped the spare tyre on the gravel. "Oh, and I have a credit card that should be good for a little while longer." She continued rummaging.

"Whoa, slow down, Kess," Hawk said, dodging as a car jack sailed past and hit the dirt.

Her voice echoed from the depths of the ute. "I'm rather sharply aware that we have reduced our transport capability by a third, and there are heavily armed and powerful people currently hunting us, who are probably in more of a hurry now we've killed one of their trackers. We need every advantage, tool, and type of supply we can get." Her head popped into view, and she tilted her eyebrow. "So, is anyone going to help me strip this car of everything useful, or not?"

Waving my hand in the air, I re-coiled my plait on top of my head, out of the way, in what H-slash-Falcon called my Business Bun. "I will!"

With only the occasional brief argument — that Kestrel and I almost always won — the seven of us got to work, frequently pausing to listen for anyone sneaking up on us. Soon, Falcon's truck and Marcus's car were crammed full, and their tanks had been topped up with the siphoned fuel from the abandoned yellow ute. It was finally time to stuff ourselves in as well.

"Who's coming with me and Falcon?" I said, handing an old rag to him. He stopped trying to wipe his hands on his shirt and gave me a smile.

"How about I go in the sedan, then poor Raven won't be squashed to death by three giant winged males," Kestrel said, grinning.

I laughed. "Cool. Hawk and Miguel, you'll have to fight over who gets to ride in the ute – I mean," I quickly corrected, seeing their confused reactions, "the pickup with me and Falcon, and who has to squeeze into the back of the car."

"I don't mind the back seat," Miguel said.

Hawk sighed theatrically. "Guess I get shotgun with Fal, then!"

"Nope, that's my seat, bro," I said, and made him climb into the middle. "I need the window, especially with Falcon's driving."

Falcon huffed and puffed in pretend protest, jokingly elbowing Hawk much more than necessary as he took the driver's seat, dark brown wings banging into mid-brown.

"Any time today, Fal," I said. "Every minute we wait is another minute those *poaka* get closer."

Falcon saluted with enthusiasm. "Yes, ma'am!"

Groaning, I tried to get comfortable with my folded wings digging into my back and hips. As the ute turned around, and roared back out onto the main road, I knew it was going to be a long drive.

15

HAWK

Despite Tui and Falcon's natural good humor, and the sense of purpose we'd developed during the rendezvous, tension filled the air as we left the shelter of the trees and returned to the open road. But the two-car convoy continued southeast with no further interruptions.

The sedan and the pickup wound along the long highway, putting as much distance as possible between us and the guys in black. The weather was depressing, gray skies with low-lying cloud, but for some reason that felt safer than driving in bright daylight.

"So," I said eventually. "How did it happen for you guys?"

There was a pause.

"I had a back injury playing basketball earlier in the year, so I thought it was just something to do with that," Falcon said, at last. "I didn't want to say anything to my parents because Mom … she'd been so busy at work, hardly ever home. Dad's been sick for a long time, and our health insurance was already causing problems. Then one day my back was itching like crazy, and yeah … it was like a horror movie."

Nobody said anything for a few moments, and then Falcon continued. "I kept it a secret until you turned up on the news. So

I came looking for you, hoping you'd have a better idea of what the hell was happening to us."

"You weren't the only one," I said. "Sorry to disappoint."

Fal smiled. "It's still better than being stuck at home freaking out. I thought if I got out of the way, it'd be one less thing for Mom and Dad to worry about. I'd been planning to move out for a while, I was just waiting for my eighteenth."

"You're seventeen too?"

"Yeah."

I waited for a second, but that seemed to be that. "How about you, Tui?"

She shrugged one shoulder. "It just kinda happened, same as you guys. There was a lot of drama going on at home. Mum had been on night shift for a few months, and her lazy *pākehā* boyfriend cheated on her. She kicked him out, and then my little sister, Ria, had a meltdown when her daddy buggered off. I had major exams going on at the same time. Then when I started getting sick, I tried to ignore it. By the third day, when I realized how serious it was, I went to the emergency room."

I stared at her. "You went to the hospital? What did they say?"

Tui's fingers twisted the hem of her hoodie. "I made it as far as the ER door. Then I don't know what happened, I just ... freaked." She sighed. "I'd never been scared of hospitals before, didn't have an issue with needles, I'm usually sweet as with medical stuff. But it was like a switch flicked in my brain. The thought of anyone finding out about ... whatever it was ... scared the crap out of me."

I took a sharp breath as I remembered the same fear had made me conceal my 'sickness' from my own parents.

As the suspicion grew in my mind, Falcon said it out loud. "Do you think it's part of whatever's happened to us? The instinct to hide? To keep it secret?"

"I don't bloody know. I guess it's possible." Tui's feathers rustled under her sweater. "The only reason I could hide it at all was because Mum was on night shift. Then when the wings broke out, I just … went into shock, I think. Kept hiding. Spent several days on the internet trying to figure out what the hell had just happened."

"Then I showed up online," I said, sourly. I tried slouching down in my seat, but my wing bones were so long now, it was really uncomfortable. Stubbornly, I stayed like that, glaring out the front windscreen at the infinite scroll of road.

Tui sighed. "If the first instinct was to hide, then the second was to migrate, or flock together, I guess." She tried to keep her voice light, but the pain was a thick layer under her drawling accent. "As soon as I knew you existed, I just had to find you. In less than twelve hours I was on a plane. Used the money I'd saved to go to nursing school. If I'd waited an extra day, the urge might have faded, but by the time I realized what a crazy idea it was, I was halfway across the Pacific."

"I don't think it would have faded," Falcon said, his voice low. "It took a couple days before we met, and once we did, there was no question of splitting up again. Same with Marcus and Raven. Soon as we ran into them, we just stuck together. No one asked, it just happened."

"What do you know about them?"

"Not much," Falcon said, as he steered us around a corner. "Tui and I only ran into them early this morning, on our way to the Angelist rally."

I frowned. "How did you figure out they're like us?"

"Obviously we were on red alert, going into the heart of birdkid-hunter territory."

Tui waved a hand. "You can't help but notice every hunch or slouch and wonder what that person is hiding now, right? And the eyes are a dead giveaway."

Falcon nodded. "We don't know anything more than you, man. They don't say anything unless you ask them straight out. We know he's from South Africa because I asked about his accent, and he confirmed that Raven's Chinese. Only other thing he's said is that they're both seventeen, but there's no way she's that old."

"Raven hasn't spoken once," Tui added. "They're a little antisocial. Sometimes it feels like they're watching you, waiting to see what you do before they make a move. But they haven't done anything too strange. Not yet, anyways."

"It's so weird we've all just kind of turned up at the same time," I said. "It was just me, then there was Miguel, then Kestrel, and now there are *seven* of us."

I didn't want to voice the fear that maybe this whole thing had been remotely triggered somehow. The weird instincts were disturbing enough, without adding in an unseen, unknown, genetic puppet master.

"Do you know anything about what the hell is going on?" Falcon asked.

"There is one theory we've been discussing," I said. "Do either of you know if you were conceived by IVF?"

"You mean test tube babies? Isn't that expensive?"

"I think so, but my mom and dad said they got it done in Beijing. Maybe it was cheaper there? I don't know, I didn't really have the time to get all the details."

"So, you think you were experimented on there?" Falcon asked, sharply.

"Damned if I know. It could have been dodgy machinery that caused an accidental mutation, or anything. But if we were all from in vitro fertilization, and that's part of the how, then it's a good place to start figuring out the why."

"Hell, I don't know." Falcon frowned ahead at the road. "I wouldn't have thought so, because my folks wouldn't have had the money, but if it was a cheap job in a dodgy clinic … But what the hell would they have been doing in Beijing?"

"My dad died before I was born, bro," Tui said, slowly. "I don't know exactly when. From what I *do* know, Mum didn't even know she was pregnant with me at the time, that's how early it was." She hesitated, fidgeting with the long braid that was knotted on top of her head. "I couldn't be IVF if Mum didn't know she was pregnant."

No one had an answer for that, and we slipped back into silence.

The worst part of the ride was stopping at a small-town gas station, hoping like hell we could fill up, pay, and then get out again without raising suspicion. The day's events had us all on edge, but luck was on our side. The few people we encountered seemed too absorbed in their own lives to look twice at us.

By the time the light grew dirtier and dimmer, my nerves were frayed. Even the long hours of travel with a soundtrack of terrible local radio hadn't made a difference to my hyper-awareness. Those few days in the forest with Miguel, and then Kestrel, seemed a lifetime ago. Yet we had only left that morning. Even so, I was grateful that I had the others around. It made me feel like less of a freak, and more hopeful.

Tui had slumped against Falcon's shoulder in exhaustion, having finally agreed to a change in position, and my head was resting on the window. For miles, my eyes had been glued to the wing mirror, watching for pursuers. A change in the vibrations in the glass jerked me out of my trance.

I straightened and stretched as Falcon followed the sedan into a parking lot. "What's going on?"

"Guess we're going shopping," Falcon said, turning the engine off. He popped the door, stiffly unfolded his legs, and staggered over to Marcus and the others.

Tui hugged herself and sighed, before sliding out of the cab after Falcon. I was just happy to stretch my legs.

We'd stopped in the middle of a small country town in the gray twilight, somewhere near the border between California and Arizona. The whole place was deserted. The shops were all in darkness and even the streetlights weren't on. We couldn't see a bar but there were all the other usual places, including a mechanic's and a diner. Our target was the largest building, a department store that hadn't seen an open bucket of paint since the eighties.

During the argument that followed, only Marcus and Raven kept quiet.

Unsurprisingly, Miguel was totally opposed to 'acquiring' what we needed without paying.

"My credit card won't get us everything we need, Miguel. If we're going to survive, we need to bend a few rules," Kestrel said, stubbornly.

"You didn't complain when I swiped a tent from those wannabe bounty hunter jerks," I reminded him. "And if I hadn't taken that, we wouldn't have these tails and we wouldn't be able to fly."

"And we're still being hunted, man!" Falcon said. "Only now we're being chased by dudes with guns. Kestrel's right. It's a matter of survival. Everyone and everything are out to get us."

"The Angelists aren't—"

Tui cut him off. "The Angelists aren't here, bro."

Finally realizing he was the only one opposed, and that there was nothing he could do to stop the rest of us, Miguel resorted to crossing his arms and wearing his most disappointed look while Falcon, Tui, Kestrel and I discussed strategy.

Breaking in was the easy part. Breaking in without being betrayed by any security systems, now, that was the challenge. We agreed not to do a smash-and-grab, and to avoid unnecessary damage. We'd only take what we needed to survive and, after some heated discussion, decided to leave some money on the counter.

Shockingly, Kestrel turned out to be suspiciously knowledgeable about security hardware and how to get around it. I was dying to know more, but decided to save that conversation for later. We needed to get in and out as smoothly as possible. She was quietly confident there was nothing she couldn't handle in this run-down part of nowhere.

As we schemed, Miguel and Raven were appointed lookouts. Privately, I wondered what use a mute and a conscientious objector would be, but I hoped that if it came down to it, they would have our backs.

After moving the cars around to the store's rear loading dock, which was nothing more than a roll-up metal door, Kestrel gave Falcon instructions on how to disconnect the phone line and thereby disable the unsophisticated burglar alarm. She then quickly picked the lock on the back door. I was starting to realize how little I knew about my fellow freaks, but I brushed any uncertainty aside. All we had now was each other.

Once inside, our faces covered with hoods and caps, Kestrel pointed out two security cameras. Their little red recording lights glared at us.

Falcon picked up a spirit level off a nearby shelf and went to deal to the cameras, but Marcus stopped him.

"I will delete it," he said.

Falcon frowned. "How?"

"I will delete," Marcus insisted.

Not entirely convinced, Falcon put down the level and moved further into the store.

Night pressed in like it was trying to see what we were doing. I shivered, my wings rustling under the bomber jacket. *So much for not feeling guilty.*

In the gloomy darkness, we spread out in search of useful loot. *It's going rather well*, I thought, as I considered the merits of solar lights. Then I turned a corner and walked straight into a trolley, bruising my shin and pushing it into a display.

"Ow!"

A small stack of tins collapsed, tumbling and rolling across the floor in all directions. I grabbed a few but couldn't see where they all went, so, I continued down the aisle. Two steps later I was flat on the floor.

A small pool of light flicked on at the end of the shelving.

"You're not exactly a natural at this breaking and entering business." Kestrel laughed quietly as she moved toward me, carefully avoiding all obstacles with the help of a flashlight. "Need a hand?"

The combination of stress and hours of being cramped up in the pickup seemed to have made me physically incompetent. I nearly smacked skulls with her as I struggled to my feet. She dodged sideways, bumping into the shelving. There was a nasty wobbling noise, and I reached up just in time to stop a big jar falling on her head.

"I really don't like this place," I said, pushing the jar safely back onto the shelf. I found myself staring at her as she shyly smiled back, her nose about three inches from my chest.

My left hand was still resting on the shelf behind her. I could see flickering emotions in her beautiful gray eyes, but couldn't read them. I struggled to think of something to say. After long seconds where I could hardly breathe, I finally dropped my hand and stepped back. "Sorry."

"Don't be," Kestrel said softly. "Thanks."

I watched her move off down the aisle, wondering what the moment had meant. Rehashing the encounter in my head, I tried to find any clue that might reveal what she thought of me, and whether I had just come across like a total dickhead. Had that been a flirty moment? Or was it just the sudden rush of adrenaline and hormones? I shook my head, impatiently, trying to dislodge the thoughts. The middle of a burglary was hardly the time to start thinking about a potential relationship. Even if Kestrel was smart, and funny, and...

Stop it, I ordered myself, and imagined Dad was standing over my shoulder instead. What survival supplies would he put on an emergency shopping list? What would he prioritize?

Some minutes later, with a parka-full of camping food in one hand and two sleeping bags suspended from the other, I met my fellow looters by the loading bay door. We pooled our prizes and took stock.

Along with sleeping gear and enough dehydrated meals and preserved food to feed an army, we'd collected flashlights, batteries, fuel for the camping stove, a compass, more large water containers and individual water bottles, a couple of first-aid kits, hunting knives, and seven pairs of sunglasses. Everyone had also acquired extra desert-appropriate clothing as well as sewing supplies for tails and repairs. At Kestrel's suggestion, we'd also each selected a pair of 'flight boots' — sturdy knee-high biker boots that would, as she pointed out, add a critical layer of protection between our muscles and the tight tail straps. Tui had added rolls of toilet paper and soap, Marcus had found smaller but no less useful things like matches, Swiss army knives and other tools, and Falcon produced—

"No way," I said. "We are *not* taking a gun."

Falcon scowled. "*They* have guns." He tightened his grip on the pistol.

"They weren't shooting to kill," I said. "What will happen if they realize that we're armed as well?"

Falcon waved the gun around in the harsh glow of the flashlights in the loading dock. "Maybe they'll leave us alone if they know we're dangerous!"

Kestrel looked frightened as its shadow crossed her face. "Where did you find it?" she asked. "This place doesn't even sell guns."

"Found it at the back of a drawer underneath one of the cash registers."

I couldn't tell what the others were thinking. I sighed.

"I don't like it. But I'm not in charge. What should we do, vote?"

"Ammunition?" Marcus said.

Falcon produced a box and opened it. There were only half a dozen bullets in there.

"Doesn't seem worth it," I said.

"But it's six shots they won't expect!"

"They'll expect more after the first," Kestrel said quietly.

Falcon grinned. "Then I'll have to shoot quickly."

"Then what happens when they start shooting back and you've run out of ammo?" she snapped.

I interrupted. "How many people want to take the gun?"

Falcon raised his hand. There was a pause, and Tui half-heartedly put hers up too. Surprisingly, Marcus also voted yes. So, it was just me and Kestrel against.

"What about the others?" I asked. Falcon grunted, annoyed, and Kestrel ran to fetch them.

When Miguel and Raven joined us, they both voted against, Raven shyly raising her hand to waist height, and Miguel defiantly waving his hand high.

Falcon glowered.

"We've still got knives," I said.

Kestrel added, "And wings."

"All right, all right!" Falcon turned to take the gun back, muttering to himself. I watched him go, using my new super sight to make sure he actually did return the thing to where he found it. Thankfully, he did so. He didn't even seem to consider sneaking off with it anyway, as he put it back without a single glance in our direction. He respected the will of the group, which in turn made me respect the guy even more. My natural instincts to trust my fellow freaks was, so far, proving to be a good choice.

In the meantime, Miguel had found paper and a pen.

Stomping back to re-join the rest of us, Falcon peered over his shoulder. "What are you doing?"

"Can you hold the flashlight? Thanks." Miguel resumed his scribbling. "I'm making a list."

"Why?"

"So the owners know exactly what we took and can claim it from their insurance," Miguel said with finality in his soft voice.

Falcon rolled his eyes. Kestrel stepped around the mountain of loot to help Miguel. "Twenty packets of dehydrated potato flakes, seven sleeping bags, seven sunglasses, two boxes of sunscreen…"

"Do we really need the sunglasses and sunscreen?"

"We're going to the *desert*," she said.

Miguel sighed. "Okay, okay."

"I will delete the video," Marcus said.

"Ooh, show me how?" Falcon thrust the flashlight at Kestrel and followed him.

Raven and Tui scooped up supplies and carried them out the dock door after Miguel had recorded them.

I extracted our wad of cash and roughly recounted it. It was less than a quarter of the value of the stuff that we'd taken, but the guilt was starting to ease. After all, it wasn't our fault that we were on the run and without the means to survive.

But I hoped Miguel was right about the insurance.

There was a muted thud from a distant corner.

"What's up?" I called softly.

"Just getting into the back office," Falcon said, curtly. There was a creak as a hinge protested, and then Falcon and Marcus reappeared.

"That was fast."

"Magnets," Marcus said. When I remained blank, he added, "Magnets delete the tapes."

"If you say so."

"We're lucky it was ancient, and not digital. And that there were magnets in the hardware section." Falcon grinned. "It's about time we had some luck."

I shrugged. After all, did it even matter if they caught us on camera? We were already on the country's most-wanted list.

Tucking the list and the money under the foot of the ancient cash register at the front of the store, I saw the note that Miguel had added at the bottom of the page.

We are truly sorry that we can't pay for everything we took, but we have no other way to survive.

16

HAWK

Once we'd transferred the remaining loot into the vehicles, I swapped places with Miguel. He climbed into the dark red pickup with Tui and Falcon, while I drove the sedan. Kestrel rode shotgun, and Marcus and Raven tried to get some sleep in the back. Kestrel and I didn't talk much, not wanting to disturb the others, but it was a comfortable silence.

After a while, though, I couldn't help myself. "So, Kestrel. How did you know all that stuff?"

"What stuff?" Kestrel said softly.

I kept my eyes on the gently curving road. "The satphone, the credit card, then at the store ... How come you know so much about security?"

"And getting past it, you mean?" Kestrel said, sounding embarrassed, but also amused.

"You don't have to talk about it if you don't want to."

"No, it's okay." She heaved a sigh. "It's on my police record, so I guess I can't keep it a secret forever."

"Now I *have* to know," I said, laughing. "I won't tell."
Kestrel smiled cheekily. "Cross your heart?"

"It's that serious?"

"Normally you'd have to put your hand up and take an oath, but you are driving, so—"

I put my right hand up. "It's not like we're doing the Indy 500 right now."

"Okay, repeat after me. I, Hawk, solemnly swear to never reveal that Kestrel was arrested and charged with multiple counts of breaking and entering, cross my heart and hope to die."

"You what?" I dropped my hand in surprise.

Kestrel screwed up her nose. "Cross your heart first, then I'll explain."

Obediently I held up my hand and began repeating the oath, trying not to laugh. As I came to 'cross my heart', Kestrel leaned past my hand and gently traced an X on the left of my chest. Her head was right next to mine, and I could feel her breath on my cheek. I nearly faltered as my pulse accelerated, but managed to finish the oath without hesitating.

"There," she said, looking up into my eyes from an incredibly short distance for the second time that evening. I smiled uncertainly, my gaze flicking from hers to the road and back again.

After a long moment, she ducked out from under my oath-taking arm, settling into her own seat. A glance into the rear-view mirror showed Marcus and Raven fast asleep. Either that, or they were extremely good actors.

"Okay, now it's time to spill," I said.

"Remember how I mentioned the evil stepfamily thing going on at home?"

I nodded.

"My stepsister, Stephanie, is Miss Perfect Popularity and a complete nightmare. She didn't like me from day one, because I was an English nobody and she's the sort of rich princess who's only interested in people with money to burn. She constantly mocked everything about me. My accent, my clothes, my interests, even my name. She accepted my mum because she's a world class suck-up and even Stephanie knows that Gavin gets whatever he wants. Gavin is her dad. A total jerk. He made a fortune through his security firm, and was always boasting about how his systems had never been beaten, and—"

"I think I can see where this is going," I said, glancing over with an understanding smile.

She blushed. "One thing led to another, and I decided to take down Gavin's 'unbeatable' security system." Her fingers made air quotes around the word.

"And did you?"

"I did," she said, proudly, no trace of embarrassment left. "Living in a snobby, gated community only made it more enjoyable."

"But how did they catch you if you beat the system?"

"Simple logic, in the end." Kestrel sighed. "I didn't have any desire to steal anything. I simply wanted to prove that the system could be hacked. Once I was inside the target house, I'd move things around. Mess with their minds. I never broke anything, or did something that couldn't be reversed. I even earned a nickname."

She paused and smiled. "The Gremlin."

I chuckled.

"Eventually they realized it had to be an inside job and began combing through the whole enclave. I had access to Gavin's systems, I had the motive, and I had the opportunity. All it took was a few people who remembered seeing me near the burgled houses around the right time, and I was in the frame."

"And they arrested you?"

"Mum was so embarrassed," Kestrel said. "Gavin, of course, was absolutely furious. No one believed I could have done it by myself, and I admitted nothing. In the end, the police had no solid evidence and were forced to drop the charges and let me go. But Gavin locked me in my room until I told him how I'd beaten his system. I wasn't even allowed to go to school. He kept me like that for weeks, but I refused to tell him. I was still in there when my wings started growing. That's why I couldn't hide from them." Her voice cracked in pain and she turned away, pressing her head on the window.

"How did you escape?" I asked, gently.

Abruptly, the happy, playful Kestrel was back. "The Gremlin had a few tricks up her sleeve that even the evil Gavin couldn't predict. I guess I could have left earlier, before my wings came through, if I'd really tried. But once that happened and Gavin chained me to the floor—"

"He *what*?!" I yelped. Marcus and Raven shifted, and I swallowed the rest of the outburst.

Kestrel's smile was thin. "I think he was trying to negotiate a price with the Evolutionaries at the time, as well as waiting for me to cough up the Gremlin info. The point is, that made it a little more difficult. But I escaped on my first try. All I needed was the right incentive."

"And what was that?"

Her voice was soft. "You."

My breath quickened and I couldn't think of what to say. A shiver ran through my wings, tickling the root of every feather.

After a moment she added, "They didn't know about the improvement to my hearing. I managed to keep that to myself. So, I overheard the news reports about your accident from the TV downstairs, and Gavin talking about the Evolutionaries taking me away. So, I escaped. Safety in numbers, right?"

I shook my head. "Makes my life seem pretty tame."

"Doubt it!" She turned in her seat and pulled her knees up to her chin, looking at me expectantly.

If there was one thing I found hard to resist, it was an audience. "I guess there was that time when I was six that I put on Dad's uniform cap, and scared the hell out of Mom by jumping off the roof with cardboard wings…"

Kess and I continued swapping stories until we forgot about the others and laughed too loud. Marcus grunted in his sleep, and we fell silent, sharing conspiratorial looks.

I thought about how much I enjoyed Kestrel's company. She wasn't just a pretty girl. I felt — hoped — that we were developing a genuine friendship, something that had once seemed impossible after puberty kicked in. I continued stealing glances at her, and was encouraged to see the faint smile remaining on her face as she absentmindedly played with the ends of her feathers poking out from under her jacket.

After a while, Kestrel insisted that I let her drive. Falcon stopped the pickup behind us and followed our example, swapping drivers. Gratefully, I climbed into the seat behind Kestrel, Raven giving me a brief smile as she scooted over. Marcus moved into the front passenger seat as it was too cramped in the back for two tall guys with wings to rest comfortably. With Kestrel and Tui behind the wheels, our convoy returned to the road.

Soon I was dozing. Some hours later, I was vaguely aware of the car stopping again for another changeover, but I nodded off before I could take in any details.

Soft voices woke me from a restless dream. As I stirred, the muted discussion stopped. I peered through heavy eyelids and saw Marcus was driving again, with Raven in the front passenger seat.

I tried to shift position, but there was a warm weight holding me in place. Blinking, I found Kestrel had put a folded sweater on my lap as a pillow. She had one hand under her head, and the other trailed on the floor by my feet. The wing-lump under her jacket was pressed into the back of the seat, and my hand was resting on her shoulder.

Confused, I glanced forward, and noticed Marcus watching me in the rear-view mirror. Just as that was starting to feel really weird, his pale gray eyes flicked back to the road, and he made no further acknowledgement. It felt so surreal, I wondered if I was still dreaming.

Hesitantly, I brushed some of Kestrel's long blonde hair off her face. She smiled in her sleep, and I quickly looked out the window. *Okay, before this gets any more awkward, I'd like to wake up, please.*

Instead, Kestrel jerked awake as Marcus turned off the highway and the car bumped across extremely rough ground. She scrubbed at her eyes. Suddenly remembering where she was, she struggled upright and gave me a sheepish grin. I smiled back uncertainly.

The sedan jolted over the rocky, scrub-scattered ground, revealed in sharp splashes of color and shadow by the headlights. The sky was barely beginning to lighten in what I assumed was the east, almost directly ahead of us.

"This car is – not built for – off-f-f-f-roading," Kestrel said, as we were bounced around.

"Where are we?" I asked quickly, between jolts.

Marcus didn't look up. "Arizona."

When nothing else was offered, I guessed it didn't really matter. We could always check on the satphone later, if we needed to.

After a bruising half hour or so, during which time we couldn't have gone more than a few miles, the lightening sky revealed a range of rugged hills rising from the desert scrub ahead. The tallest one in the middle barely qualified for the title of 'mountain'. By the time the sun was squinting over the top, the car had bounced into the mouth of one of the countless canyon-like valleys slashing into the foothills.

I was looking ahead in some dismay at the rising ground and increasing piles of broken rock, when the sedan jerked around a particularly jagged outcrop and crunched to a halt. The pickup followed, and parked next to the steep stone wall.

Everyone emerged, stumbling as they stretched, and the first hunger rumbles seemed to echo off the rocks.

Laughing and commiserating about our endless new appetites, we worked together to make our first proper meal as a group. The packets of food we'd consumed on the drive already made a significant pile of trash in the back of the pickup, but there was something more meaningful about cooking and eating together.

As we got to work, we peeled off our jackets and stretched out our wings. Black, gold, multiple shades of brown. Feathers much richer in color, pattern and texture than I had been able to see before. And everyone's wings matched their natural hair color. I felt a slight thrill of satisfaction as the evidence for my keratin theory stacked up.

Sitting on a rock next to me, Kestrel extended her golden wings as far back and as straight as they could go, the tips of her feathers reaching about eight feet behind her. I had to consciously turn my eyes away so she wouldn't see me staring, and caught Miguel looking at her too.

A surge of rivalry rose in my chest, but I stamped on it quickly. I might have only known Miguel for a few days but, somehow, I knew I already had a stronger connection with him than any other guy I knew, even Nico. Maybe, I mused, because our situation stripped away all the petty problems that dominated high school friendships. Out here, our priorities were aligned through necessity, and now there were seven of us learning to hang out and work together. I wasn't going to let my attraction to a girl ruin that.

Not yet, anyway.

17

KESTREL

As we ate a strangely satisfying breakfast of rehydrated scrambled egg and potato mash with a side of cereal bar, the sun skipped higher and the shadows shrank back as if they were seeking shelter in the rocks too. The temperature was already climbing. The dry heat of the desert air was a sharp contrast to the damp chill of the forest.

I put my empty plate on the ground and sighed. "That feels so much better."

"Hell, yeah." Hawk flexed his brown wings vigorously. There was a loud ripping noise, and he froze.

"What was that?" He tried to turn and see what had happened.

I started laughing, and some of the others joined in. "You've ripped your shirt."

As Hawk experimentally moved his wings, he discovered there was more air brushing across the skin of his back than a few moments ago. The two slits in his t-shirt were now ragged tears from his shoulder blades to the hem, leaving a dangling strip between his wings, and the sides flapping open.

"Oh, damn," he said, disgusted. "I'm going to run out of clothes."

I grinned. "You'll have to go native and wear a loincloth. Very angelic, or so I hear."

Falcon wolf-whistled and Hawk flipped him the bird. "I refuse to cast off civilisation just because civilisation has cast *me* off," he said with great dignity, which was undermined by his efforts to tuck the end of the new strip and two corners of his shirt into the waistband of his jeans.

I saw that this attempt to control his clothing wouldn't last long, and wondered what on Earth we'd do as our wings kept growing and complicating the mechanics of simply pulling on a T-shirt. Regular clothes clearly wouldn't be practical for much longer, and I had a brief vision of the seven of us running around like feral children in the torn remains of human fashion.

Then, the loincloth joke suddenly blossomed into a new idea.

"Hawk, turn around," I said, gesturing in a small circle with my finger.

Looking bemused, Hawk obeyed. Then he yelped in protest as I grabbed the loose strip and ripped it free from the rest of his shirt.

"What the hell, Kestrel?"

"Stand still, I'm not finished yet."

Later, I was impressed with myself and how bold I'd been, but at the time I was too focused on the experiment to think about how close I was standing behind Hawk, or how confidently I nudged his large brown wings aside as I reached forward to wrap the strip around his belly, stretching it as far as the material would give. It wasn't *quite* long enough to tie off at the back, and I stood there for a moment between his wings, holding the ends closed and frowning. Then Tui appeared beside me with some safety pins from the kit we'd lifted from the department store.

When I finished, I stepped back and dramatically brushed off my hands. "How does that feel?"

"Weird." Hawk tried to look over his wings to see what I'd done.

"Not too tight?"

He snorted. "How tight is it supposed to be?"

"Snug enough to keep your clothing on, but loose enough so you can breathe and move, you spoon."

"Oh."

Tui chuckled, but her face was full of speculation as she eyed Hawk's new fashion.

Hawk experimentally flexed his wings and twisted from side to side. "Seems to be working, so far."

"You're welcome," I said pointedly. "It'll do for now, but if our wings keep growing like this, then we'll have to find more practical, long-term clothing solutions."

"How big will our wings get?" Tui asked. "How long do you think our bodies will be able to handle it before they're just *too* big?"

Falcon grunted and stared at his own wing, resting on the dirt next to him. "I don't think there'll be much of a weight issue. Isn't it the feathers growing longer, rather than the bone and muscle? Feathers don't weigh much."

"But if you feel down to the end of your wing arm," Hawk said, trying to demonstrate without whacking anyone in the face, "it's much further away than when they first popped out, don't you think?"

"Where's the end of your arm?"

"Under those feathers." Hawk pointed.

"Which ones?"

"The ones near the end ... not those sticky-outy ones, the *top* ones. On the front edge." Hawk gave up. "Damn it, what do you call different types of feathers?"

"I don't even know what to call *myself*, let alone the parts of my wings or different types of feathers," Falcon said, throwing up his hands in exasperation. "Or even different parts of a feather."

As I quietly pulled out my phone and typed 'bird wing diagram feathers' into Google, Tui leaned forward on her knees and tapped her mouth, thoughtfully. "What do we call ourselves now, bro?"

"I don't think we technically count as human anymore." Despite his smile, there was a trace of sadness in Miguel's voice.

I looked up from the phone, suddenly remembering what we'd overheard at the rally. "What about the name that Evolutionary guy was using. Icari?"

"What does that mean?" Falcon demanded. Hawk and I took turns explaining, and Fal was unimpressed. "They've named us after some old myth?"

"It doesn't sound that bad," Hawk said.

"Yeah, but you just said he *died*. His wings weren't so great. Why would you want to be named after him?" Falcon said.

"His dad didn't die though," I said. "And he was the one who made the wings."

"Yeah, but he was the reason they were locked up in the first place," Tui pointed out.

Miguel shrugged his wings. "Why not take it as a morality tale instead of a bad omen?"

"Don't fly too high?" Fal snorted. "Not much of a motto."

"It's a warning not to take our wings for granted."

"We still don't know why we've got these frickin' things in the first place." Falcon began pacing, his dark wings flexing. "Doesn't it bother any of you? Don't you want to know why, and how?"

"Of course we do, bro!" Tui said. "We've just been a little distracted trying to survive. But where the bloody hell would we go for answers?"

Hawk slowly raised a finger, frowning as he thought. "What about the other thing that guy said?"

"What *now*?" Falcon turned on him, his feathers flaring.

Hawk held up his hands. "Whoa, dude, relax. I'm not the bad guy, remember? I'm just as confused as you."

Falcon subsided, looking slightly embarrassed but still defiant. "What are you talking about?"

"When we were eavesdropping at the rally thing outside the bookstore, Kestrel, Miguel and I heard that Evolutionary guy say something. When he was talking about the 'Icari', he said some guy's name."

"Goldberg," I said. "He said, Goldberg's Icari."

Falcon frowned again, slumping back down onto his boulder. "What does that mean?"

"Not a clue." Hawk spread his hands. "I'm guessing it's the name of someone, but who, or what he's got to do with us, I've no idea."

"Does the name mean anything to anyone?" I asked, gazing around. Hawk shrugged and Falcon and Tui shook their heads. Miguel kicked moodily at the ground, and Marcus and Raven remained blank. They hadn't looked up at all during the entire conversation, hadn't fidgeted or shifted or anything. It was almost unnatural.

I did a quick search on the satphone. Nothing. Nothing useful, anyway.

"There's still the IVF idea," Hawk said. "Marcus? Raven? Do you know if you were IVF babies?"

After a pause, Marcus and Raven nodded silently.

"So, if we were all IVF, and from the same clinic," I said, "I wonder how many others are out there, still hiding."

Hawk sat up straighter, as did the others. "What do you mean?"

"Well, for whatever reason, after our wings came out, we all chose to leave our families. How many more might have done the opposite? Stayed with their families, who took them to the doctor. Or kept them in hiding."

"If anyone went to the doctor, they could be locked up in a lab by now." Hawk shuddered.

"There must be others," Falcon said, brightening. "It can't be that there are only seven of us in the world and we all happened to coincidentally hide and then run to the same place."

"I was on the other side of the planet," Tui said. "So, there might be more in other countries too."

"It all sounds great, but there's not enough evidence." Hawk slumped back on his wing elbows. "Only four of us were IVF for sure, two of us have no idea, and Tui was apparently a surprise so couldn't possibly have been IVF."

"Sorry," Tui said, shrugging.

"Another dead end," Falcon said. "God, I hate this!"

Miguel twitched. "Maybe it's a test," he said, carefully.

Falcon frowned. "Some freaking test. How do we know if we pass or fail, then?"

Miguel jumped to his feet. "We'll find out when we're meant to. In the meantime, we have to do our best." He softened his agitation and tried to smile. "I'm sure we'll find out that it's a blessing, in the end. There must be a reason for this."

"Yeah? Well, I wish we knew what it was." Falcon also jumped up and resumed pacing. "It was torture growing these things, not knowing what the hell was going on. I tried strapping them down, hoping they'd stop. I even thought about cutting the frickin' things off, but I'm too much of a chicken to go through with it."

There was another long, awkward silence after Falcon's outburst. He stopped pacing and stared at the rock wall of the little valley. Eventually, Tui reached up and took his hand. "Everything's going to be okay, Fal." She coaxed him back down onto the rock beside her.

Miguel remained standing, his hand playing with his crucifix. "It will be worth it."

Falcon glared at him, but I jumped in quickly. "The flying does make it worth it. Once you can fly, it's just ... I mean, we can only fly for like a minute at a time, and it's still incredible."

Immediately Falcon perked up, and Tui smiled. "I can't wait to fly," she said, and the longing in her voice was something we all understood perfectly. "Weren't we going to make some tails?"

I started explaining what we'd learned in the forest, and carefully drew Miguel into the conversation. Much to my relief, he and Falcon seemed to get along okay again, discussing how to construct the four new sets of tails with increasing enthusiasm.

Hawk leaned back and gazed around the group. "What do you call a group of bird-kids?" he asked. "Or Icari, or whatever. A herd? A gaggle? A flock?"

"A flight," Marcus said.

"What?" The others paused the discussion to listen in.

"Not a flock," Marcus said, although it looked like he was regretting drawing attention to himself. "A flight."

Another pause.

"That, I can live with," Falcon said at last. For the first time, there was general agreement.

Looking around at my new family, the Flight, I felt a moment of complete happiness, a moment of total peace and belonging, for the first time in a long time. When I crossed gazes with Hawk, I saw a slight crooked smile on his face too. I didn't know how or why we'd ended up together, but the important thing was that none of us were alone.

The Flight worked hard all day to make four new tails. Our only breaks were to eat or work on our flapping technique, while waiting for the next website to load on my phone. We were desperate for every drop of information that might help us, and eager to learn which feathers were primary (the big end ones), secondary (the medium-sized middle ones) and tertiary (the smallest ones). Covert feathers covered the base of our other feathers, making the whole wing more aerodynamic. And so on. It was fascinating.

We finally finished up not long before sunset, and then had to concentrate on making camp for the night.

"We have enough water for another day or two, and then we'll have to find a fresh source," Tui said, lining up all our containers and bottles.

"Yeah, and I wouldn't go near the current latrine for a while," Falcon said, grinning, hooking a thumb over his shoulder and pointing up the little canyon. "We're gonna need a better system."

Tui and I were suitably disgusted, but Hawk and even Miguel seemed to find that hilarious. As usual, Marcus and Raven stayed silent, watching the rest of us, though every now and then there'd be a hint of a smile on their faces as jokes were cracked and food was shared.

The stars flickered on one by one, then ten by ten, and finally by the hundreds and thousands. The conversation became slower and quieter. It was as if we'd been camping together a dozen times before. Miguel even felt comfortable enough to kneel nearby for his regular evening prayer.

As we spread the sleeping bags in a circle around the small camping stove, Hawk took the spot on one side of me while I talked to Tui on the other. Miguel took his place just beyond Hawk, Falcon kept close to Tui's other side, and Marcus and Raven completed the circle opposite me.

"One night, I want to fly under the stars," Falcon announced from his sleeping bag.

There were murmurs of agreement as we stared up at the stunning night sky.

"It's going to take a lot of hard work," Hawk said, "but it will be totally worth it."

"We're not that far ahead of you, so it won't take long for the rest of you to catch up," I said, yawning.

"Speak for yourself," Hawk muttered, and chuckled.

I rolled over and gave him a look. "You better watch your tail, Hawk," I said, poking one finger over the edge of my sleeping bag at him. "This Icarus girl's got plenty more tricks she hasn't told you about, yet."

"That sounds like a challenge."

"That's because it is."

"You're on." Hawk winked at me.

I giggled, and wanted so badly to stay awake and flirt with Hawk some more. He was the only person on the planet who knew exactly what I'd done in my past, and he hadn't judged me at all. The complete opposite of everyone else in my life to date. But I couldn't fight the exhaustion from multiple disrupted nights, extreme stress, and growing two new limbs at a ridiculous rate.

Still smiling, I crashed into sleep.

I was the first to wake the next morning. It was still so early, there were a few stars faintly visible in the blush of dawn. Around me, the heavy breathing and snuffling of my new friends, my new family, the Flight, was comforting. I smiled to myself, snuggling deeper into the sleeping bag. *Maybe I should try get another half hour of dozing*, I thought.

Then someone rolled over, snorted, and farted in their sleep.

I thought I would pass out from trying to hold in my giggles. I didn't want to figure out who it had been, because I needed to be able to look the Flight in their mutated eyes for the rest of the day. There was certainly no rolling over and trying to doze off again after that.

However, as the rough ground wasn't exactly the type of surface to encourage sleeping in, and a lack of curtains – as well as windows, walls, doors, and a roof – meant that the growing light was nudging everyone else awake too. Soon, seven teenagers were up and about with far more energy and enthusiasm than we'd probably ever felt at that time before, and there was only one topic of conversation on everyone's lips.

Today we would finally fly. Properly.

As we ate our rationed (but huge by normal standards) breakfast, I pulled up a satellite map of the area on my satphone. We needed a new campsite. Although we were all city kids, Hawk turned out to be a closet survivalist. His years of cadet training and a tough military dad meant he was a mine of useful information, such as where we were most likely to find water in a desert.

"There," he said, zooming in on the map. Sure enough, there was a glint of water in the satellite photo, although it wasn't high res.

"There isn't much gas left in the tanks," Falcon reminded us. "When we move the cars, it'll probably be for the last time."

"Then when we do finally leave, it'll be under our own power," said Hawk.

The rest of us took a moment to absorb that incredible thought. Falcon broke the silence, waving his hands and wings in excitement.

"Imagine flying long-distance, like geese!"

"We'll have to try formations," Hawk said, just as enthusiastically.

Tui coughed loudly. "Yeah, but how about we actually learn to fly first, before we start counting chickens or whatever?"

Despite everyone's desperation to climb straight up the mountain and launch ourselves into the air, we decided to first relocate the camp and allow the desert thermals time to 'power up', as Falcon put it. Even with our sharp eyesight, the interstate was barely visible on the horizon, and we felt safe enough to travel in broad daylight.

After picking our way along the lower reaches of the hills, the two vehicles eventually bounced into the mouth of a deeper, narrower valley. A trickle of water flowed through it. But it was not to be so easy. The terrain was rugged, and we soon had to abandon the pickup and sedan, continuing up the valley on foot. After a fair bit of moaning and significant effort, during which I fervently hoped that Hawk knew what he was talking about, we finally reached a flat area near a shallow pool in a bend of the desert stream. The tall rock walls protected the site and kept the harsh sun off the water for long enough to avoid total evaporation. It was perfect.

"And right up there should be our take-off platform," Hawk puffed as he dumped his load in a pile on the ground.

"Now can we start flight training?" Falcon pleaded.

Hawk's eyes brightened. "Setting up camp can wait, can't it?"

I laughed as Tui and Miguel nodded eagerly.

"Let's fly!"

Scrambling, slipping, and flapping our way up the valley wall, we emerged on a small plateau into a light breeze. High above, the local birdlife was already taking advantage of the massive columns of air rising from the sun-cooked rock. On one side, the head of the mountain watched over us. Stretching into the distance on the other side, the cracks in the ground became wider and more frequent, revealing the presence of the developing canyon system. At some point, I was sure, it reached all the way into the system of rivers that eventually formed the Grand Canyon. I made a mental note to check on the satphone as soon as it recharged in the sun.

We were too eager to fly to stay gawking at the view for long. Hawk, Miguel and I helped the others strap up, and we all took turns falling over as we practised the new hooking system of twist-rotate-attach. The new flight boots not only made the tails more comfortable to wear, they were also a more stable surface to strap onto.

Then, after a quick recap of flapping technique, Hawk scrambled up onto a nearby boulder.

"Here goes," he said. He took two steps back, then sprinted and dived off the rock.

As the Flight cheered, his wings flapped down confidently and powerfully. A massive gust of wind and dust swirled around us. His legs straightened, the tail hooked together, and I could feel my own muscles gently tightening and twitching in time with Hawk's, watching each stage of the technique and imagining my own wings doing the same.

Before he reached the end of the plateau, he rolled sideways, letting his right wing angle down and lifting his left wing high. There were a few wobbles, but his flight curved around, losing only a metre or so of height before he quickly resumed flapping, heading straight back for us.

We scattered as he came into land. His flapping became rougher and ragged as he tried to convert forward motion into a gentle descent. He brought his legs down but didn't get his tail unhooked before his feet hit the ground, and he flapped frantically to stay upright before collapsing in a heap.

Before the dust had cleared, we could hear him laughing.

"Again!" he yelled as Falcon hauled him to his feet.

"Wait your turn, flyboy," I said, grinning.

Miguel went next, and before he'd even completed his first turn at the far end of the training ground, I had scrambled up onto the boulder.

This time, I felt no hesitation. Opening my wings, I felt my ribs expand, and as I sucked in a deep breath of dry desert air, I began to run.

I jumped and flapped. The powerful surge of energy that swirled through my body made me gasp, and then laugh. For a moment I was weightless. Then I swept my wings forward again. Stretching my legs, my flapping faltered as I spent too long hooking up my tail. But it clicked, and my legs lifted. I beat my wings again and again, as fast as I could, to regain the height I'd lost in those precious few seconds. My heart pumped my blood at top speed, making my head light and my body tremble with adrenaline. My chest and back already ached, but I pushed through the burn.

In a few moments, I was shooting toward the large ravine, a gaping crack in the rock that sliced off the end of the plateau.

As I entered empty space, I lifted one wing high and pressed the other down, trying to roll sideways. In those few seconds I stopped flapping, gently sailing in an uneven curve. I felt the centrifugal force pull my legs outwards. Looking down into the ravine, I saw it was much deeper than I had realised. *If my wings failed me now, I wouldn't survive the fall.*

I flapped again and shot back over the plateau, leaving the deadly drop behind in my dust.

I saw Falcon jump into the air, yelling in triumph as his wings kept him there. As soon as he was clear, Tui followed.

I didn't want to land, but I needed a rest. Even the massive breaths that I drew into my lungs every time I flapped weren't providing enough oxygen, and my muscles were burning too hotly for me to ignore.

Remembering Hawk's mistake, I unhooked my tail before I changed the angle of my wings. I hit the rock hard, hissing as the ground-shock stung my feet through my flight boots, but I stayed upright.

"Nice flying," Hawk said, jogging over. He held up his hand and I slapped a high five.

"Everyone's doing brilliantly," I said, panting, as I turned to watch the others awkwardly circling the plateau.

"If it wasn't for the extreme physical effort and brain-draining concentration, I'd say it was almost easy," he said.

We laughed. Tilting my head back, I looked up at the distant blue sky. Hawk followed my gaze. Only the faintest hints of thin feathery clouds were visible. "We'll be way up there, soon," I said. And his smile told me that day couldn't come soon enough.

The rest of the Flight landed one by one, collapsing on the ground with faces flushed, chests heaving, and eyes bright. It might have been short, but it had been sweet. The adrenaline and sheer joy were almost tangible in the hot air.

And within half an hour, after a quick snack to refuel, we were ready to go again.

18

KESTREL

By the end of the day, the whole Flight had completed multiple laps around the plateau. Hawk and Miguel managed more than the rest of us, having had those few extra days of training in the forest, but even they were visibly exhausted as we slowly climbed back down to camp.

"This is crazy," Falcon said as his butt hit his rolled-up sleeping bag. "I thought it'd take much longer to learn to fly."

"I'm knackered," Tui said, sitting down next to him. "But it's bloody amazing."

I smiled and stretched my aching muscles. "Our wings are already big enough for a short flight with a lot of effort. Imagine how easy it will be when they're full size, and we're not only fitter but actually know what we're doing!"

Falcon opened his dark-brown wings out wide, almost knocking Raven over. "Sorry, Raven. How big would you say my wings are now?"

Hawk called her over. "There's room here, Rave, out of Falcon's way." When she edged over to sit next to him, he totally failed to hide his surprised-but-pleased look. I turned away, ashamed to admit that I felt … jealous. But, when I glanced over again, I saw something different in the way Hawk was speaking to the small, mute Chinese girl. And I remembered the way he'd talked about his little sister that night in the car. How protective he'd been of her. And my heart ached for him. Unlike Hawk, I was actually enjoying being away from my family.

Miguel cheerfully stretched his black wings against Falcon's dark feathers, and an intense discussion about size and length occupied the next half hour. Finally, we agreed that, on average, the boys' wingspans were roughly fourteen feet from tip to tip, with each segment being about a quarter of the overall length. When their wings were in what Hawk was semi-jokingly calling the 'angel fold', their longest feathers nearly touched the ground behind them. In the 'full fold', the tips tickled the back of their necks.

We girls were all much smaller in frame, so our wings measured about twelve feet (or about three and half metres, as Tui and I grumbled) but our primary feathers still nearly touched the ground when in the relaxed fold. It still felt a little weird allowing my wings to be so free, instead of hiding them away as tightly as possible.

As night fell, we couldn't rest, because we had to clear the ground for our campsite. After moving dozens of stones and pebbles, enough dust and sand was left for a thin carpet on the bedrock. There was some scrubby vegetation around the place that we could use as firewood. A deep crack, far downstream and protected by several big boulders, was appointed as a latrine. After spotting a few creepy crawlies, we shoved some of the surrounding rocks away so they had fewer hiding spots within stinging range when we literally had our pants around our ankles.

The entire Flight was feeling the strain as we came down off our high, but that didn't stop the excited chatter and eager discussion about how to improve our flying technique, which continued as we set up camp.

"My eyes are dried out," Tui complained eventually. There was a chorus of agreement.

Scrambling up, I dug through the supplies. "It had crossed my mind, but I forgot about it this morning. Hopefully these will work." I handed out the sports sunglasses I'd insisted on taking, goggle straps and all.

I blushed as the Flight, including Miguel, congratulated me on my stroke of genius. We'd now be able to fly faster and teach ourselves to dive without worrying about desiccated eyeballs or, as Hawk pointed out, bug strike.

As I glanced around the Flight, I saw that Raven's pale features were very pink. Marcus was burnt as well. Hawk, Tui, Falcon and Miguel, with their melanin-richer skin, were fine. Using the front camera in my phone to check my face, I groaned. "I wondered why I was still feeling so hot."

"It doesn't look too bad," Miguel said, comfortingly.

"At least I also grabbed the sunscreen. I'll have to remember to actually apply it, though!"

Tui peered closely at my pink face. "Nah, it's not bad. If we were in New Zealand, you'd be a crayfish by now."

"Crayfish?"

"You'd call them lobsters." She grinned, her teeth white against her Polynesian skin. "You'd be red *as*, mate!"

Marcus and Raven were fascinated by the new colour of their faces, and discreetly checked themselves in their shared phone more times than seemed necessary. I wondered if they'd ever been sunburned before.

Then someone's phone beeped, sounding like a radar ping. It was just a novelty tone, but it still made me flinch from the sudden flash of the obvious. The GPS in my satphone was theoretically protected from being hacked, but I had no idea what sort of security — if any — Marcus and Raven, Falcon, Miguel, and Tui had on their devices. Hawk was still phoneless, but didn't seem to mind.

"Hey guys," I said, casually. "Just thinking about our phones. Shouldn't we put them into—" I paused to grin in anticipation of the pun, *"flight mode?"*

I was rewarded with a muddle of groans and chuckles, but after I explained why, everyone quickly agreed it was a good idea. Hawk pointed out that it would not only avoid inadvertently giving away our position, but also would help conserve battery.

As Hawk and Tui swapped stories about phones going off at awkward times,Falcon kicked a trash-stuffed plastic bag towards Miguel. "Come on, show me what you got, Mexico!"

I could see Miguel was caught between following through on his promise to help Tui with dinner and his obvious desire to have some fun.

"Go on, I'll help Tui," I said, taking the can of stove fuel from him. "Just don't expect the girls to do all the cooking all the time!"

With increasing skill and confidence, Miguel fielded every kick Falcon sent his way.

"You'll have to do better than that to get past me," Miguel said as Falcon groaned at his fifth failed goal attempt.

"Hawk, help a brother out!" Falcon called.

Miguel laughed. "That's not fair!"

"Marcus, how about you?" Hawk beckoned the big quiet guy. "Want to join Miguel's team?"

Marcus looked at the 'ball'. "Raven is better," he said, twitching a pale gold wing.

"Go on, Raven, represent the girls," I said, cheering.

The Flight whooped as Raven shyly got up, and took her place behind Miguel. With the boys taunting each other, the game resumed.

Raven was doing quite well, usually managing to make foot-contact with the ball when it came near her, but then she saved a goal with a quick whip of her wing.

Falcon blew a loud whistle with his fingers. "Time out!" he yelled. "Doesn't that count as hand ball?"

"It's a wing, not a hand!" Miguel said, laughing.

"But it's *foot*ball."

"We need clearer rules."

Falcon tried to bounce the ball on his knees, then transfer it to his wing. But he hit it too hard and it sailed straight at me and Tui, and the dinner we were heating on the camp stove. Tui easily deflected it with a quick hand, and it landed harmlessly into the dust.

"Whoops, sorry, babe!" Falcon shouted.

With a little sigh and slight smile, Tui tossed the ball back to Raven, who immediately kicked it past Falcon. Delighted, Miguel declared another goal, while Hawk dissolved into laughter at Falcon's face.

"So, Tui ... are you and Falcon, like, *together,* together?" I whispered.

Tui snorted. "Yeah, nah. He thinks so, but we aren't."

Falcon, having obviously heard, mimed taking a shot to the heart. "I'm wounded," he announced, falling dramatically to the ground. Miguel immediately kicked the ball past him and awarded his team another point.

"Stuff this, I'm on Miguel's team next time," Falcon said. "Sorry, Hawk, but I like to win."

"That's okay, I'll join Raven's team, if she'll have me!" Hawk grinned. "She's going to make a great goalie."

Blushing from both embarrassment and the effort, Raven nodded and tucked a loose strand of hair behind her ear.

While the boys kept messing with each other, she slipped back to sit next to Marcus, who touched her hand as they shared a glance.

"What do you think about them, then?" I murmured to Tui. "You reckon they're a couple?"

"Why does anyone have to be in a relationship?" Tui sighed. "We're only seventeen, it's not like it's the bad old days when we would have all been married off already."

"Didn't date much at high school, then?" I asked.

"I didn't have time, sis. Too busy with study, working part-time and training with the St. John ambulance cadets so I could get into nursing school." Her face was serious as she clunked the pot around. "Even though I'm only seventeen, I'd just been accepted. My division leader had nominated me for a full scholarship. All my hard work was finally paying off. Then this happened." She flicked a wing irritably.

"You could still be a nurse, one day," I said hopefully.

She rolled her eyes. "Yeah, right."

"Okay, so maybe not in a regular human hospital. But we're going to need specialist Icarus doctors and stuff, I guess. Maybe you could be the first."

Tui's face lost the fierce scowl and softened into something more thoughtful, the light from the camp stove's flame playing across her skin and feathers in the gathering dusk. "I guess we really don't count as human anymore. But where the hell would I go to train?"

"We're still mostly human!" I protested, gesturing to my body. "Arms, legs, organs, brain. We might have a few extra limbs, and really good senses, but we're still going to break and get sick at some point."

"Hmm." Tui ladled the food into the bowls I'd set out on the rock. "I guess all the basic principles of first aid and biology and chemistry and stuff haven't changed. We can't fight the laws of the universe." She smiled slightly.

"I'd bet money that most of our DNA is still human, just with a few extra bits." I flexed my wing. "A few brilliant bonus bits."

"Our bio teacher made our class debate how to define a human, once. It got loud."

"Why's that?" I asked. As the rest of the Flight gathered around, drawn by the smell of the food, they listened in.

"The question actually was: *How do you define a member of a species?*"

Hawk scraped his spoon in his bowl. "Can't you tell by looking?"

"What about caterpillars and butterflies, bro?" Tui countered. "Same species, totally different appearance."

"DNA, then," Falcon suggested.

"Yeah, but everyone's DNA is different, that's why we aren't clones. At what point do you say it's different enough to be a different species?"

Hawk thought hard. "Is it the ability to reproduce? Different breeds of dog look totally different but they're still the same species, right?"

I remembered something from my own science classes at early high school in England. "Horses and donkeys are different species, and they can mate and make mules. But the mules are infertile because of the DNA clash."

"And then people with infertility issues wouldn't be considered 'human' either," Tui said. "That would include a huge number of people."

"My head hurts," I pleaded.

Hawk groaned in sympathy. "Mine too."

Tui smiled thinly. "Now you know why the classroom debate didn't go well. Especially with an extremely Christian teacher aide in the mix."

In the increasing gloom beyond the glow of the camping stove, I saw Miguel's distressed face, and the way he was clutching his cross. Across from him, Falcon and Hawk were more thoughtful than upset, and Marcus and Raven seemed almost disappointed that the discussion was stuttering to a halt. For a moment, I thought maybe Marcus was about to say something, but he kept his mouth firmly closed.

"I know one thing for totally certain," I announced brightly, determined to cheer everyone up before bedtime.

"What's that?"

"I don't care how we define it, but I know that we belong together." I gestured with my arm and my wing. "We might not be human, but we are us."

"Ick-are-us," Hawk added, grinning.

An appreciative chuckle rolled around the Flight and the tension eased. I knew it was a discussion that would return, probably soon, but I had said what I honestly believed to be true. And I would defend that conviction with everything I had in me, mutant DNA and all.

In the morning, the Flight woke to find Marcus quietly working on a series of diagrams drawn in the dust. Next to him, he had laid out our tails.

"Better lift," he said, not meeting anyone's eyes.

"Worth a shot," Falcon said, and I noticed Marcus's quiet surprise and a hint of pleasure as the Flight worked to incorporate his suggestions; tightening a strut here, twisting a curve there, enhancing and strengthening the overall aerofoil shape.

The improvements were noticeable as soon as we were in the air, and we showered him with praise and thanks. Eventually, it got too much for him, and he retreated from the group a little way, until we were distracted by food.

But the Flight didn't forget, and over the coming days we came to rely on his opinion when discussing adjustments in technique and gear. Slowly, Marcus became more confident. Although he still spoke with as few words as possible, he occasionally began to offer a thought or suggestion before he was asked, like a quiet but watchful older brother. And whenever he did, it was always with such insight or meaning that one night Tui chuckled.

"You're such a wise old owl, Marc," she said. "You just sit there, watching us with those big blinking eyes and then suddenly you'll say something that no one can argue with."

"What do you say, Marc? Do you think you're an Owl?" Hawk said, also laughing. "Do you want to take a new name?"

Marcus considered that for a moment. Then he shrugged. "New names, new beginnings."

Then the whole Flight was laughing. Even Raven smiled, ducking her head. The newly christened Owl blinked, a smile twitching at the corners of his lips. After a while though, he retreated beside Raven, keeping out of the spotlight for the rest of the evening.

Raven spent much of her downtime doodling in the dirt, practising elegant Chinese calligraphy. She still never spoke, but she'd willingly join in the occasional trashball game, and it was eventually noticed that whichever team she was on tended to win.

"You're a good luck charm, aren't you, Rave!" Hawk said, as he high-fived her after their third consecutive win. She blushed, and her smile was more open than it had ever been before.

"Everybody loves Raven," I murmured to Tui as we sat obsessively tidying the feathers on our tails.

"Of course they do, she's like the Flight's little sister," Tui said. "I wish my real sister was that chilled out and fun. And quiet."

"Do you miss her?"

"Yeah, nah." Tui sighed and leaned back on her wing elbows. "I don't miss having to look after her. It's hard enough looking after me sometimes."

"And Falcon." Smiling, I glanced sideways. The African American Icarus was wrestling with Hawk in the dust, while

Miguel and Raven kicked the trashball back and forth between themselves, patiently waiting for the two boys to come to their senses.

When Tui didn't reply, I turned and caught the secret smile on her face. "Oh, come on, spill!" I whispered.

Tui glanced around, then leaned in. "Don't you dare tell anyone else, but I let him kiss me yesterday."

"I don't believe you," I said. "There's no way that could have happened and he wouldn't shout it to the world!"

Tui sniffed and held her head high. "Don't care if you believe me or not."

"When? Where? How? Did he ask first?"

"You lot were busy, we went for a walk, we were talking and then he just kind of asked, and I said yes." Tui shrugged. "What do you want, a blow-by-blow replay?"

"What are you girls whispering about?" Hawk demanded.

"Tails," I said, immediately. "Trying to keep the feathers in line is hard. I keep kicking mine against stuff when I land."

"Me and Miguel talked about grooming, once," Hawk said, dropping beside me, shedding a layer of dust. "Birds do it all the time. Though I have no idea how we would."

Daintily, I brushed the dirt from his blast radius off my tail. "Birds have beaks for the job."

"We made tails. Maybe we can make beak things too?" Tui suggested.

The suggestion turned into a planning session, which turned into an experiment. Eventually we had a Flight set of beak-shaped handheld grooming tools, fashioned from hard plastic rubbish reshaped over the camp stove flame. Even after our first inexpert effort at feather combing, it was clear the 'preeners' had made a significant improvement in the aerodynamics of our wings, reducing the energy we had to spend on each flap. Just like that, we could fly better and longer.

Grooming became a regular ritual. Most of us took turns to partner with others to get those hard-to-reach spots, and I couldn't help but feel an extra thrill every time it was my turn to pair with Hawk. The feeling of his hands on my feathers sent tingles through my skin. I wondered if he felt the same, but I was too shy and wary of rejection to ask. He never seemed to seek out my company especially, like Falcon did with Tui.

And I reminded myself of what Tui had said. A relationship was not the primary goal of my life at that moment — but flying was.

And, for a while, so was the question of clothing. Being in the hotter environment meant we were sweating more, even with our higher core temperatures, and that meant we had to change our clothes more often. The extra two limbs sticking out of our backs was now an issue for everyone. Trying to slide a shirt on over such big 'arms' and then trying to get the feathers out through the holes was almost impossible without destroying the fabric.

Inspired by my improvisation with Hawk's shirt, Tui shredded several of her own shirts into rectangles which she then stitched into one long strip. Raven and I watched in fascination as she experimented with different ways of winding this around herself, finally settling on a strapless wrap that left her wings and arms completely unhindered, and showed off the elegant jade pendant at her throat.

With a confidence that I had lacked even six months before, I eagerly copied Tui and soon found my own preference was for a two-strip criss-cross design that worked like a halter neck and twisted down between my wings before wrapping around my body. It took some practice to get it sitting right, but once it was arranged properly, it was surprisingly comfortable — and, more importantly, was practical for flying while preserving modesty.

Although Tui and I offered to help Raven, she disappeared for a while before returning with her own style. Her full-length shirtsleeves had been left intact with long thin 'straps' of fabric tying around her chest over top of a second shirt that had been sliced into a halter neck with a generous upper back hole. This helped her look older than twelve, and was, I assumed, to protect her ultra-pale skin from the harsh desert sun.

Owl also always wore long-sleeved shirts, and these were gradually getting tighter on his lean frame. He and the other two guys had gradually adopted Hawk's holey-shirt-with-cummerbund improvisation but, judging by Falcon and Hawk's grumbling, they would soon be developing their own male Icarus fashion line. In the meantime, they were more concerned with flight training, and occasionally went shirtless — which both Tui and I quietly found very distracting. Especially as the days went by and their muscles became even more well-defined with the ten-hour-a-day workout.

In fact, we all were becoming visibly toned. There was some good-natured teasing around the campfire, but it was clear the entire Flight was totally committed to doing whatever it took to get properly airborne.

After more than a week of strength conditioning and flight training close to the ground, we were finally confident enough to try flying at altitude. At last, the Flight stood on a shoulder of the mountain, a cliff dropping away from our feet. The summit still towered over us, but we were a good half mile or more above the plain. The air shimmered and I was already sweating.

"And I thought it was warm yesterday! I'm glad it's not the height of summer," Falcon said.

"It should be powering some great thermals, though," I said, flexing my blonde wings in anticipation. "Look at that."

A lazy swirl of hot air was rising just to the north, like a shimmering column of heat.

"That's a *long* way down," Tui said, peering over the edge, her dark wings flexing nervously.

"Why does it make any difference?" Hawk said, surprisingly gently. "If you can fly at ten feet, you can fly at a thousand."

"Yeah, but I'm less dead if I fall from ten feet than a thousand, eh, bro."

"Actually, higher is better because you have more time to correct and recover. More room for error, not less."

"You sound like you've had experience with this," Falcon said, grinning, but his wings were shifting with equal anxiety.

Hawk chuckled. "With machine-powered flight, yes, not—"

A patter of feet on the rock. Raven ran past us, aiming at the edge of the cliff. Diving off the mountain, her wings outstretched and steady, her legs quickly straightened to hook her tail pieces together. She leaned, raising her left wing high. A moment later, she caught the edge of the thermal and began to rise.

The Flight whooped and cheered as Raven moved in wide, easy circles, her wings now flapping regularly, her legs supported by the mini hang-glider tail, arms invisible against her torso. It was a mesmerising sight. She wasn't just swooping around just above the ground, she was hundreds and hundreds of metres in the air, and rising. As she climbed, the Flight took it in turns to follow her lead.

Miguel tried to insist that I go before him, but I refused. I wanted to see all my friends safely in the air before I threw myself into the void. For some reason, which I couldn't explain even to myself, I didn't want anyone watching me in that moment.

Finally, it was just me and the mountain and the beckoning air. I backed up against the rock face.

"Here goes, Kestrel," I said. "Time to earn your wings."

Pulling on my flight goggles, I ran.

Empty air accelerated toward me. As my boots hit the edge, I pushed off as though diving into water. The instinct even made me clap my hands above my head as my feet and tail snapped together. My wings scooped out as wide as they could stretch. There was a heart-stuttering moment of weightlessness, like at the top of a swing's arc. Then the air caught under my feathers.

I yelled for sheer joy, arms spreading out like a second pair of wings. Looking straight ahead at the visible tower of air, I risked that first flap. The hours of practising smoothed out the movement, so I barely felt a reduction in momentum or lift at all. Ecstatic, I flapped again, easing into a steady rhythm of *sweep forward-twist back*. Already familiar, the subtle surging motion was barely noticeable as my feathers sliced through the air, lifting my body higher, propelling it forward.

I was *flying*.

Finally, I glanced down. I was hundreds and hundreds of feet above the unforgiving rock. All that was holding me up was a pair of giant, golden, bird wings somehow grafted onto my body, and all I could feel was pure exhilaration. Enraptured, I gazed at the model landscape until the flicker of the others' tiny shadows distracted me.

Eagerly, I looked forward into the breeze and worked to catch up, the quicker wingbeats stretching and compressing my ribcage with more force, dragging my breath in and out equally rapidly. Soon, I glided into the warm circling air of the thermal. It felt like I was suddenly floating in a warm pool, and I experimentally slowed my pace. As I'd seen with the rest of the Flight, the ascending air pressed under my feathers, reducing my weight and slowing the natural fall that began whenever I stopped flapping. Rolling slightly to my right, I lazily stroked my wings through the rising current and began spiralling up with the thermal to join the others, several hundred feet above.

Although the incredible landscape was a vast expanse of raw natural beauty, and I was certain I could see the edge of the Grand Canyon in the far distance, I kept being distracted by the sight of my own shadow. Tiny but distinct, it flicked up and over the undulating rock, keeping pace with me as I winged my way back and forth between thermals. Despite all the evidence from all my sharp senses, it was still almost unbelievable that I could actually *fly*.

I don't know how long the Flight spent simply circling the mountain that day. We'd ride the first thermal as high as it would go, and then glide over to the next one, not fighting the gentle descent as we did so. No one had the energy or strength for aerobatics, although I knew Hawk wasn't the only one itching to try out some fancy manoeuvres, he was just the most vocal about it. Instead, the Flight basked in the warmth and the bliss and the sheer freedom. No one could catch us, control us, or hurt us. It was everything I ever dreamed flying could be.

And I knew it would only get better from here.

19

MIGUEL

As the days turned into weeks, the Flight trained for longer and longer every day, until we were in the air for most of the daylight hours. The nights were cool and stunningly clear. One night when I climbed the valley wall, away from the small sphere of light cast by our campfire, the whole of Heaven spread out above me, inviting me to soar among the stars. I wondered how much closer I would feel to God if I did. I already felt something bordering on religious ecstasy each time I took flight. But despite our enhanced night vision, everyone was nervous about being too tired to land properly in the dark and too impatient to remain grounded during the day. So, the evenings were for relaxation.

After those first few days, we avoided discussing where our wings came from because it always descended into a pointless, circular argument. Most of us didn't want to talk about our past, myself included. It was still too painfully close. However, as the days flew by, the absence of any visible threat meant that the Flight started to really live again. It was no longer just about survival. We were hanging out together like regular teenagers on an extended camping trip; inventing new games, taking selfies with each other on our 'Flight mode' phones, playing mild pranks, telling spooky stories around the fire.

Ironically, it was the first time I'd ever felt like an ordinary teenager. Since I'd left New York, and all the dramas that followed, I'd been so tied up with the hard grind of work and caring for Abuelita, that I had forgotten how much fun it was just being with friends.

One reason we grew so tight so quickly was, I assumed, because of the sheer physical closeness, the fact we were totally dependent on each other for survival, and the intimacies of the regular grooming sessions. Loose feathers of all sizes were piling up to one side, and it was fascinating to sit with my friends, turning the vanes over and over in our hands, and marveling that we had grown them from our own skins.

Falcon, in his latest enthusiastic effort to make Tui laugh, picked out a few of the smallest feathers (still many inches long), stuck them in his growing afro, and began pulling fierce faces. Or trying to.

She sighed, looking unimpressed. "Not like that, you bloody idiot. You look like a dick." She swiped a couple of the feathers and tucked them into her own hair. After a brief hesitation, she grabbed some charcoal from the fire pit, blackened her lips and drew some swirls on her chin. "Now *this* is how you show who's the warrior." Her face morphed into the most intimidating stare I'd ever seen, her eyes wide, chin lifted and jutting, with her arms lifted and strong and her hands vibrating.

Enraptured, Falcon dropped dramatically to his knees. "Teach me, oh goddess!" Tui snorted but couldn't hide her grin.

While Tui mostly-patiently tried to convert the wannabe into a warrior, and Hawk laughed at his efforts, I glanced around to see where Kestrel had gone.

I found her watching as Raven used a combination of charcoal and damp sandy clay to draw patterns on one of Owl's discarded feathers. Owl himself was close by, as always, silent and protective.

I hunkered down to look closer. "Wow, Raven, that looks incredible."

The tiny Chinese girl glanced up, a faint blush tinging one of her cheeks. The other had a dark smear of black from her stained hands.

I grinned. "You've got a bit of—"

"Don't wipe it!" Kestrel interrupted. Gently, she reached over and added another matching line of charcoal to Raven's other cheek. "You look almost as fierce as Tui," she said, giggling.

As Raven blinked, and Owl handed her their phone to check herself in the camera, Kestrel jumped up. "My turn!"

Hawk came over to see what was going on, and stopped in mid-step when he saw Kestrel applying the thick black lines around her eyes.

"Whoa," he said, and I agreed loudly.

Kess blushed a little as she admired the smoky eye effect in her phone. "You know what else we could do, though," she said as she clicked the device off and slid it into her pocket. "Look at what Raven's done on Owl's feather. Imagine if we put designs on our entire wings."

"I spend too much time grooming already, I don't want to deliberately add more dust and crap to my feathers," Hawk said, groaning.

Kess laughed. "True. All right, we'll save it for a special occasion, then. In the meantime..." She pointed at me. "Miguel would totally suit warpaint, don't you think?"

Even Owl and Raven were drawn into the ensuing tribal face-decorating session, with Kestrel gently applying thick black eyeliner to Raven's wary but hopeful almond eyes, while Hawk and I encouraged Owl to experiment with different patterns on his own fair skin. With Falcon and Tui also 'painted' up in their own unique styles, I lost count of how many photos and selfies and poses the Flight went through over the rest of that afternoon. We were starting to get quite a good collection of action shots too, as our confidence in flight was growing.

It was just more evidence of how strong our new family was — and further proof, as far as I was concerned, that it had been divinely willed.

A few nights later, Tui was playing pop music on her phone while she was taking her turn at making dinner. The acoustics in the canyon, and our good hearing, meant the small inbuilt speaker was more than enough. At first, she was just humming along, but then it seemed one of her favorites came on and she started singing along to the power ballad. By the time it reached the swooping chorus, she was letting rip at full volume and her amazing voice was filling the whole canyon. As we broke into spontaneous cheers, she jumped up on a boulder and belted out the epic climax with a spoon as her microphone, and finished with her arm in the air, her outspread wings casting massive shadows on the rock face behind her, and her voice echoing away down the narrow gully. The Flight filled the space it left behind with enthusiastic applause, and Falcon's wolf-whistling.

Tui bowed. "Thank you, thank you."

She leaped lightly down from the rock and resumed stirring the pot of stew with an airy *What are you looking at?* expression.

"Were you a singer, before?" I asked, over dinner.

Tui shrugged as she swallowed her first mouthful of rehydrated potato. "Not solo. I was in the *kapa haka* group at school. We won a few competitions, it was sweet as."

Falcon turned to face her. "A what?"

"A traditional singing and dance group, I guess, although that makes it sound so old and lame." She made a face. "It was actually really popular. All the cool kids were in the group. Brown, black, white — didn't matter."

"White kids dancing? Whatever," Falcon said.

Hawk shook his head. "Don't look at me. I'm only half white but my sister's got all the moves in our family. I am a master of the meaningful sway but that's where my dancing ends. And don't get me started on singing."

We all laughed hard. Especially Kestrel. While Hawk and I still got on well, I noticed more and more of his attention was shifting toward her. Not that I could blame him. Her English accent stood out from the jumble of the Flight's voices, and she was always everywhere helping everyone. I sometimes wondered if my own attention was increasingly focusing on her just because she was the only unattached girl in the group. But I couldn't deny that the more time I spent with her, the more I wanted to know about her. She was cute, clever, and funny, and she wasn't afraid to stick up for herself.

I tried to tell myself that it was just friendship, but the truth was, I was rapidly falling head-over-tail into infatuation.

I did my best to hide it. The Flight's happiness was more important, and introducing myself as a rival for Kestrel's attention would only cause problems.

I wondered if perhaps Hawk was thinking the same thing, and that was why he never acted on his obvious attraction to her. He certainly showed off more when she was looking his way, and the rate of his joking increased when she was nearby. But he never made a move, and I began to doubt my intuition. Perhaps he really was just being his friendly self, and because of my own feelings I was oversensitive.

But then one morning, when Hawk was the last to wake up, I watched the way his eyes opened and focused on me and Kestrel, taking our turn to make the breakfast.

Abruptly, he shoved his way out of his sleeping bag with a disconcerting tearing sound. Pulling on his boots and grabbing his tail and a granola bar from the communal stash, he stomped away from the campsite without a word to anyone.

My smile faltered as I watched him go.

Kestrel followed my gaze. "Did he get up on the wrong side of the sleeping bag or something?"

I shrugged, although I was certain I knew what was bothering him. Glancing around the campsite, I saw it again. Owl and Raven, Falcon and Tui, me and Kestrel. And then Hawk, by himself.

"Did you hear how his shirt ripped again?" Kestrel said, giggling. "His wings are still growing. They're already the same size as Owl's and he's huge."

"Do you think maybe Hawk's wings are different to ours then?" I asked, moodily stirring the oatmeal some more. I couldn't imagine my wings getting any larger. *And Hawk's are already bigger than mine, and still growing.*

Kestrel looked at me oddly. "Don't tell me that guy thing about size applies to wings as well?"

I blinked at her, then realized what she meant. Blood flooded my face, and I stared determinedly at the pot. "I couldn't say," I said as calmly as possible. Kestrel regarded me for a moment more before the giggles burst from her lips. I liked her laugh, but I was too embarrassed to join in.

As the rest of the Flight gathered around the pot for breakfast, I sat back and tried to sort through my feelings. *Why do I feel so guilty about liking Kestrel? Maybe it's because she isn't Catholic, or even Christian ... I don't think Abuelita would approve.* I glanced sideways at Kestrel, sitting a few feet away. *Besides, I don't think she even likes me in that way.* I sighed.

"Penny for your thoughts?" Kestrel asked softly.

"Worried about Hawk." I avoided her eyes as I admitted this half-truth.

She bit her lip. The expression was incredibly cute, but my heart tripped over itself when I saw the anxiety in her face. *Will she ever be as concerned about me?*

I forced myself to think about the day ahead instead.

"More training today?" I asked, scraping up the last of my breakfast.

Kestrel smiled, the anxiety fading as she visibly made an effort to perk up. "Of course. But later, I think you boys will finally have to commit to sorting out your wardrobes."

"If you say so."

The Flight cleared up and geared up, and soon we were on the plateau. The sun was already high in the sky and so, I realized, was Hawk.

He was clearly experimenting with speed, as he used a thermal to soar higher, and then tucked in his wings and entered a steep dive as he jumped out of the column of air. At first, he didn't dive for long before his wings snapped out again, but he was quickly gaining confidence, diving further and faster each time.

As the Flight watched him dive for the fifth or sixth time, he suddenly lurched to one side. Some of us gasped.

"What was *that*?" Tui asked from where she was sitting on the rock, checking the straps on her tail.

Kestrel didn't take her eyes off Hawk. "Sudden sideways gust of wind, I guess." Whatever it was, he'd pulled out of his dive early, and was now circling above us.

One by one, the Flight launched from a handy ledge of rock, sedately circling up to Hawk's level. That day, there was also a steady updraft from the desert wind, so there was plenty of lift to be borrowed from the air around us with minimal effort.

Not much was said while we slowly circled before beginning the day's training. I simply enjoyed the support of the warm morning air and let my gaze pass over the dry, rocky terrain, scattered with dark bushes. Occasionally a car or truck crawled by on the distant highway, but the Flight was too far away to look like anything but birds in the cloud-scattered sky. Soon I stopped noticing them altogether.

After a while, Hawk led the way by starting to dive again, showing off what he'd learned. One by one, the others took the plunge, diving for as long as they dared before flaring their wings and riding the air elevator back up to a comfortable height. Watching the rest of the Flight practicing did little to reassure me about my own abilities, and it took me a good five minutes to talk myself into trying it.

As I prepared to dive, I instinctively shut my eyes and sucked in a huge breath, sending a prayer to Heaven. Every feather seemed to shiver as I relaxed my outspread wing arms, drawing the elbows close to my back, where I could feel them trembling against my spine. A moment later, gravity noticed me, my head tipped forward, and I began to fall.

My stomach flipped with the sickening feeling of the ground rushing up to hit me. Freefall hummed in my chest and limbs. A few short seconds later my self-preservation reflexes kicked in. My wings snapped out, the air slamming into my feathers and wrenching on my chest. I gasped in relief, thanking God that I was still alive and still airborne, but that taste of adrenaline had been enough. I needed another rush.

Soon I was diving for as long and as fast as the others. Gradually becoming more and more daring, each member of the Flight was soon pushing their personal limits, challenging themselves and each other. After some initial fear that the sheer wind force might tear our wings off, we were beginning to realize that, although our bodies might be the first of their kind, we could trust them as instinctively as we had before the abrupt Change.

The revelation was intoxicating.

Amazingly, as soon as they were in the air, Kestrel and Raven matched Hawk dive for dive. I could tell Hawk was enjoying himself and didn't seem at all bothered by the friendly competition. He hadn't said a word, letting his actions speak for him, but he whooped aloud after each particularly exhilarating or challenging dive.

When we all agreed it was a real effort getting back up to cruising level, the Flight began to descend in a large spiral. No one wanted it to be over, even though we'd been in the air for hours.

I was above everyone but Raven as we descended. Looking down, I admired my friends' outspread wings as they circled slowly lower and lower. Falcon and Tui's dark wings were in stark contrast to the lighter spreads on Kestrel and Owl. Reluctantly, I noted that Hawk's mid-brown wings did look slightly bigger, although now I had a good view, I could see subtle differences in shape and size that were difficult to distinguish when they were only half-open on the ground, or moving in the air. Hawk's wings weren't only wider, they were broader too, as the long feathers along the lower edge of each wing stretched down his thighs. But perhaps he was going through another growth spurt the rest of us had yet to reach.

I was distracted when Kestrel crossed through the air above Hawk. Her long blonde hair had been half-torn out of her ponytail by the wind, and it fluttered in her slipstream, glinting in the sun.

"Hey, look out, man!" Falcon's shout jerked my attention away from Kestrel and I realized I'd nearly flown into him.

"Sorry," I yelled. "Tired."

The Flight landed, wings flaring, bringing our legs down carefully beneath us and alighting within a few hundred feet of each other on the rocky shoulder above our canyon. Remarkably, despite our exhaustion, there were only a few stumbles, and no one fell over.

Falcon's voice broke into my musings. "I wonder how high we can go." The Flight turned and began to gather, picking our way carefully and tiredly over the rough, slightly sloped rock.

Hawk scratched his brown hair as he gazed up at the sky. "If it was just a matter of will, I'd fly as high as a fighter jet."

"You and your planes," Kestrel said, smiling at Hawk fondly.

I was startled by a sudden rush of jealousy in my chest, and turned to look out over the desert to hide my face.

"How high do you think we were, though?" Falcon persisted.

Tui sat down on a jutting piece of rock. "Does it matter? It was high!"

"What's our ceiling, though? As high as we can go without running out of oxygen?"

"I think it would get too cold before that," Hawk said.

"Our feathers would freeze, bro," Tui said. "The opposite of Icarus's problem, really."

"Ironic," I said, in a pathetic effort to join the conversation.

"I'm keen to try out more stunts." Falcon flexed his wings, one lifting high and the other flaring wide. "Diving is great and all, but not very impressive. What about barrel rolls, and loops, and ... and stuff?" He floundered for more examples.

"Aileron rolls first," Hawk said. "Easier than barrel rolls."

"Formations," Owl said. "For long distances."

"You mean in a V, like geese?"

"Yes. Reduces drag, all fly longer."

Tui nodded. "And we take turns being the leader. That makes sense."

"We should definitely practice that," Falcon said enthusiastically. "Then we can fly anywhere we want to go, and no one can chase us."

There was a pause.

"What about all our stuff, though?" Kestrel said. "Food, survival gear, clothes and so on?"

"We could try flying with our front packs," Hawk said.

Kestrel's nose wrinkled thoughtfully. "What if we have to leave in a hurry again? Wouldn't that slow us down?"

"I'm sure we can still fly faster than we can drive. We wouldn't be stuck following the road," Falcon said confidently. "As the crow flies, so to speak." He laughed.

"Carrying stuff would tire us quicker," Tui said.

Fal shrugged. "We'd get stronger quicker."

"And could take turns carrying the supplies," Hawk added.

I shook myself and turned to pay proper attention to the discussion. "We should practice first, then decide later."

Falcon nodded. "I guess it's pointless arguing till we know if we can do it or not."

"Maybe we could pack lighter, if you boys would finally fix your fashion statements into '*I am an Icarus*' instead of '*I am a hobo*'?" Kestrel suggested with a giggle, tugging on a loose strip of my shirt, causing half of it to flap open.

I flushed and brushed the fabric back into place, trying to tuck it in and forget the sensation of her fingers on my skin. "That would probably help, yes."

The rest of the day was spent on clothing. After several shirts were sacrificed in the name of experimentation, we found that cutting a single large hole in the middle-upper back was the most straightforward style. Then we could step into that hole from the back, pull it up to our waists, then slide our arms into the sleeves while lifting the neck hole over our heads. While it looked normal on the ground, it was still a bit breezy on the back, and we could tell that it would ride up annoyingly while flying.

After messing around with strips of cloth like the girls had, and Falcon loudly moaning about how it didn't look 'badass' enough, Hawk dug through the dwindling pile of loot from the department store and produced several belts, some with utility pockets and loops attached.

"I thought these would come in useful while flying," he said, slinging them around his upper body in an X that followed the current arrangement of the shirt wrap. After several readjustments, he struck a pose. "How do I look?"

"I want one," Falcon said immediately.

Tui and Kestrel also demanded their share, and I had to admit that I really wanted to try my own version too.

After some friendly arguments about the fairest way to allocate the handful of belts that Hawk had grabbed, each of us soon had our own new 'Flight harness' — some with a single diagonal strap, others with the loops around the shoulders or a double circle around the waist.

"Okay. Now we are *Bad Ass*," Falcon announced, grinning, and I chuckled.

As I was adjusting the belt across my chest, I watched Raven reaching up to help Owl, and as her arm lifted, her sleeve slid back.

"Raven! Are you okay?" I ran over. "What happened?"

Her eyes widened and she stepped back, her other hand hastily tugging down the sleeve and locking around her wrist. Owl stepped in front of her protectively and I skidded to a halt, raising my hands.

"Is she all right? What happened?"

Owl's face tightened slightly, and after an excruciatingly long moment, he lifted his own arm and pushed back his sleeve.

There was a hissing jumble of gasps as the Flight saw the dark red scars and faded marks that must have come from many years of some form of abuse. It was the same kind of damage I'd glimpsed on Raven's arm, but now I could see it wasn't a fresh injury.

Suddenly, her muteness and their awkwardness made even more terrible sense.

"I'm sorry, Owl," I said, my voice low.

He dropped his arm and shrugged. "No more," he said.

Kestrel appeared beside me. "Never again," she replied, firmly.

The slightest hint of a smile tugged at the corner of Owl's mouth, and Raven peered around his pale gold wings.

"Hey, Rave? I think you'll like this, check this out," Kestrel said, and turned to show off her latest piece of Icarus fashion, as she insisted on calling it. She had cut away the sleeves of a sweater, leaving them joined with the upper back strip, turning it into something she said was a 'shrug'. "Do you want one too?"

Hesitantly, Raven nodded, and Kestrel drew her away and distracted everyone with further adjustments to their clothing. The awkward, horrible moment had passed, but the Flight would never forget.

As the rough outfits were refined, combining our knee-high flight boots, multilayered shirt wraps, and now the variety of flight utility harnesses, I realized how strongly the Flight was drawing together. I touched the cross around my neck and whispered a brief prayer of thanks.

Evening came and night fell. After another odd combination of preserved food for dinner, everyone crawled into their sleeping bags and quickly fell asleep.

Except me.

I lay awake for a long time, staring up at the glowing strip of stars visible between the rock walls towering above us. I tried to say my evening prayers, but I couldn't find the words. The thrill of flying, the horrific glimpse of Owl and Raven's past, the excitement of designing new clothes and the Flight growing ever stronger. Kestrel's kindness. It was almost too much to process.

Finally, I whispered to the sky. "Why am I here, God? What do You have planned?"

Kestrel shifted and sighed in her sleep. Holding my breath, I waited for her to wake up. After a long moment, and no other sound except the others' breathing, I relaxed again.

Please, Lord, all I'm asking for is a sign to tell me I'm doing the right thing, that I'm following the right path. And please, keep us safe. Amen.

The next day was focused on expanding our flying skills. It seemed everyone in the Flight had something they especially wanted to try and, by the end of our flight session, each of us had successfully pulled off an aileron roll (spinning on our long axis with our wings tucked in, which Hawk explained was different to barrel rolls) as well as a backward loop. Although no one was particularly good at them yet, we knew it was only a matter of time — and it was already obvious how useful the utility harnesses were for keeping things safe and accessible, regardless of how many loops and rolls we flung ourselves through.

Right at the end of the session, the Flight tried flying in the V formation, and each of us practiced moving up into the point position as well as dropping out of it without knocking anyone else from the sky. There were a couple of close calls, including a time when Kestrel tried to drop back and nearly flew into me, but I brushed off the fright as casually as I could. Embarrassed, Kestrel kept apologizing, her accent thickening in her distress. Unfortunately, it only made me like her more.

By the time we landed, the Flight had spent nearly an hour longer in the air than the day before, and everyone was excited by our rapid progress.

"It's like we're just relearning something, rather than starting from scratch," Tui said.

Hawk frowned. "Genetic instinct?"

"I thought that took generations to evolve," Kestrel said, twisting a strand of golden hair.

Hawk shrugged, distracted by Falcon picking up the trashball.

I was relieved when the conversation didn't go any further, as I knew I was the only one who thought there was a divine purpose guiding us. Keeping my evening prayers simple and unassuming, I tried to relax while I waited for God to give me a nudge in the right direction.

In the meantime, the Flight was completely focused on learning to fly. Everything else was secondary.

That was almost our downfall.

20

MIGUEL

I realized the full extent of my feelings for Kestrel while she was helping Hawk groom his feathers one afternoon. Hawk's face looked almost feline in his satisfaction as her gentle hands scraped the oils and dust from his feathers, and then it was his turn to groom her wings. He definitely took longer than necessary, and although Kestrel chatted cheerfully with Tui nearby, I could see the flush in her cheeks and the dilation in her silver eyes as Hawk caressed the golden feathers at the shoulder of her wings.

I could no longer deny that Kestrel was attracted to Hawk as strongly as he was to her.

As I continued making dinner, I tried to push the heat of jealousy out of my chest and into the little kerosene stove. It was probably my imagination, but perhaps the pot did boil quicker than usual.

To my surprise, however, Kestrel offered to groom my wings. She was just as gentle and deft as with Hawk, and the sensation of her hands running through my dark feathers was intoxicating. I struggled to focus on the conversation, and was almost relieved when she was done. Almost. I knew she hadn't taken nearly as long with my wings as Hawk's, and I knew why. She didn't see me in that way. I was a good friend. Nothing more.

The hurt was so much sharper than I anticipated, but did nothing to dull my ever-growing feelings for her.

It was hard because she was always around, whether it was joining in a game of trashball, adding illustrations to Raven's elegant calligraphy, getting Tui to teach her the graceful movements to some of her *kapa haka* songs, or insisting that I show her my sleight of hand tricks over and over again until she'd figured them out. Her constant presence made it impossible to get her off my mind even for a minute.

Hawk, for his part, never seemed to make any particular effort to talk to Kestrel, not like I did. I tried to be subtle with my attentions, but Hawk was so casual it was almost annoying how he seemed to be nearby so often. I rarely had a chance to be with Kestrel on my own — which, I realized, was possibly his intention.

It was frustrating, to say the least. I prayed to God for some help, but obviously this was something I had to find the strength to deal with myself.

The Flight was relaxing as dusk crept over the sky. Kestrel announced she was going for a walk to use her legs instead of her wings for once. Falcon and Tui were celebrating their first successful double loops, while Hawk, Owl and I were talking about the different hand signs we were developing for communication in the air as I helped Raven with her share of the chores.

Then Falcon butted in.

"Hey, Miguel, are you ever going to take a bird name?"

I lost my voice. I had no idea what to say.

Hawk jumped to my defense. "He doesn't have to if he doesn't want to."

Falcon shrugged. "It seems kind of weird that everyone has a bird name except him now." He glared at me accusingly. "Are you part of the Flight or not?"

"There aren't any rules, Fal," Hawk said, starting to show his irritation. "It's not like any of us chose to be here."

"Yes, we did. We all came here because we wanted to find others with these." He stretched his dark wings out as far as he could before refolding them with a rustle. "Why would you do that, and then not join in when we're trying to make a new life for ourselves?"

"Hey, chill, dude!" Hawk's own brown wings flared briefly. "Why is this suddenly so important?"

"Why don't you let him answer for himself?"

I swallowed.

"I'm still waiting," I said, finding my voice at last. I wasn't sure what had happened to it while it was gone, but it had suddenly gained a strength and certainty it hadn't had before.

"What are you waiting for?" Fal demanded.

"For a reason. A purpose." I waved a hand. "I know we've got one. I'm just waiting to find out what it is."

"Why do we have to have a purpose? Don't *we* get to decide what to do now? Life was hard enough as it was!"

I stood up, fighting to keep the anger out of my voice. "Then don't you think we should be doing something to make the world a better place?"

"What, like superheroes?" Falcon looked like he couldn't decide whether to mock the idea, or consider it seriously.

I shrugged. "We do look a lot like angels."

Falcon stared at me for a long moment and then began laughing. "Oh man, I am *not* an angel. No way, no how."

Hawk smiled at me. "Don't worry, Miguel, there are good and bad angels, right? Maybe you're the good one sent to stop the rest of us from falling any further."

Falcon just laughed harder at this, despite Tui punching his arm, but I appreciated what Hawk was trying to say. He held my gaze for a long moment, and a wash of strange relief passed through me. I knew I could count on Hawk to have my back, to still be my friend, no matter what we might feel about Kestrel. At last, I nodded. He nodded back, then returned to the discussion like nothing had happened.

"Hey, guys?" Kess called from above. The Flight glanced up and saw her silhouette leaning over the edge of the plateau above. "I thought you'd be interested to know, there's a rather large camp being set up in the desert."

Everything else was instantly driven from our minds.

"The Evolutionaries," I guessed.

"Or the Angelists." Hawk slapped his hands together in frustration, and I winced as it bounced off the rock walls into our sensitive ears like a gunshot. "How in hell did they find us?"

Falcon crossed his arms. "Could just be some Scouts."

Kestrel's shadowy wings flicked. "I can't see enough detail in the darkness. Why don't you come look for yourselves?"

As we scrambled up our usual path — take-off from flat ground was still too difficult and energy-draining, especially in the confines of the canyon — I couldn't fight the surging anxiety. "We would have seen them if they'd arrived when we were flying, right?"

Hawk grunted. "I sure hope so."

"We couldn't have missed them in the daylight," Kestrel said, waiting for us nearby. "Come on, you can see best from over here. But keep your voices down. Sound carries way too easily out here."

Trusting in the dark of night to hide us, the Flight peered at the distant circle of lights on the plain below. I counted a dozen tents, but it was impossible to be sure how many people were moving around the campsite. I couldn't see a flag or smaller figures that might be children if it was a Scout camp, but there was also nothing that hinted at the Evolutionaries or Angelists.

"They obviously won't do anything tonight," I said eventually, my eyes tiring from the strain. "We won't see any more by getting closer."

"What if they come looking for us during the day, bro?" Tui said, agitated. "If we hide, and they find us, we're trapped in a bloody dead end."

"If we kept watch, we could escape over and around the mountain before they got anywhere near us," I said.

"Maybe if we listened in on their conversation, we could figure out why they're here," Falcon said. "That would give us the advantage."

Tui nodded and stretched a wing. "But not all of us should go. They're less likely to catch two or three of us, and even if they do, the rest of the Flight can get away." Her tone made it obvious she thought capture was extremely unlikely.

"They won't expect someone to come snooping round at this time of night, even if they are out hunting for us," Falcon added.

"Who's going then?" Hawk said, before any further argument could be made. I shut my mouth and glared at him in the darkness. Something was telling me this was a bad idea. But I couldn't let the others take the risk, especially as Hawk and Falcon were the type to act first, think later. My hand was one of the first in the air.

As everyone except Owl and Raven volunteered, we settled it by a quick round of Rock Paper Scissors. Tui and Kestrel complained that the boys had cheated as Hawk, Falcon and I prepared to fly.

Raven said nothing, as usual, but Owl was also silent. They seemed unusually agitated as the rest of the Flight formed the reconnaissance plan, but still, they didn't speak.

It was decided that Hawk, Falcon and I would fly a little closer, then land and sneak forward until we were within earshot, which would be a reasonable distance with our enhanced hearing. We'd hang around for ten or fifteen minutes, if it was safe, and listen in on the campfire conversation or anything else we could hear. As soon as those fifteen minutes were up, we promised to head back.

"What do you think, Owl?" Hawk asked, sounding hopeful.

The tall blond Icarus paused in his pacing. "Not good."

"Well, what would you do?"

"Not go." His wings, looking silver in the starlight, rustled. "Fly away."

"We can't just leave in the middle of the night, where the hell would we go?" Falcon demanded. "What if they're harmless? Maybe they'll just move on tomorrow. We'd be giving up all this for nothing."

"But if we just wait and see, we lose valuable time, and we'll have to stay out of sight, so that means no flying till they go," Kess said.

"Better to find out now," said Hawk. "Then we can get out of here tonight if it's bad news."

"Let's recon first, then we can make an informed decision," Falcon said, defiantly. "Come on!"

"Be careful," Kess said quietly, as the three of us stepped away along the ridge so we could take off. I wasn't sure, but I thought I caught Kestrel flashing me a brief smile in the darkness. I hoped I wasn't imagining it.

"See you soon," I said and followed Hawk and Falcon as they dove off the plateau.

Even if my sharp eyes hadn't been able to pick out their shadows in the dull glow from the clouded moon, I could have identified Hawk and Falcon easily from the subtle sounds of their wings. Having spent so much time together, the Flight was beginning to appreciate each other's individual flight rhythms and the differences in the sounds that our feathers made.

To make sure the campers didn't hear us, we landed a few hundred yards from the nearest tent. Sand, soil, and stones shifted under our feet as we touched down, but luckily no ankles were turned, and we successfully avoided the low scattered shadows of spiky bushes.

Falcon took the lead, creeping closer to the campsite with Hawk and me right behind him. On our hands and knees, we took cover behind some rocks a hundred feet or so from the large campfire.

Hawk leaned closer. "I count seventeen people," he whispered.

I frowned. "I can only see a dozen."

"Shut up, guys, I can't concentrate," Falcon hissed, a few feet away.

Falling silent, Hawk and I strained to eavesdrop on the muted conversations occurring in the campsite, but they were all mundane, boring, practical things, like the expected weather tomorrow, and which crate had the toilet paper in it.

"They're harmless," Hawk murmured. "Let's go home before my stomach digests itself."

Reluctantly, Falcon began crawling away from the campsite. Hawk was already some yards ahead. I glanced back one more time, and saw nothing out of the ordinary.

Suddenly, dozens of bright lights bathed the desert in a white glare. My shadow stretched out in front of me, fleeing in fear.

The people in the camp started running. Toward us.

They knew we were here the whole time.

Hawk hollered. *"Get up and run!"*

Scrambling to my feet, my tail flapping, I started to sprint. There were shouts behind us and a burst of loud pops. I swerved and ducked. Small projectiles hit the dirt around me, glinting in the harsh white floodlights.

The darkness reached for me as I zigzagged toward it. Hawk and Falcon were flapping, trying to take off, and I stopped dodging and weaving so I could too. I jumped, flapped hard — and something stung me in my leg.

Yelling, I hit the ground again and my leg crumpled, numb. Stubbornly, I tried to rise.

Falcon dashed back and grabbed my arm. "Come *on!*"

"Trying!"

"Hawk, get the hell out of here!" Fal bellowed, dragging me with him. "Get the Flight out!"

"I'm not leaving you—"

The edge of the darkness was only a few feet away. Falcon and I were about to cross the line — and something stung me, even harder, in the middle of my back, right between my wings.

My body stopped responding and I crashed forward, taking Falcon with me. Hawk tried to grab me but Falcon shoved him away.

"Warn the Flight!"

Just before my eyes closed, I saw the tiny syringe-like dart hit Falcon's arm. He bellowed in pain, his words beginning to slur.

Then darkness took me.

The first thing I became aware of was the horrible thirst.

As I struggled to generate some spit in my mouth to unstick my tongue from my teeth, I climbed closer to consciousness.

What ... happened?

Trying to roll over and rub the crust from my itchy eyes, I found my hands were tied together. Peeling open one eye, and then the other, I squinted in the gloom. My wrists, ankles, and wings were bound, and I was lying on my side in an empty utility van.

The effort made my head pound, but I confirmed I did still have all the right body parts, and that Falcon was with me. I couldn't roll over to check, but we seemed to have been laid out wing-to-wing, facing the walls of the vehicle. Judging by his breathing, he was still unconscious. My throat was too dry to even say his name.

At my feet, I could see the faint outline of two darkly tinted windows in the back doors of the vehicle. Otherwise, the metal walls were featureless. There wasn't even a window into the cab.

As my thoughts became clearer, so did the pain of being tied up so tightly. I ached where I'd probably been dropped on the floor. There wasn't even the slightest give in the straps around my limbs, and there was no way I could loosen, nibble, cut, or otherwise erode through the rope.

Should have focused on escapology, not sleight-of-hand, I mused, feeling a twinge of hysteria. *Would it have been too much to ask for a pair of handcuffs instead?*

I rested my head on the floor to ease the pounding in my skull. To distract myself, I listened to the muffled sounds that were growing in volume outside the truck.

A couple of people walked past, and I concentrated to pick out their words from the background noise.

"Did you get a good look at them?"

"Yep. They're exactly what we expected. They're the same as the others."

"How did Goldberg do it underneath the boss's nose, though?"

"Who's to say it was Goldberg?"

"Who else could have done it?"

"You know, come to think of it, there were all those rumors. I remember one of the interns was positive she'd seen Goldberg in LA about a week after the funeral."

They walked out of earshot, and I cursed. Filing the information away for later, I began reciting the Lord's Prayer in my head, first in English, then in Spanish. Over and over again, the familiar words and rhythm helping me stay calm.

A chorus of slamming car doors began. It sounded like the whole camp was on the move. Suddenly, the van was unlocked and opened just long enough for a person to climb in.

"Are you awake, dears?" a soft, kindly voice asked from the restored darkness.

Falcon responded with a soft, "Uh."

A firm hand lifted my head. "Here's some water for you, dear." The terrible dryness seized me by the throat, and I guzzled as much as I could before the bottle was taken away.

I slumped back to the floor. Falcon was taken through the same routine.

"We're going on a little trip now, dears," the woman said as she returned to the door. "As long as you're both good boys and lie nice and still, you should be quite comfortable. Mr. van Scholtz is quite anxious that you aren't harmed in any way, don't worry."

She knocked on the back of the van, and I steeled myself. It swung open, allowing in a blast of daylight. Before the door slammed shut again, I glimpsed a male silhouette, and on a vehicle in the distance behind him, a familiar logo.

It is the Evolutionary Corporation. Who the hell is van Scholtz? And Goldberg? And what 'others'?

"Migueeeeeel?" Falcon slurred.

"Here," I tried to say, but my throat was still sticking. I coughed. "I'm here."

"Sucks."

"Uhuh."

"Flight?"

"Don't know." *Please, Lord, let the Flight be safe...*

The van lurched. Door slams vibrated through the metal floor and into our stiff bodies. As the engine roared into life, the vibrations became continual, almost comforting. But only if I didn't think about the fact that we were being taken to who-knew-where to have who-knew-what done to us.

"They'll come," Falcon grunted. "Tui won't let us go without a fight."

I was sure Hawk and Kestrel were the same, and had a feeling Owl and Raven were too. The Flight was too strong to give up so easily. They all knew I'd come after them ... didn't they?

Please don't let them be captured coming after us. Please.

The van shifted into gear and began rolling across the stony desert floor, jarring every now and then. Falcon and I had no choice but to endure it silently, until finally the tires bumped onto something flat, and the truck accelerated smoothly.

"We're on the highway."

Falcon grunted. "Hope they can keep up."

That was it. We didn't speak of the Flight again.

Fal finally broke our silence, and the monotonous hum of the engine. "That woman was weird."

"What is she doing with the Evolutionaries?"

"Just because she's old doesn't mean she can't be an evil scientist. She might be an expert in evolution and genetics and crap. Maybe she's the one who'll be experimenting on us."

I shuddered. "Whatever happens now ... at least the Flight had some good times together."

"Why do the good times always have to end?" Falcon sighed. "And it always happens so freaking quickly."

"Yeah. I know exactly what you mean."

"When I was a kid, like real young, life was great. Mom and Dad had good jobs, school was easy. Then, *bam*. Mom gets fired." Falcon's voice was low but unstoppable in the gloomy van. I could feel the tension in his bound wings, shoved against mine. "Dad had to work overtime, and because of that he had this massive accident. Major brain damage. Suddenly, life was hell."

"I'm sorry," I said, but Falcon didn't appear to hear me.

"Took a while, but things were finally starting to get better at home, and then, *bam*. Wings. So, I work through that, and the Flight happens, and that's all starting to be awesome, and then, yet again, another *bam*. Kidnapped." He wriggled, apparently trying to free his hands. "Seriously, what the hell?"

"Do you know why your mom got fired?"

"I don't know, her boss was having a bad day or something. Why do rich white guys need an excuse to do anything?"

"Sounds like my dad," I murmured.

"What did he do?"

"Betrayed Mom." The anger still made my voice shake, even five years later. "She left him, straight away. We walked right out of our cushy lives and back to my Abuelita, in Mexico City, where Mom had grown up. Found Abuelita living in poverty. A couple of years later, Mom was dead."

"What happened?"

"I don't know for sure. I was just a kid and the doctors told me I wouldn't understand, just said she worked herself to death. Abuelita wouldn't talk about it." I tried to shift into a less agonizing position. "Some of the other kids taunted me, and said my mom had been a whore. That was why God punished her." The words hissed. "I know she wasn't."

"Jeez. Sorry, man."

I sighed, trying to let the old anger fade. "Not your fault, Falcon."

"I just … I don't get why people can be such dicks to each other, you know?"

"I know." I inhaled slowly and deeply through my nose. "We just have to be better than them. We really have a chance to make a difference."

"As long as it doesn't involve singing *Kumbaya* and driving flower power Kombis, then I'm in."

I smiled at the wall. "Hey, Fal?"

"Yeah?"

"Thanks for coming back for me."

He grunted. "You'd have done the same for me."

The silence returned as the truck wound through a series of tight corners, and we tried hard not to roll into each other.

"Where do you think we are?" Falcon asked.

"I don't know. Probably still in the desert."

Finally, the truck gently straightened out and we tried to resettle ourselves, Falcon grumbling about the poor in-flight service on this crate.

Then…

THUD!

21

TUI

"Are you guys ready for this?" I asked.

Kestrel, Hawk, Owl and Raven all nodded, faces set.

In the dull light of the overcast morning, with our flight harnesses stuffed full of supplies, we ran off the side of the mountain and into the air. Quickly, we aimed for the low cloud ceiling, only a few hundred metres overhead.

Look out, you bloody Evolutionary dickheads. I'm coming for my boyfriend. Did you buggers really think you could steal him from me so easily?

It was hard to believe how badly these people wanted us, but I knew it wasn't to take us to a magical land where everyone had wings.

All we wanted was to be free.

Is that so much to ask?

We were completely aware that the only reason the Evos had hung around in the desert all night was because they were trying to trap the rest of us. The boys weren't only their prize, they were bait.

But the Flight had a plan.

As I climbed, I had a weird moment of claustrophobia as the cloud layer seemed to press down on me. The wind picked up, making it harder to breathe. Then the current abruptly changed direction and slapped the side of my face, before lurching underneath my wings.

"C'mon, Tāwhirimātea," I muttered, addressing the Māori god of the wind. "I could use a little help here."

Trying to ignore the chafing of the supplies and extra clothing strapped to, and threaded through, my harness, I struggled to maintain a steady course in the turbulent air. There was no definite line between clear and cloudy sky. One moment I was flying just below the threatening grey ceiling, in the next it felt like my vision was getting a little hazy, and then gradually the haze thickened and became a puffy fog. The air within the cloud swirled and moved much faster than was obvious from the ground. It was like swimming in a rip current without the issue of trying to keep your head above the water. Every time we dropped a few metres with the trough in the airwaves, we could see through the haze to the ground below, while we still stayed well camouflaged.

"This is weird," Hawk said, somewhere off to my right. His voice was deadened by the cloud, but I could still hear him okay. I even caught the occasional shadowy glimpse of him, keeping pace with me.

"We can do this," Kestrel said determinedly, from my other side.

I rearranged my wrap a bit, trying to protect my skin from the cold sticky fog, and took a deep breath. "Time to hunt, sis?"

"Definitely."

Dropping out of the cloud layer and into the calmer air, we came around in our practised formation.

Hold on, Falcon. I'm coming.

I ended up on point with Hawk as my right wingman and Kestrel on my left. Owl and Raven were behind us, completing the long V. Swinging back towards the mountain just beneath the cloud layer, the dull rocky landscape tilted below us. It wasn't a perfect move, but it was solid.

With the Flight following, I climbed back into the turbulent cloud when the camp came into view. That is, where the camp had been. In the short time we'd been out of sight prepping to fly, they'd packed up. Now seven vehicles were trundling along the desert floor like a line of beetles. The van that held the boys was smack in the middle.

"They're heading northwest," Kestrel said, checking the satphone that was safely tied to her chest harness. It was likely to be a long time until the right moment came up for our hit-and-run mission.

Apart from our regular wing beats, which never quite fell into rhythm, everyone was silent. We flew hard to catch the convoy before it reached the road. As soon as it did, the lead vehicle picked up speed, and the line of cars stretched out behind it.

Although we couldn't fly as fast as they could drive, the convoy stayed well below the speed limit, and there were enough bends and wide curves in the road that we could cut corners above them and catch up whenever necessary.

"Do you think they're deliberately driving slowly so we can keep up?" Hawk asked, finally.

I wiped cloud from my flight goggles again. "Yeah, that's my guess."

"But they don't know what we're going to do, right?" said Kestrel, hopefully.

"*We* don't know what we're going to do," Hawk said. "How can they?"

"We do have a plan, bro," I said defensively. "It's just ... flexible."

"Will be suspicious, but not sure," Owl said from the back.

With shared bloody-mindedness, the Flight managed to trail the convoy. The initial rush of adrenaline had already worn off due to the sheer slog and rough wind. I wasn't exhausted yet, but I was definitely getting tired.

Come on, Tui, you've been more tired than this before, and you got through. You've always done what you gotta do. You always wanted to save people. Now you actually have the chance. Falcon and Miguel are counting on you.

A few times, the road rose and fell in more rugged terrain, but never cut deep enough or wound tightly enough to give us a chance to put the plan into action.

I was worried by the quickly-growing smudge of dark forest on the horizon. We were approaching the edge of the desert and running out of options.

"The plan will work in the forest, eh?" I asked.

Hawk said grimly, "We'll make it work."

"No," Owl said. "There."

Ahead, several flat-topped towers of rock thrust up from the wrinkled desert floor, guarding a maze-like band of ancient rock formations. As the Flight approached, I began to appreciate the size of them. The best part was that the road was heading straight towards them, and appeared to wind its way past, over, and between the columns of the huge natural fortress.

"Stage one," Owl said.

This is it.

We pushed ahead nearly twice as fast, or so it felt. Even better, the road had to curve away and around a smaller tower-mountain, while the Flight could fly right over it and gain some time.

While the convoy was out of sight, the Flight plunged down from the clouds, the air whooshing past and snatching oxygen from my lungs. As the rock rushed up at me, my wings flared. I scooped just enough air to pull up, skimming less than ten metres above the ground, gravity pulling at my body as I swooped out of the dive.

I heard the air swish behind me as the others followed hard on my tail.

We skimmed beside the road as it cut deeper into the rock, scanning the steep slopes on either side for what we needed.

Kestrel pointed. "There."

One by one, we dropped onto an overhanging outcrop, and quickly dumped all the extra supplies behind a large rock.

"They're nearly here," Hawk said, hovering some metres above us, buffeting us with his downdraft before he dropped lightly back to the rough rock platform.

Quickly, we all gathered an armful of rocks and stones, and spread out along the rock that towered over the ribbon of road.

After only a few moments, Hawk hissed, "Get down!"

Lying flat with wings extended behind us, Kestrel and I wriggled forward to the crumbling edge, the grit scraping at my hands and eardrums. I peered over as the first car purred past, then ducked back as the next two followed, a less-than-generous gap between them.

"They've closed up with less visibility," Kess said, her voice trembling.

I grunted. "It'll work."

Cautiously, Kestrel and I peered down again as the prison van passed below us. I caught a glimpse of two bodyguard types in the cab, one driving, the other cradling a couple of guns. But it was the back doors I was more interested in.

Memorising everything I could see, I watched the van disappear around the next corner. "No padlocks or chains."

"Bet it'll be tough glass," Kess said.

"What do you think?"

"I just hope I can do it."

There was no time for second thoughts. "Ready, sis?"

"Let's go."

As the next vehicle came into view, Kess and I launched off the edge of the plateau, hurling rocks at the dusty black car, aiming for the windshield.

The car weaved on the road as the driver flinched. Loud cracks and bangs left holes and dents in the windows and roof of the car.

"Last one!" Kestrel shouted. "Now!"

Side by side, we swooped low and heaved our biggest and heaviest rocks directly at the windshield. A huge web of cracks exploded across the weakened safety glass. The car missed the corner, plunged off the road onto the shoulder, skidded on the loose gravel, scraped the stone wall with ear-shrivelling shrieks and finally crunched to a halt, wedged between the road barrier and the rock.

Kess and I hauled our feathered butts out of there. Trails of shattered glass and plastic led to more Evolutionary cars crumpled into the rocks, courtesy of the Flight.

Ahead, we saw Hawk trailing the prison van.

He glanced round as we caught up. "Stage two," he said. The three of us fell into formation and gave chase.

We shadowed the van for a few corners until it entered a rare straight in the road.

This would be the hard part.

Hawk went first. He dropped low, keeping pace with the van, until he folded his wings and fell onto the roof with a loud THUD. The driver instinctively slammed on the brakes and Hawk snatched at the tie rails, his body and feet swinging in a big arc as the vehicle sharply decelerated.

"Hurry up!" he bellowed at me and Kestrel.

As though the driver heard him, the van suddenly surged forward as it tried to outrace the attack.

Kestrel folded her wings and dived straight for the roof, thudding onto the metal in the middle. Hawk grabbed her shoulder before she slid past him.

My turn. There was a hell of a lot less room on the van now, and I was running out of straight road.

"Shit!" I groaned, and dived.

As the van curved to follow the road, I tucked in my wings and hit the roof, colliding with Kestrel's boots and tail.

She and I were now facing the same way as the van while Hawk was looking back at us from the front. Kestrel and I tried to ease ourselves backwards while Hawk commando-crawled closer, the slipstream flicking some of his feathers up the wrong way.

My boots slid off the end of the truck. Kestrel clung to one tie rail while Hawk crawled beside her and grabbed my hand, anchoring me as I eased backwards, over the edge.

My toes slid down for a horribly long way before I found the footboard beneath the double doors. Suddenly, the van lurched as it took a tight corner, and my wings automatically snapped out in survival reflex.

It almost killed me.

My wings caught the wind, nearly lifting me off the van. All the breath was wrenched from my lungs, my fingers slipping along the dusty metal. Kess yelled, Hawk swore, his fingers digging harder into my arms as he began to slide along the roof. Kestrel lunged sideways and grabbed his belt, straining to halt both of us. Beneath my feet, the road whizzed past, hungry to rip me into pieces.

All this happened in seconds. I quickly flicked my wings straight back and folded them in. Thudding against the rear doors, I clutched the tie bar with one hand and a door handle with the other, my feet firmly on the wide patterned aluminium tray that served as a bumper.

Without waiting for me to recover, Kestrel came next, Hawk's fingers visibly white as they gripped her arm. Her boots hit me in the head as the van rounded yet another corner, but she avoided my mistake. Finally, both she and I clung to the back doors.

It was simultaneously terrifying and exhilarating.

"Hurry up," Hawk shouted.

As I acted as her safety line, Kestrel began to pick the lock with one hand. First with the knife, then some long bits of wire she'd scraped together, but it resisted her every effort.

"Where the hell are the others?" I yelled through the wind. We'd only been clinging to the back of the van for a minute, but our tiny window of opportunity was rapidly closing.

Kess jammed a pared-down fork into the lock, and tried the handle. It still didn't move. In frustration, she smashed her fist against the door.

There was an answering bang from the inside. Kess and I stared at each other. Then I rapped twice. There were two answering knocks.

Hawk yelled over the noise of the wind and road. "We got company!"

I glared. "You come up with that one yourself?"

A dented sedan came racing around the corner behind us, flashing its lights and sounding its horn.

I groaned. "The others must have missed it. Where the hell are they?"

"Going up!" Hawk launched himself off the van, leaving us exposed to the Evo car that was catching up fast.

"Thanks, bro," I snarled and started smashing my fist against the blacked-out glass.

Guns emerged from the car behind us. I flinched as a dart ricocheted off the van near my head.

"We just ran out of time," shouted Kess. "Why isn't the van stopping?"

"Maybe they're trying to force us into another trap?" I swore. "Where are the others?"

The van rounded a few more tight corners, forcing the car to drop back, but then it burst onto a downhill straight. We were coming out of the mountains.

I flinched again as something bounced off the van, but then realised it wasn't a dart or a bullet.

"Finally!"

Hawk, Raven and Owl swooped overhead, dropping more rocks onto the sedan. The van driver picked up speed.

"Give me a rock!" Kestrel shouted at the others winging back and forth above us. Hawk dropped closer, keeping pace with the truck.

"Catch!" he yelled.

Kess grabbed the rock Hawk tossed at her with one hand. I missed the first one Raven dropped to me, but caught the next from Owl. Together, Kestrel and I smashed at the window on my side. At first there was nothing. Then a tiny crack appeared.

"Bloody … safety … glass," I growled between impacts.

"Together?"

"Three — two — one—"

The rocks finally broke through, the safety glass crumbling away into the slipstream. Kestrel and I smashed out the remains of the window before she helped me wriggle through the narrow rectangle.

Landing on someone's leg, I scrambled upright in the swaying van, then remembered to turn and help Kestrel through.

Falcon and Miguel lay on their sides on the floor, their wrists, ankles, and wings tied together. The banging we'd heard was Falcon kicking on the door.

Kestrel and I pulled out our knives and sawed through the ropes, leaving a few bloody scratches in our hurry. Falcon was rambling at me, but I tuned him out, concentrating on getting him free.

As soon as I hauled on his arm and helped him upright, he grabbed me and pulled me in for a deep kiss.

For a second, nothing existed but his lips on mine. It was okay, he was okay, I had him back.

But then the van finally braked. The kiss broke as we staggered sideways.

"Hurry up, let's go!"

Scrambling for the handle, I unlocked the double doors and threw them wide open, revealing the rapidly shrinking wreck of the final Evo car and our three friends flapping hard to catch up.

"You okay to fly?" I asked Falcon, horrified at how pale he was. He glared. "I'd better be."

One by one, we lurched out of the van. Flapping furiously, the four of us struggled to make a decent height and settle into a better rhythm.

"Make for the summit," I yelled. Without looking back, I aimed for the rest of the Flight, who were swinging around and gaining altitude.

It took some minutes but, eventually, the entire Flight made it to a high tabletop mountain, where we collapsed.

We shared out some of the remaining snacks from our harness pockets. Then, I pulled out the little first aid kit and switched into nurse mode to patch up the cuts and scrapes on Falcon, Miguel, Kestrel, and myself. Meanwhile, the uninjured Owl, Raven and Hawk went off to retrieve the supplies we'd stashed on the outcrop.

"My heroine," Falcon gushed, as I covered and taped up a shallow gash on the back of his hand.

"Yeah, well, I think I was the one who cut you. Sorry."

"While rescuing me from certain *death*! Or maybe worse!" He pretended to swoon, putting the back of his other hand to his forehead.

I peered at him. "Don't worry, the drugs will finish wearing off soon, I'm sure. 'Specially with our metabolisms."

He chuckled, then his grin faded, and he took my surgically gloved hands. "I'm serious, Tui. You saved me."

"It was a team effort," I protested, embarrassed at his earnestness. Then I tightened my grip on his hands as he swayed, going pale again. Miguel wasn't looking good, either. Gently, but firmly, I got them both sitting down, leaning on a rock, their wings limply splayed across the stone. When Hawk, Owl and Raven returned, I insisted the boys ate something a little more substantial, which seemed to help. Still, I remained wary, ready to jump out of the way if one of them suddenly needed to puke.

We'd done it. We'd got them back. And I had never been as grateful for anything in my life. But, as the adrenaline wore off, reality was not looking sweet. The Flight was exhausted. We had two guys still recovering from tranquilisers, and we were stuck on top of a mountain with stuff-all resources, no idea where to go, or what to do next, and a storm was building right over our heads. Thunder rumbled in the distance.

Just because things weren't bloody hard enough, Hawk peered over the edge and announced that the Evolutionaries were regrouping and boy, did they look pissed off.

It wasn't over yet.

22

TUI

"Now what?" Falcon asked, from between his knees. His head was hanging there as I rubbed his upper back, between his wings. He had most of his usual colour back in his face, but I could feel he was a bit shaky, and when I squeezed his hand, it was clammy.

Kestrel pulled out the satphone. "We're not all that far from Los Angeles, as the Icarus flies," she said, with a forced grin. "So, the question is, do we head towards or away from civilisation?"

"We had to leave most of our stuff back in the canyon," Hawk said, dividing up our remaining supplies. "We've brought a few extra clothes, rations, and everyone's hoodies so we can hide our wings, but it won't be enough. Doesn't matter where we're heading, we'll have to stock up somewhere."

"The Evos will try to follow us, wherever we go," Kestrel pointed out. "How do they keep finding us?"

"We'll figure it out," Miguel said, grimly, as thunder growled again, not so distant this time. "But we need to leave soon, or that storm will blow us off this rock."

"I'm so sick of rock," I moaned. "Can we please go somewhere that's not entirely made of bloody rock?"

Hawk said, slowly, "What if they've tagged Miguel and Falcon somehow?"

Falcon's head snapped up. "Like we're freaking birds or something?"

Miguel examined his arms and legs, rolling up the sleeves and patting himself down. Falcon did the same. "I can't see anything that might be a tracker."

"Maybe they're not so sophisticated, after all." Sighing, Hawk slumped back.

Miguel finished checking the insides of his boots and pockets, and in his hair and feathers. "Not that sophisticated, anyway. We don't know what else they're planning."

"What are *we* planning?" Falcon demanded. At least he seemed more energetic again.

"I don't know. I was a little preoccupied with the whole rescue part," Hawk said, shrugging his brown wings.

Miguel suddenly perked up. "I found out something about that Goldberg guy!"

The Flight was instantly alert, exhaustion forgotten.

"Are you sure you'd worked off the tranquilisers?" Falcon said doubtfully, as Miguel tried to repeat exactly what he'd overheard. I smacked his arm gently, and he winced. "Sorry. But it seems too coincidental that they happened to say that just as they walked past."

"It might not have been a coincidence," Miguel said, calmly.

Falcon gave him a weird look, but Hawk was intrigued. "Doesn't matter. This Goldberg person is obviously the key. We need to find him."

"Assuming he's still alive," I pointed out, reluctantly. "They did mention a funeral."

"Either way, LA is the only lead we've got right now."

Falcon threw up his hands. "What do we do once we get there? Go door knocking all over Los Angeles? Excuse me, are you the Goldberg who made a whole lot of human-bird hybrids about seventeen years ago?"

The wind was pushing at my body, and I tried to shield myself with my wings. "And what about the 'others' they mentioned?" I asked. "Others exactly like us?"

Nobody had an answer for that.

Instead, Hawk said, "We won't find out if we stay here. It doesn't matter *where* we go, just that we go soon. Fal, Miguel, will you handle it?"

The boys nodded. "I just need to get moving," Falcon said, levering himself to his feet.

Miguel held a hand up, feeling the air currents. "The storm is blowing in from the east. We can't fly against that. It's almost like…" He hesitated. "It's almost like we're being pushed in the right direction. Let's fly west, and if we end up near Los Angeles, then we can figure out what to do from there."

We got ready to fly.

"Lucky they didn't take our tails, huh?" Falcon said, cheerfully, but with an edge to his voice, as he gently straightened a dented strut.

"Mm, yeah," Hawk said, eyeing the feathery kites, already battered from weeks of use, and now missing a feather or two from the abuse it had taken during Fal and Miguel's capture. "Let's hope it is just luck."

Despite both Falcon and Miguel checking their tails and bodies all over yet again, with the rest of us watching closely, we couldn't find anything else suspicious. So, with no other options, no reason to stay, and a tower of storm cloud looming over us, it was time to go.

We launched from the mountain and flew up through the cloud banks that were being pushed ahead of the enormous storm cell. After several minutes of anxious flapping through thick, dark fog, we rose into clear, less turbulent air.

Carefully, the Flight moved into a long-distance V formation. With Kestrel on navigation and calling out directions, we pulled off a pretty sweet turn. Almost immediately, it felt like the wind was helping us along.

As I settled into my long-distance rhythm, I let my mind relax. Flying was now as automatic as walking. Although I was tired, I'd found my second wind.

And glancing over and seeing Falcon safely beside me gave me the courage to keep going.

Kia kaha, my mum and my aunty would have said. It meant, stay strong. *You know what you want, Tui, and now you gotta go get it. The world isn't going to just hand it to you.*

Now that I had Falcon back, I could metaphorically sit down and figure out the insane rollercoaster of feelings that I'd ridden that day. Losing Falcon, even for a few hours, had been worse than when I'd thought my entire life had been destroyed by a pair of wings.

I'll have to tell him how much he means to me.

I glanced over at him again. He saw me looking, and replied with a huge smile that showed only a hint of strain. My heart bubbled.

Then I remembered thinking about him as my 'boyfriend'.

Well, that's going to make him happy. The thought kept me smiling to myself for hours.

The Flight flew on as the sun dropped lower. The clouds below began to thin out, and the occasional thunder rumble grew more and more distant. The colder air of the higher altitude was finally getting to me. I wondered if we'd have to add hypothermia to our list of Things To Worry About.

Eventually I realised we were flying over the Californian countryside, with only random swatches of cloud floating between us, the forest below, and a couple of snow-capped mountains to the south.

Falcon complained, "The sun's getting in my eyes."

"We're near the edges of LA now," Kestrel said. "But I'm about to run out of battery."

"Let's land," I said. The Flight had shuffled our formation several times, and I was on point again. "There's a park or something just ahead."

Hoping that no one was looking in our direction, we broke out of the long-distance V and began circling downwards.

When we were low enough that people might notice we were a bit too big to be birds, we took turns diving down into the large empty green space below, the air resistance pulling hard on aching muscles after the longest flight we'd ever made. Quickly, we took shelter under the trees.

"So where are we, sis?" I asked, coiling my hair back up on top of my head, and peeling my flight glasses off my face. My fingers massaged the indentations around my eyes.

"The phone just died," Kestrel replied. "I know we're near a new development, and downtown Los Angeles is in *that* direction, but that's all I can tell you. We should also keep all the other phones off in the meantime, just in case."

I continued scanning the park around us, but it was completely deserted. "Where the hell *is* everyone?"

"It's the middle of the week, so maybe everyone's just at home?" Hawk suggested.

"I'm hungry," Falcon said. It was getting dark, but the distant streetlights still hadn't turned on. "Can we eat now?"

"Shelter first," Owl said.

Nervously, the Flight approached the road. There were no cars, no people. There weren't many buildings either, just empty sections with the occasional darkened house in between.

"I'm really creeped out," I finally said. "Where the hell are we?"

Turning a corner, in the far distance I could see the fully lit city of Los Angeles. It was surrounded by bright, bustling suburbs, where people were driving home from work or out to dinner. But for another half mile or so in front of us stretched this weird, dark collection of scattered houses and empty bits of grass.

Just as I was bracing for a serial killer to leap from the bushes, Miguel pointed ahead. "There's a lit sign over there."

It was edge-on to us, so we had to walk right up to it to see what it said. When I read it aloud, a few of us laughed hysterically in relief.

In big cheerful letters it proclaimed: *Welcome to Heavenly Acres!* Below was a map of the vast suburb and adjacent park, with various helpful annotations such as *Sold!* and *Vacant Lot* and *Nearly finished, hurry before it's too late!*

"That's why there's no one here," Hawk said with satisfaction. "No one is living here yet."

"Look at this, bro," I said, pointing to a corner of the map. There was a large orange star announcing: *Show Home!*

"Perfect," Hawk said. "Let's go."

The show home was the only other source of illumination in the whole development. When the Flight arrived, Hawk slipped into the garden and found the switch that turned the spotlights off. Immediately, the house appeared no different to any of the others lining the dark street.

Kestrel quickly picked the lock and led the way into the house. "No alarm," she said after a moment.

Hawk followed more cautiously. "How do you know?"

"One, no alarm panel by the entrance." Kestrel ticked off on her fingers. "Two, no sensors in the rooms. Three, because if there was, we'd know it by now."

We took off our shoes and left them by the re-locked door. It was an upmarket, classy place, and I felt really weird wandering through it, switching on the lights and pulling the curtains as if I belonged there. We hadn't been in a proper house for weeks, and this was heaps fancier than what I was used to.

The stomach rumbles grew louder as the Flight gathered in the kitchen.

"Okay, Hawk, Kestrel and Owl, you're in charge of finding dinner," I ordered.

"What about me?" Falcon demanded.

"You're still recovering from being kidnapped. Go get cleaned up in one of those fancy bathrooms. You too, Miguel. Raven, can you make sure everyone has a place to sleep?"

"Yes, Mom," Hawk joked. "But where are we going to get food?"

"I have my credit card, but I have no idea if it still works," Kestrel said.

"So order something for delivery to a random house, and when the delivery guy goes to the front door, raid his car while the person in the house is trying to explain they didn't order anything," I said, pushing them out the door. "Or something. You'll figure it out!"

"Devious. I like it," Hawk said.

"Go!" I shut the door in his face.

Dumping the first aid kit and other supplies from my flight harness onto the kitchen bench, I decided to have a bit of a nosey through the house to see if I could find anything useful.

I'd got as far as the hallway cupboards when I heard Falcon's muffled swearing.

I ran down the hall and banged on the bathroom door. "You okay, Fal?"

He wrenched on the handle a few times before he remembered to unlock it. Then he threw open the door and dragged me inside.

"Can you feel something, right there?" he demanded.

I stared as he thrust his naked bum at me and pointed at a slight bruise on his butt cheek. His other hand clutched the towel to his groin.

My brain briefly froze up. "What?"

"I think the frickin' Evolutionaries injected a tracker into my ass, that's what! Can you tell me if there is actually something in there, or am I still high on drugs?" He grabbed my hand and tried to make me feel the bruise.

"Are you coming on to me, Fal?" I demanded. I really didn't want to believe that what he was saying could be true.

Falcon rolled his eyes. "Come *on*, babe, give me some frickin' credit. I'm *so* much smoother than some dumb 'I have a tracker in my butt' move."

"Okay." I took a deep breath. I didn't have time for a freakout. "Let's check with Miguel."

As Falcon clutched the towel around himself and dripped on the floor, I talked to Miguel through the other bathroom door and confirmed that he also had a bruise and a lump in the same place.

"I'll get dressed and go," Falcon said, dejected.

I swung around and eyeballed him. "Excuse me?"

"Well, we can't hang around here, we'll just bring the Evos down on you."

"You … bloody idiot." I grabbed his towel and pulled him close with one hand, sliding the other around his head and pulling him down for a deep kiss. "You're not going anywhere without me, and you're *definitely* not going anywhere with a tracker still in your arse! If you really can't feel it yourself, then the injection site is still numb. If we move quickly, I can get it out before the numbness wears off."

"Are … are you sure?" Falcon asked, still clinging to his towel and breathing hard.

"Have you not realised yet, Fal?" I grinned at him, slightly hysterically. "I only took on an entire Evolutionary platoon to get my boyfriend back. One tiny tracker is a piece of piss."

As Falcon stammered in shock, I yelled at Miguel to hurry up, get some clothes on, and get his arse in the kitchen.

Raven was quietly waiting with the first aid kit, more towels, soap and water, and some of the hunting knives, freshly cleaned and glinting in the bright artificial lights.

"Nice thinking, Rave. How did you know what I needed?"

She shrugged, rolling out a towel on the table as part of our emergency operating theatre.

"Okay, who's going first?" I asked as Miguel and Falcon appeared nervously in the kitchen.

"I will," Miguel said immediately. Falcon looked like he was about to protest for sake of appearance, so I ordered him to go and wait in the lounge before he could speak.

"But I want to stay and help—"

"Watching and getting freaked out is *not* helpful. Go."

As soon as Falcon was safely out of the way, I had Miguel lying face-down on the table with a cushion and a wooden spoon to bite into.

I drew in a deep breath and touched the smooth warm stone of my *pounamu* pendant for strength. "Let's get this over with."

With Miguel's pants pulled down just far enough to expose the bruise on his butt cheek, and while I drenched my hands and upper arms in sanitiser, I talked Raven through swabbing the site with antiseptic from the kitchen, soaking the knife in more of the same, and preparing to make the first incision.

"Brace yourself," I said to Miguel. "Say if it gets too much, and don't jerk around or you might end up with a new arsehole."

I heard Falcon's whimper from the lounge, but ignored him.

"Just do it, Tui," Miguel said, his voice muffled by the pillow.

He didn't react as I slid the point of the knife across the lump, making as small of a cut as possible. The skin parted easily, and Raven quickly mopped up the blood that instantly trickled out.

"Can't feel much yet," Miguel said.

"Good." I could see the whitening of the flesh where the pressure of the foreign object was pushing up from underneath, a few centimetres deep in his subcutaneous fat layer. "Last cut."

As I drew the knife point through his flesh one more time, and saw the green of the pill-like object peek through, Miguel bellowed into the pillow. Raven and I ducked as his wings flexed.

"Almost done, one more thing," I said loudly over his noise. Placing my fingers on either side of the incision, I squeezed. The tracker popped out, and Raven daintily grabbed it with gloved fingers, dropping it into a nearby bowl.

"Just got to clean it up, bro, you'll be right," I said. Miguel's yelling had stopped but his breathing was ragged.

"Uhuh," he grunted.

He yelled again as I flushed the wound with a proper medical antiseptic from the first aid kit. As I directed Raven to hold the incision closed, I applied several cloth sutures, and then a few layers of bandages and tape for good measure, making sure there was no way that the flesh could pull apart again.

"Try not to bend your bum too much for a few days, bro," I said cheerfully. "You're done."

Awkwardly, Miguel rolled off the table and stood up. "Thanks, Doc," he said, grinning weakly, and limped off into the lounge.

"*Ka pai*, Nurse Raven," I said, smiling. "Nice work." She blushed and smiled back, and continued prepping for our next patient.

Falcon appeared a moment later.

"Come on, babe," I said, putting a fresh towel on the table. "The longer you wait, the more it's going to hurt."

"Just so you know," Falcon said, easing onto the operating surface. "I won't hold this against you." He gulped. "But if I say something … uh … not very nice while under extreme stress and pain, please don't hold it against me?"

"You'll be fine," I said cheerfully. "I've had practice now, so I know what I'm doing, eh."

"Thanks," Miguel said dryly from the lounge.

With freshly sterilised tools, Raven and I got to work. Lying with his face buried in the pillow and his hands interlaced behind his head, despite all of his bluster, Falcon didn't say a single word as I made the incision. His knuckles whitened, but otherwise he stayed perfectly still.

Until I had to extract the tracker, that is.

The volume of his scream made me flinch, and it was only Raven's quick reflexes that got the object out before it slid back into the deep incision. As Falcon cursed into the cushion, his whole body trembling, and his wings shivering, I kicked myself into gear, rapidly cleaning and bandaging the wound.

"There, all done!" I said, more brightly than I felt.

Finally, his long body relaxed, and his breathing slowed as he realised the worst was over. He lay there for a while as Raven and I cleaned up around him.

Falcon finally rolled off the table when there was a loud knocking.

"Somebody order a pizza or twenty?" Hawk called through the front door.

Falcon limped down the hallway. I grinned as I overheard him demanding the password, and Hawk and Kestrel protesting there wasn't any damn password, so open the damn door or they'd eat all the damn pizza themselves.

Triumphantly, the delivery crew strode into the kitchen, with their stockpile of pizza boxes and other takeaways, but stopped dead when they saw the remains of our improvised operating theatre.

"Okay, I hate to ask. But what's with all the blood?" Hawk peered around his 'Leaning Tower of Pizza'.

Miguel, Falcon, and I kept the explanation as short as possible as the heavenly smell of fresh mozzarella and tomato sauce wafted through the kitchen.

"We have to get the trackers moving again, quickly," Hawk said, eyeing the green objects with disgust. "Or they'll start closing in."

"Fine, but I'm taking a pizza with me," Falcon said.

"I'll help," I said.

Carrying a pizza box each, Falcon and I slipped from the house with the trackers in my pocket. I walked slowly, knowing that Fal's injured butt was killing him, even though he insisted it wasn't hurting anymore. Miguel tried to come too, but Kestrel convinced him to stay behind. I gave her a grateful smile as we left. She knew that Falcon and I needed some one-on-one time.

We didn't talk much on the way out of the development. We were too busy demolishing an entire pizza each. With our wings in full fold, stuffed under our hoodies, Falcon and I walked to the nearest petrol station, trying to keep out of the brightest streetlights. As casually as we could, we wandered past a truck that was idling while its driver was inside collecting a coffee, and tossed the trackers into the heavily-loaded trailer. We waited until the truck rumbled off towards the main road east, and breathed a deep sigh of relief. By the time the Evos realised we'd sent them on a wild goose chase and backtracked, we'd be long gone.

Ditching the empty pizza boxes in a bin, Falcon and I found ourselves walking back in an awkward silence.

"Tui," Falcon said, eventually.

"Yeah?"

"Did I hear you call me your boyfriend, before?"

My cheeks warmed. "Yeah."

I *heard* his sly grin. "I don't remember you asking me if that was okay."

"You are *such* an egg." When he just chuckled, I sighed. "All right. Fair enough. Ahem." I took a deep breath. "Falcon, will you go out with me?"

He pretended to think. "Do you mean like just on a date, or like officially seeing each other regularly, or do you mean exclusively, or—"

"You bloody … *American*! You *know* what I mean."

"I want to hear you say it."

Oh, for… "Do you want to be my boyfriend, or not?"

We were back in the dark safety of Heavenly Acres. Falcon grabbed my arm and pulled me to him. I felt his breath on my face, and my heart accelerated.

"Almost as much as I want to fly."

"Only almost?" I pretended to pout.

His lips touched mine and all the blood left my head.

When he finally broke away, he said, "Well, you did just carve a new hole in my ass…"

Groaning, I tried to pull free, but he just kissed me again.

"You're *welcome*," I said, pointedly, when he let me breathe.

"For what?"

"Saving your arse. Even if I did have to let some of the hot air out first."

Laughing, Falcon laced his fingers tightly around mine, and we resumed walking, though more slowly.

"I like you," he said.

"That's good, seeing as I'm your girlfriend now."

He chuckled. "You're different from all the other girls I knew at school."

"That's because you've never met a half Māori, half Samoan girl before."

"See, that's why I like you." He stopped again. "No crap, you just tell it like it is."

I shrugged. "Never had time to waste." I glanced around. Although the trackers were safely on their way out of the city, I still felt a little exposed. "Come on, we've got to get back to the Flight."

"Just a few more minutes? What's the hurry?"

"Well…"

Falcon stepped backwards into the dark shadows under a tree. "Five more minutes, while I have you to myself for once."

"Five minutes. Or they'll come looking for us anyways."

I let him pull me into the shadow with him, and into his arms. "Deal."

23

HAWK

By midmorning the next day, the Flight was safely away from the development, and occupying the far corner of a quiet suburban park.

Being back on my home turf made me feel better and worse at the same time. In this part of town, everything was slightly familiar, but not familiar enough. To keep the weird shivers out of my wings, I concentrated on the idea I'd had the night before.

Falcon was also in a weird mood, although his was probably caused by the painful hole in his ass cheek. He'd been walking stiffly and snapping at everyone all morning. Now, he crossed his arms and glared. "This is such a waste of time. I'll bet you anything we won't find the slightest trace of a Goldberg mutant-experimenter anywhere in LA."

Kestrel shrugged. "We don't have anything else to go on."

"Yeah, but how do we even start?"

"Kess, can I have the phone for a sec?" Tui asked. Kestrel passed it to her, having recharged it overnight. Tui sat back and began tapping at the screen, frowning.

Falcon flapped a hand irritably. "From what Miguel heard, this Goldberg guy wasn't exactly friends with the Evos, especially if he was doing stuff, quote, '*under the boss's nose*'. If the Evos can't find him, how the hell are *we* going to?"

It was now or never. I blurted my idea. "I think I might have a lead we can follow."

Six pairs of enlarged irises turned to me expectantly. I took a deep breath. "My family lives in LA. In fact, my house is probably less than thirty miles away. If anyone knows who messed with my DNA, it would be them."

"You mean, they'd remember who the fertility doctor was?" Kestrel asked, instantly intrigued.

I nodded. "Or at least which clinic the IVF stuff was done in." I was hazy on the exact process, and still had problems trying to use the technical terms for reproduction in association with my parents. "When I left home, Mom was planning to dig out all that old info, so she'll have it waiting for us."

Owl said, almost apologetically, "The Evolutionaries will have ... questioned them."

His words were like a punch to my gut. "How do you know?" I demanded, my heart rate accelerating.

He struggled to find the words. "It is ... logical?"

I struggled not to hyperventilate. Now I *had* to go home, to make sure my family was okay. If the Evos had come around while Dad was away, leaving Mom and Cherie without protection...

"Then they're already a couple of steps ahead of us. Are we going to try and catch up, or what?" My wings strained against the bomber jacket, instinctively trying to flare in my agitation.

Owl barely blinked. "They will be watching."

My fists clenched and I *really* wanted to punch something. An Evolutionary would have been nice. "So, we're careful about it."

"I think it'd be a little obvious if seven teenagers suddenly walked down your street and knocked on your door," Falcon said. "We can't all go."

"Who's coming with me, then?"

"I will," Kestrel and Miguel said at the same time.

"What do we do while you're off playing detectives?" Falcon picked up a rock and began tossing it back and forth between his hands. Under his hoodie, his wings fidgeted.

Owl shifted slightly against the tree he was leaning on. "Supplies."

Tui suddenly sat up. "Guys, you gotta see this."

She showed us the phone screen and unmuted the audio.

A shaky video tilted up to the sky and jerked around, until it centered on a gliding human figure with huge white Icarus wings. There was no mistaking it. The camera managed to follow the person for five full seconds before he or she flew over a clump of trees and disappeared.

The seven of us stared at each other.

"There was no tail!" Kestrel said, upset. "How come they could fly without a tail?"

"They were gliding. The video didn't show them taking off, or even flapping."

"This must be one of the 'others' that the Evos were talking about."

"But no one has naturally white hair ... do they?"

Unnoticed in Tui's hand, another video automatically queued, and began to play.

"Lord, we have heard Your call, and we await Your messengers!"

Miguel grabbed the phone. Reverend Carter's familiar face appeared. He was in his long white robes, with a backdrop of fluffy white clouds, standing with arms outstretched behind a pulpit. It was apparently a video produced and released by the Angelists, on their own evangelical YouTube channel.

"We have sought them out, but they are rightly wary of humanity, and of what we have become. We pray that they evade those who would desecrate Your Innocents, and seek us out in return so that we may become closer to You and know what it is You would have us do…"

Scrunching her nose, Tui paused the video. "Bunch of wackos."

"But what about White Wings?" Kestrel twisted her fingers together.

Miguel was stroking the cross around his neck thoughtfully. "It is a sign."

"Of what?" Falcon demanded.

"There are more of us. We should find them." Miguel stood up. "What else should we do, just keep running all the time?"

"I'm still going to talk to my parents, though," I said, quickly.

"Of course," Miguel said. "That's important. But what if they can't give us any more information and it's a dead end? We need to have something to aim for."

Tui stretched out her legs, staring past her feet into space. "I think it would be good for the Flight to have more people in it," she said. "That is, assuming they want to join."

"They don't necessarily have to become a member. We're not a gang," Miguel said, amused.

Falcon snorted with laughter. "We're the weirdest-looking gang, like, ever."

Miguel ignored him. "But to reach out the hand of friendship and reassure them they're not alone — well, if I was by myself, I would definitely appreciate it."

"Okay," Kestrel said, "so while we're at Hawk's house, Falcon, Tui, Owl and Raven can acquire replacement supplies." She patted a bulge in her pocket. "I still have all the cash my credit card let me take from the ATM last night."

"What do you think, Owl? Raven?" Miguel asked.

"Finding others is priority. Your … our … origins will not change."

"Straight from the wise old Owl's mouth," Tui said, grinning. "Raven, you agree too?"

Raven gave her single darting nod, not looking at anyone.

"I'm keen to keep moving. This long-distance flight stuff is good fun." Falcon stood up and stretched. I could hear the creak and rustle of his restrained wings, and mine itched in sympathy.

Tui copied Falcon's stretch. "The four of us will plan for tracking down the other Icari, and locate more supplies. You three go discover the meaning of life, and we'll rendezvous tonight."

Other details of our different missions were quickly agreed and then, a little dazed at how fast everything was moving, I followed Kestrel and Miguel toward the nearest bus stop.

By the time we'd crossed the city, which took hours on different buses, my wings were aching, and my dislike of public transport had evolved into a strong repulsion. But we had no other way of safely traveling in daylight. Our wings were in full fold under our hoodies and our eyes were hidden behind our sunglasses, but I knew we still stuck out. I just hoped it was no more than the other weirdos that came and went through the bus doors.

As I began recognizing familiar landmarks, my stomach twisted and my pulse accelerated. Kestrel reached over to stop my hands from strangling each other. Her touch jolted me, a surge of intense emotion briefly overpowering the building apprehension. I gave her a feeble smile.

"Everything's going to be fine, Hawk," Kestrel said softly. "Miguel and I will be with you all the way."

I nodded. "This is our stop," I said, surprised at how calm I sounded.

Only minutes later, I was staring at my parents' house. It hadn't changed at all. I couldn't think why it would have, but it still felt strange. I guessed because I'd changed so much so quickly, it seemed odd that the rest of my world hadn't done the same.

Miguel broke me out of my trance. "Do you think your parents are home?"

I checked my watch. "Mom probably will be. I don't know about Dad — he could be anywhere."

"I guess we'll find out," Kestrel said. She took my arm and my skin fizzed under her touch. "Come on, Hawk."

Kess pulled my unresisting body up the driveway to the front door, positioned me squarely in front of it, and knocked firmly. Then she stepped back beside Miguel.

I heard my mom's voice inside, calling to Cherie as she approached the front door.

Then the door opened.

Mom looked at me and went white.

"Hi, Mom."

Her hand shot out. She dragged me inside, threw her arms around me and squeezed. Kess and Miguel quickly stepped in after me.

"Where have you been? What happened to you? How did you get home? What's been going on?"

"Mom, Mom, it's okay, I'm okay," I said, not entirely sure how to deal with my hysterical mother. She still hadn't let go of me, but then I realized my arms were just as tight around her. I buried my head in her hair and tried not to cry when her familiar smell filled my nose.

I jumped as a high-pitched shriek cut into my sensitive hearing. "TY-WER!"

Something small and pink with brown curls hit my legs at Mach One. I let go of Mom and reached down to Cherie.

"Hey, Cherie," I said shakily. "I didn't think you'd miss me."

"Tywer, Tywer!" Apparently, Cherie had regressed from six to three in the few months I'd been gone. I detached her from my leg and lifted her up for a proper hug. She couldn't stretch her arms around me and clamped to my shoulders instead.

"What the hell is going on?" My father strode in and ground to a halt. "Tyler?"

My relief at seeing him home, and in regular clothes, nearly choked me.

"Hi, Dad."

He looked at Kess and Miguel, who were trying to blend in with the wall. "Who the hell are you?"

"I'm Miguel, sir, and this is Kestrel."

Mom rushed over to them. "You brought him home! Where did you find him? How did you do it? How can we ever repay you?"

Miguel held up his hands uncomfortably. "Um, Mrs. Owen, can we talk to you first? We have some questions too."

Mom drew back, uncertain. Miguel and Kess took off their sunglasses.

Mom and Dad stared at Kestrel and Miguel's abnormally large irises, and their unusually hunched shoulders, and back to mine. Mom's hand covered her mouth again.

"Are you ... is it ... how...?"

I put Cherie down. "Mom, Dad, we need to talk. Quickly. I can't stay long."

Mom shook her head and reached for me again. "Don't be silly. Where are you going? Where have you been?"

"I don't know how much time I've got, so if we can sit down somewhere, I'll try to explain."

"Kess and I will keep an eye out," Miguel said. "We won't intrude."

"I'm sure Cherie would like to show me her room," Kestrel said, smiling at my little sister. Enthusiastically, Cherie grabbed her hand and towed Kestrel up the stairs at top speed. Miguel nodded to me and moved off, placing himself in the living room where he could see the road without himself being seen.

Before he shut the front door, Dad leaned outside and scanned the street. He then slammed and locked it with the multiple deadbolts.

Meanwhile, Mom pulled me into the kitchen, where I finally realized she had giant, silent tears rolling down her face.

"I'm so sorry, Tyler," Mom whispered, thick tracks of mascara staining her cheeks. She pulled me into her embrace. "We missed you so much. We were *so worried*."

My dad entered the room and wrapped his strong arms around me from the other side. For a few long seconds, I felt completely safe.

Mom was kissing my head and Dad was rumbling away comfortingly. It took me a moment to register what he was saying.

"No matter what, Tyler, you are our son and we love you. We don't know why this is happening, but we'll get through it. Somehow."

"Who wants a drink?" Mom asked, forcefully cheerful. She pulled away and started making coffee, working around the abandoned half-made dinner as she began firing questions at me again. "What have you been *doing* all this time? Where have you *been?*"

"Settle down, Julia. Give Ty a chance to speak," Dad said gently, but he gave me a stern look. "You couldn't even have called or texted to tell us you were okay?"

I flushed and ducked my head guiltily. "We were a bit busy," I mumbled.

"Doing *what?*"

"Learning to fly."

"You can *fly?*"

"Yeah, turns out these things actually work." I carefully pulled off my jacket and sweatshirt, revealing the fully folded lump of my wings. Hissing a little with the cramp, I straightened my wing fingers and eased one wing away from my body, the other keeping my tail clamped against my back.

"Wow, those are … bigger," Mom said in a bright, brittle voice.

Dad moved behind Mom and rested his hands on her shoulders. "Where have you been?"

"We were camping out in the desert for a while. The thermals helped us to train."

"Us? How many of you are there?"

"Well, there's me, and Miguel, and Kestrel — I mean, Victoria — and then there are four others. Seven in total ... so far."

My dad frowned. "Kestrel-you-mean-Victoria?"

"Most of us have taken bird names. The others call me Hawk."

Mom and Dad digested that for a moment. "How come there are so many of you?"

"I don't know. I was hoping you could give us a clue. I know you told me I was IVF, and the clinic was in Beijing, but ... does the name Goldberg mean anything to you?"

Mom bustled over to a drawer. "While you were away, I found all the old records." She pulled out a page of hand scribbled notes, wiping impatiently at her eyes. "They took every piece of evidence with them, but I wrote down what I could remember."

Instantly it felt like all my feathers were standing on end. "*They*? Who's *they*?"

"They claimed to be from the state government, but I couldn't verify their credentials," Dad said, his voice tight. "I followed them after one of their visits and they went into an unmarked building. After a bit of snooping, I found out that it belonged to the Evolutionary Corporation. The next time they tried coming around, I was waiting in full uniform with a police officer and a restraining order against them. Haven't seen them since." He folded his arms, looking self-satisfied. "I extended my leave to make sure that I was home to protect your mother and sister."

Despite the relief that Dad had been as prepared as always, I couldn't stop the blood draining from my face. *The Evolutionaries have been in my house?* I had known that it was likely, but it was still terrifying. I fought to keep my voice steady. "What evidence did they take?"

"The information leaflets from the IVF clinic, receipts, all your old x-rays, that kind of thing." Mom handed me the piece of paper a little fearfully. "I don't know anything about a Goldberg, but I re-read some of the old paperwork before those people took it away."

I stared down at the single piece of paper in my hand.

Dr. Kris Schmidt. Golden Goose Fertility Clinic. Beijing.

"You never told me what you were doing in Beijing?" I asked, numbly.

Dad shrugged. "I was sent there on short-term diplomatic duty with a few other delegates from various arms of the government and the Forces. Partners were allowed to come too. There were several big international conferences going on at the time, and I do remember there seemed to be a lot of international couples at the clinic."

"In fact, we heard about it from one of the Navy reps," Mom said. "He and his wife were considering taking advantage of the cheaper price and newer technique."

"And did they?"

"They did, but we don't know if they got pregnant or not." Dad shrugged. "While you were gone, we wondered if they had, and if their child had also … uh … changed. So I tried tracking him down, but they seem to have fallen off the grid. Can't find a trace of him or his wife anywhere online, or through any channels and contacts at work."

Mom sat down with a cup of coffee. "As for the clinic, I've trawled the internet for hours with every search term I can think of, but it's like it never existed at all."

I tried to sort through the thousand questions swirling through my head, but before I could line up the words in order, Miguel burst into the room.

"Sorry to interrupt, but we have a problem."

24

HAWK

As Miguel sucked in a deep breath to explain, there was a huge smash at the front door.

"Cherie!" Mom screamed, her chair crashing to the floor as she leapt up.

A second later, Kess dashed into the kitchen with Cherie clutched in her arms.

"The whole street is filled with Evolutionaries!" Kestrel's eyes were wild. "What the hell do we do?"

"Back door, get out of here, now," Dad ordered. As there was another smash at the front door, he grabbed his wallet and thrust a wad of cash into my hands. "Julia, take Cherie to the neighbors. Any of them. The further down the street, the better."

"I'll call the cops." Mom snatched her cell off the table and reached for Cherie.

As Kestrel peeled my little sister off her body, Miguel peered out the window in the back door.

"We have at least two men in combat armor in the backyard," he said, his voice low. "They're trying to flush us out."

The front door crashed open, and heavy footsteps echoed down the hallway. Dad swore and pushed hard on my shoulder. I dropped to the floor, quickly followed by Kestrel and Miguel.

"Basement?" Kestrel asked.

I shook my head.

Dad had already jammed the kitchen door with a chair. Now he grabbed the table and flipped it on its side, sending paper and plates flying. I helped him shove it into the corner, away from any windows. Mom huddled behind it, protecting Cherie with her body. My little sister was so terrified, she was absolutely silent.

"Weapons?" Dad demanded.

I showed him the hunting knife. Kestrel and Miguel spread their hands helplessly.

Dad grunted and pulled a pistol from the back of his belt. "Get behind me." With the evening pressing in on the windows, he flicked off the lights.

As my sensitive eyes quickly adjusted, I knelt to strap on my tail, and listened hard. Kestrel and Miguel did the same. The Evolutionaries were closing in on the kitchen. We could hear them working their way through the house, muttering 'clear' as they passed each room.

"Hello?" Mom whispered. I glanced over and saw her clutching her cell to her mouth, Cherie's dark curls trembling just below her jaw. "I need police, right now. We have armed intruders, I repeat, multiple armed intruders…"

As she continued pleading to the 911 responders, I tried to concentrate on the hints of hostile activity behind the closed kitchen door and the walls of my home. My feathers and skin crawled with fear and fury, my chest burning.

"Miguel!" Kestrel muttered, pointing behind him.

Our friend took one glance and nodded. Silently, his hand reached up onto the kitchen counter and closed on the handle of a large knife. Kestrel took one too, and in her other hand she picked up the gently-steaming kettle. Her golden feathers fidgeted with fear.

"*We know you're in there,*" a harsh male voice announced through the kitchen door. "*If the mutants come quietly, nobody will get hurt.*"

Dad released the safety on his gun and took aim at the door. "I'll give you one minute to leave my house, or *all* of you will *definitely* get hurt." He urgently motioned for us to get down.

Pressed against the upturned table, I took a deep breath.

The door crashed aside. Dad opened fire. The barrage of gunshots carved holes in my ears. I cried out involuntarily. Several men dropped in the doorway, moaning and clutching at leaking wounds. Their colleagues took cover in the hall and, as the gunshots paused, through the echoes in my ears I could hear someone muttering rapidly into a radio.

"Back door," Miguel said. I glanced over. Three men were running through the yard, weapons ready.

"Tranquilizers," I said, recognizing the adapted air barrels.

Kestrel inched along the wall. "And bullets," she whispered. She pointed through the window, careful not to expose herself. Two more men were attempting to hide in the twilit yard, covering their colleagues' approach with semi-automatic rifles.

With Dad defending the hallway door, taking a shot at any hint of an Evolutionary, Kestrel, Miguel and I turned to the back door. In the corner behind the table, Cherie whimpered. Mom shushed her, starting to rock and hum, her voice shaking.

Just before the new Evos arrived, I had an idea. I grabbed the heavy roasting pan off the counter, sending raw potatoes flying, and jumped beside the back door. A moment later it was broken open. As the first man entered with air rifle held high, I smashed the pan into his face. Bone crunched, and he fell to the floor with a groan.

Darts shot through the doorway. I heard the slight whistle and vibration in their fletching as they passed me. I raised my knife, ready for the next man, but Kestrel got there first.

As he peered around the doorframe, she hurled the kettle. Scalding water hit him a split second before the appliance. He screamed and disappeared into the yard. The man who appeared in his place flinched as Kestrel and Miguel threw their knives at him. One gashed his sleeve and arm as it bounced off. He yelled and fell back, dragging his colleagues with him.

I rolled my neck and resettled the hunting knife in my hand. "Three down, two to go."

"Assuming they don't have more reinforcements," Kestrel said, her voice trembling, and looking for more weapons.

"How many could they have sent?"

Miguel shifted in his crouched position. "As soon as we clear the back yard, we should fly for it."

"But my family—"

"They want you, not us," Dad interrupted, his voice flat. "I'll cover you. Get your mom and sister into the neighbor's yard, and then you put those wings to work. Haul ass out of here."

"But—"

Dad turned to me. "DO IT, TYLER!"

As he raised his hand to order me out of the house, there was a single gunshot. Time slowed. I heard the bullet hit. I saw the shockwave of the impact ripple up from his back into his neck, his eyes turning blank. In slow motion, he fell to his knees, then slumped forward. His outstretched hand hit my foot.

My breath scraped so loudly, I could hear nothing else.

"Dad?"

I dropped beside him, the knife clattering to the floor.

My mother screamed. She appeared on Dad's other side, grabbing at the creeping stain of red in the back of his shirt.

I felt the words falling from my mouth. "I'm sorry, I'm sorry, it's my fault…"

She stared at me, and I waited a heartbeat for her to say it wasn't, that everything was going to be okay.

But she didn't.

She shook his body, crying out his name. Miguel and Kestrel appeared, shouting, but I couldn't understand what they were saying. Kestrel tugged at my shoulder, and Miguel wrapped his arm around my mom.

In the distance, I heard Evolutionaries shouting and retreating. A far-off throbbing was growing in the air.

Slowly, Miguel's words came into focus.

"Mrs. Owen! Mrs. Owen, you must get Cherie out of here! Now!"

Gently but firmly, Miguel pulled Mom away. Cherie was screaming. Mom's eyes slowly tore away from Dad, and turned to her daughter. Grabbing my little sister, she jumped to her feet and fled through the back door, with Miguel right beside her.

"Hawk!" Kestrel shook my arm. "Hawk, look at me!"

I felt myself mutter through the daze. "It's my fault."

"No, it's not, he's not—"

"IT'S MY FAULT!"

Kestrel instinctively dropped my hand and leapt back, her eyes wide, and her breath heaving.

"This is ALL my fault!"

Turning, I ran from the house and into the night. In a dozen steps, I was in the air. Kestrel kept shouting, but I couldn't listen.

Tears burning my eyes and horror ripping me apart, I flew for the sky as hard as I could. Other dark shapes darted through the night above me, and I recognized Tui, Falcon, Owl and Raven. They'd found us. The Flight was okay.

Then, a sharp white light pinned me to the sky like an insect.

Twisting in mid-air, I saw the shadow of a helicopter closing in, following the spotlight that had me in its clutches.

I heard yells from the Flight.

Fierce determination burst into flame. "NO!" *You are NOT taking anyone else from me!*

Rolling over, I started to sprint away from the helicopter, flapping as fast as I could. I had to lead them away from the Flight, from my mother and sister, from...

With a roar of pure misery and rage, I accelerated into the night with the chopper hard on my tail.

As my wings flapped harder, and the burning in my muscles began to drown out all other pain, I slipped away from emotion and into a place of cold logic. In that moment, I knew I had to make a distraction. Something huge, to draw *all* the Evos away, not just the chopper. It had to be big, it had to be loud, and it had to be irresistible.

Behind me, the helicopter rose higher, away from the dangers of trees and powerlines. I kept low, zigging and zagging, my feathers clipping streetlights and dodging signs. The few people who looked up in time to see me flash past could only gape. But the spotlight never lost me for more than a few seconds.

The glow of downtown LA was only a few miles away. Exhaustion was already creeping into my muscles, the lactic acid eating at me. But I couldn't slow down.

To one side of the city was an even brighter glow. As the buildings grew taller, I worked my way higher, and angled for a better look.

As the helicopter closed in, I realized it was the baseball stadium. There was a game on. The place was packed.

I didn't stop to think, or I might have chickened out. Tucking in my wings, I spun through an aileron roll and banked toward the cauldron of light. The helicopter was slow to respond, and I accelerated away, leaving the spotlight behind.

Seconds later I was nearly blinded, and I was thankful for my tinted glasses. Turning in a tight, upward spiral, I flapped hard to a point high above the top tier of the stands. As the Evolutionary helicopter approached, rapidly climbing to match my height, I paused in mid-air. I hovered for a moment, almost weightless in the hot updraft rising from tens of thousands of people, and hundreds of thousands of watts pumping into the night air.

Then I folded my wings.

I plummeted headfirst, flashing straight past the helicopter. Just above the stands, the huge thump of my full wingspan catching the air made the entire crowd look up.

The startled shrieks and cries whipped past my ears. Fighting to keep steady, I rocketed down the tiers, just above the crowd. With a massive effort I pulled up above the startled players, zoomed across the ballpark with the momentum, and swooped partway up

the other side before I had to flap. Catching a glimpse of the huge
TV screens frantically zooming in on me, I heard the announcers
yelling hysterically into their microphones.

I left the stadium and shot toward the central city, flashing across
the freeway and aiming for the canyons between skyscrapers.

As I slalomed around the first giant building, another helicopter
appeared right in front of me.

"Whoa!"

Instinctively diving, I flashed under it, and narrowly avoided
becoming the Icarus equivalent of bug strike.

Now everyone on the street was looking up, arms pointing,
mouths working, chaos spreading like a virus. My adrenaline was
pumping so hard, I was incapable of fear. Just because I could,
I did another roll and took off down the steel-and-glass-walled
canyon. The heat rising from the asphalt after a hot LA day lifted
my wings as I flapped harder and harder.

At the next intersection, I threw my left wing high and turned
sharply to the right, the breeze dragging on my tail as my legs
swung around the corner after me. I caught a glimpse of a third
helicopter pacing me along a parallel street. It was a news copter,
and the cameras were rolling.

Slipping into a higher gear, I began weaving back and forth. I
rolled and swooped, sliding around corners like a drifting car. The
thick, hot city air swirled under my feathers and in my throat like
warm seawater, and I let the unpredictable currents take me with
them.

Two black vehicles appeared below me, racing dangerously
through the streets and causing multiple crashes with oncoming
traffic. There was mayhem as pedestrians ran for cover.

One helicopter tried to cut me off as I barreled down a boulevard. I twisted, tucking in my wings and spinning past as it swung to target me. In that brief instant, I saw it was carrying people armed with tranquilizer guns. I knew if they darted me from this height, I'd be roadkill when I hit the ground.

A distorted amplified voice ricocheted down the street. Cop cars were catching up with the Evolutionaries. I was winging my way through Downtown LA, with both helicopters on my tail, and the news bird circling above. I wasn't sure if the cops were yelling at me, the chase cars, or the invading choppers. It didn't matter. I wasn't listening anyway.

Swerving, I took a corner way too fast and nearly smeared myself across a skyscraper. I recovered in time, but I'd lost both height and distance. Exhaustion crept deeper into my muscles.

I might not make it out free, or even alive.
The realization brought me no fear. I was beyond emotion.

As I swerved around another corner, I nearly hit a stop light. I fought hard to gain height, but the Evolutionaries' black helicopter was right overhead and forcing me down. The chase cars had picked up a couple of cops each, but they were tailing me while completely ignoring the flashing lights behind them and the chaos in front of them.

Bluntly, I couldn't see a way out.

"You flew too close to the sun, Icarus," I said. "Time to taste the salt."

25

KESTREL

"HAWK!" I screamed. "HE'S NOT DEAD!"

But Hawk, already fifty feet in the air, didn't hear me.

I swore and ran back into the house, dropping to my knees next to his dad. The bloodstain was a little bigger, and Colonel Owen's pulse a little weaker, but it was still there.

Miguel shouted from the yard. "They're safe, let's go! Come on!"

I heard distant sirens growing louder, racing towards the scene. There was nothing I could do to help Hawk's dad, as he was still unconscious, and I knew if I tried to move him, I'd probably make him worse.

Gazing frantically around, I saw the Evolutionaries had gone, taking their wounded with them. The kitchen was a warzone. Bullet holes in the walls, the overturned table, scattered potatoes and broken dishes. Blood oozing across the floor. Hawk's abandoned bomber jacket. His knife.

With shaking hands, I picked it up and slid it into the straps on my flight boot.

"KESTREL!"

"I'm so sorry," I said to Hawk's dad. "Help is coming."

Then I turned and ran into the back yard. Miguel was waiting with his wings open, ready to take off.

"Hawk's mom and sister are safe with the neighbours and an ambulance is on the way," he said. "Where's Hawk?"

"He thought his dad was dead and just ... flipped out."

Something tickled my cheek. I brushed it away, vaguely surprised to find large tears staining the back of my hand. "Where the hell did the Evolutionaries go?"

Miguel pointed up. Against the dull glow of the city-lit clouds, I saw the shadows of the Flight circling. "Not sure, but it was something the others did. Let's get out of here before the Evos come back."

Sucking in a deep breath, I tensed every muscle in my body and jumped into the air at the same time as I swept my wings forward. Miguel's downdraft battered my head but I kept flapping, my legs hooking together and the air gradually lifting me higher.

"About time," Tui said, as we approached their altitude.

"Where's Hawk?"

"See that crazy dot being chased by a helicopter, straight toward the middle of the freaking city?" Falcon said, his voice tense. "That's him."

I swore.

"Police here," Owl said.

At the end of Hawk's street, several cop cars and an ambulance swerved around the corner and raced toward his house. A moment later, I saw movement in the dark yard below us. I flinched, thinking it was the Evolutionaries, but it was Hawk's mom, sprinting for her house and her wounded husband.

"Hawk thinks his dad is dead, and that it's all his fault," I said to the circling Flight, my voice surging with each flap. "He's

possibly suicidal right now. We have to get him back before
the Evos take him out."

"How, exactly?" Tui demanded.

"How did you scare off the Evos from here?"

Falcon snorted. "Wasn't us. We were on our way to the
rendezvous, saw the chaos, and headed over. But then Hawk
came blasting out and the helicopter took off after him. The
others ran away from the cops."

"Okay, then it's our turn to distract them from Hawk. There
are seven of us, and one helicopter. It can't chase all of us, and
if we lead it on until it runs out of fuel, then we're skyfree."

Falcon sighed loudly. "Worth a try."

I rolled over, pointed myself toward the receding helicopter,
and began to accelerate. Five other pairs of wings quickly fell
in behind me. Together, the Flight sprinted after Hawk.

With my blood pounding and my wings burning, the city
air raced past my face. The thickness and stench of it was
choking after the thin dry atmosphere of the desert.

Ahead, I saw the tiny dot that was Hawk, spiralling above
a giant stadium. As the helicopter closed in, he suddenly dived
straight down. I shrieked as he disappeared. Then he swooped
up the other side and began sprinting straight for the city. The
Evolutionary helicopter, its pilot probably as stunned as we
were, was slow to respond. Hawk vanished into the maze of
skyscrapers before it had finished turning to follow.

I thought I knew what his plan was.

*Okay, Hawk, the cavalry's here. You don't have to do this on
your own.*

"When we get to the city, split up!" I yelled. "Make the biggest scene you can without getting caught, then fly and hide while the Evos are tangled up with everyone else!"

"You're insane!" Falcon shouted. "I like it!"

Tui laughed. "Count me in!"

"Works for me," Miguel said, his voice low but strong.

"Owl? Rave?"

As I glanced back, they made the 'okay' sign with their hands.

I resettled my glasses over my eyes. "If you cross paths with Hawk, try to get it into his thick skull that his dad *is still alive*, and get him out of there."

"Roger that!" Falcon yelled, excitement obvious even through the strain of flapping so hard and fast.

"Let's do this!"

As the Flight followed me into the city, they split up, peeling off in different directions, searching for Hawk.

I continued carving a path straight down the middle, trying not to think about the thousands of people and their phones now watching me. My blonde wings continued stroking through the air, forward-twist-back, again and again. My chest and back burned with the effort, my breath rasping with each powerful compression of my wings. But I didn't slow down.

Within minutes of our arrival, the city was in absolute chaos. Cars sideswiped each other as the drivers gaped upwards, or just stopped in the middle of the road to stare. The crowded pavements stopped flowing, and pedestrians jostled to get a clear view for their phone cameras. I glimpsed another helicopter, or maybe two, through the forest of buildings. My feathers prickled and itched with the feeling of being exposed to millions of eyes, but I kept flapping.

As I swung around a skyscraper, gravity tugging on my tail and wings, I saw Falcon and Tui cross paths as they wove through the streets. As they sped toward each other, Tui held out her hand. Timing their flaps, they spun past each other and slapped a high five, and shot away in opposite directions, the helicopters behind them struggling to avoid each other and keep up.

Then one helicopter turned and spotted me. Forgetting Falcon, it began to accelerate in my direction.

All right, Kestrel, remember this was your idea. Turning, I flew as hard as I could the other way.

At first, the helicopter stayed level with me, and its spotlight swung wildly from side to side as I zigged and zagged, ignoring the crowds below, concentrating only on charting a random course through the city, keeping my eyes open for Hawk.

Then the helicopter's spotlight broadened as it gained height, and I couldn't shake it for more than a few seconds at a time.

"Kestrel, incoming!"

I dodged. Miguel swept past so close I felt his slipstream tug on my feathers. The spotlight swung to follow him, and I rolled and raced in the other direction.

After a few moments, I realised I was alone in the air, and there was no sign of pursuit on the ground. Just a throng of ordinary people staring and pointing as I zoomed past. Panting, I ignored them, taking advantage of the brief respite to gain some height.

Just above the skyscrapers, I scanned the streets for my friends. Tui and Falcon were leading a helicopter on a circular chase around and around one particular block, Falcon clearly laughing his head off at the dumb doggedness of the Evos. Raven and Owl were darting in and out of view as the news helicopter struggled to keep them in shot. I couldn't see Miguel.

After circling a few times, I gently dove towards one of the taller buildings. I dropped my feet and unhooked my tail, touching down a little heavier than usual thanks to the fatigue in my bones. Shaking the ache from my wings, I paced along the edge of the building, peering at the city below, waiting for any sign of Hawk.

Briefly, I was struck by the absurdity that I was standing on the verge of a several-hundred-metre drop, without paying the slightest attention to the fatal void.

"Kess, you okay?"

I looked up as Miguel soared past. "Any sign of Hawk?"

"A couple of flashes, but I keep losing him."

"If you see the others, might be time to start pulling back," I said, as another batch of cop cars screamed along the streets. "Maybe we can flush him out."

"I'll let them know. We'll head back toward the baseball game."

I waved as Miguel banked away. In the distance, on the other side of the city, a helicopter swung wildly as it tried to chase two tiny dark specks between the skyscraper spires. I watched the silhouettes of my friends evade the helicopter with extreme turns and tight tricks in the terrifyingly limited airspace.

Suddenly, Hawk's distinctive mottled brown wings flashed past me. I broke into a run, dashed along the edge of the building and dived off the other side. For a second, I hung in the abyss, reaching out.

Then my wings opened wide, my legs hooked together. The air gathered underneath me, and I sprinted after Hawk.

Multiple Evolutionary and cop cars were on his tail, and the original helicopter was closing in on him. I tried screaming his name, but he didn't hear.

I paced the chase from above, unable to overtake but refusing to give up. Hawk was getting tired. I could tell from his uneven flapping and the slow descent as he raced along the streets.

"Hawk, look out!" I shrieked uselessly as he drifted far too wide around a corner. The helicopter was directly over him now, and trying to force him down.

I watched, my heart sinking, as he folded his wings and dived towards the traffic jamming the street. There was nowhere for him to go.

At the last second, he twisted and shot between two lorries. For a heart-piercing moment, he vanished.

I gasped.

He burst into clear air, still spinning from the effort of slipping through the narrow gap. My wings flapped in time with his as I watched him accelerating towards clear air, the Evo cars crashing into the stationary traffic, the helicopter struggling to regain height in the limited space. I banked sideways, trying to take a shortcut between the buildings and head Hawk off down the next street. He seemed to be aiming for the edge of the city.

But then another helicopter erupted from a side street and cut him off. His wings fluttered in the downwash, the violent wind robbing him of lift and throwing him sideways.

"No!" I shrieked, flapping harder.

I was too late.

The Evolutionaries began firing tranquiliser darts from the open door of the helicopter. One went through Hawk's wing.

Adrenaline surged again, my breathing rasping as I tried to set an air speed record. My flight glasses fogged. Clenching my teeth, I squinted through the haze. Hawk was falling from the sky, his flapping rough and ragged.

The deep blast of an air horn nearly scared me out of my feathers. Hawk was over the motorway, struggling to stay above the hurtling vehicles. He was swiped sideways by the slipstream of a massive lorry, then knocked in the other direction by another random gust of air.

Then I saw the bright tail of a tranquiliser dart hit his shoulder.

I screamed.

26

KESTREL

Hawk's wing slowed, flapping spasmodically. Another air horn blasted. Hawk desperately swung around. A whole convoy of trucks was roaring unstoppably towards him.

One was a fully loaded car carrier. Hawk twisted in mid-air, and began to dive.

"*What the hell are you doing?*" I shrieked from hundreds of metres away, helplessly watching the lorry close in on him. The three pickup trucks on the upper deck of the trailer seemed to flicker as they passed under the streetlights. The first pickup edged past him, then the second. Suddenly, Hawk dropped the last metre and smashed into the bed of the third pickup. He ricocheted around before crashing into the tailgate. I screamed again.

Swerving to follow the lorry and its new Icarus load, I realised the helicopter was doing the same. I stroked upwards instead, my chest burning and wings aching with the effort. But they roared past underneath me, apparently without noticing I was there.

Terrified, I followed the chopper as it tailed the lorry with its spotlight. Two Evo vehicles caught up, forcing the car carrier to take the next motorway exit and pull over on a random suburban street. Hawk hadn't moved since the crash. I couldn't see his face under his crumpled wing. I *knew* it was bad. Fear stung every nerve. *Don't you be dead, don't you DARE be dead…*

"Where the hell is everyone?" I cried. "I can't do this by myself!"

Miguel called from above. "Right here, Kess."

With brief relief, I glanced up to see his black wings a few dozen metres above me. Behind him, the four others flew in formation.

"Is he okay?" Tui called.

My feathers shivered. "I don't know."

"Look," Falcon cried. "He moved."

"It was just the downdraft from the chopper," Tui said, uncertainly.

We circled above the scene. A dozen armed Evolutionaries were advancing on the lorry and its driver, who'd emerged bright red and bellowing. The hovering helicopter was battering Hawk's limp wings with the turbulent wash from its rotors. There was nothing we could do. In a matter of minutes, they'd have climbed the lorry and taken him prisoner.

"We have to take out the chopper somehow," Miguel said.

Owl cleared his throat. "Rocks," he said.

I looked at the others. "Will that work?"

"Worked last time," Tui said.

"Yeah, but on *cars*."

Falcon frowned. "It's all we've got."

"But we *don't*—"

Fal pointed at a nearby backyard. "How about that?"

"Okay, but hurry!"

As we struggled back into the sky with hands and pockets full of ornamental rocks from someone's garden feature, an expensive black sports car pulled up next to the lorry. The Evolutionaries noticeably tensed as a man in a dark business suit emerged and glared at the scene. We couldn't hear a word he said over the thudding roar of the helicopter, but he was clearly angry as he gesticulated at the lorry. As he finished yelling, I thought I lipread the words: *Don't screw this one up!*

While a team of Evos prepared to scramble up the car carrier's ladder, the helicopter's spotlight blinked off. It banked away, taking the flattening hurricane from its blades with it, then carefully positioning itself to land in the centre of a large intersection.

"This could be our chance—"

Suddenly, Hawk burst into life. He rolled upright and scrambled onto the cab of the pickup truck. Two bounds and he leapt off the lorry into the air. His wings were out of sync, but they were both moving, flapping frantically to gain height.

The Evolutionary boss pointed, and clearly bellowed, "Get him!"

"Come on, Hawk!" I screamed, along with several other cries from the Flight.

Hawk glanced at the head Evolutionary and paused long enough to pull both middle fingers at him.

"MOVE IT, HAWK!"

The helicopter swung around, nearly clipping a power pole, and began to chase him.

"Now!" I shrieked, and the Flight dived for the chopper, hurling rocks at its finely-balanced rotor blades. Most missed, but a few connected, chipping the fuselage and flicking off into the night. The helicopter jerked, but it kept going after Hawk.

Behind us, Evolutionaries pointed and yelled, bringing their guns to bear, but we were already in the next street and drifting further. Frantically, the Evos tried to chase us around the block.

Beyond and below, Hawk was faltering, limping through the air only metres above the suburban rooftops. Dumbfounded locals stared at the scene taking place in their evening sky and at the black-uniformed mercenaries swarming past them. A siren began to wail in the near distance.

"Hawk!" I yelled, trying to get ahead of the chopper to where he could see me.

He glanced around, but not up, swiping at his flight glasses. He was barely crawling through the sky now. A rock bounced off the helicopter and past his head. Hawk's gaze followed, too slowly. His wings thrashed.

CRACK! A large rock smashed a rotor blade, shrapnel whizzing in all directions. The helicopter screamed like it was fighting for its life, its rotor rhythm broken and stuttering. It began to fall sideways towards the street – towards Hawk.

I had to get there first.

I dived. Folding my wings, I aimed straight for him.

I hit his body at full speed, knocking him sideways and down. His arms curled around me and we smacked into the branches of a tree. The helicopter's out-of-control tail passed through the patch of air we'd occupied a split second before, then struck the road with an enormous crash.

Hawk hit the ground hard and I landed on top of him.

Gasping, I struggled upright, twigs and leaves tangled in my feathers and hair.

"Hawk! Hawk, are you okay?"

Frantically, I felt for his pulse and breath, pressing my ear to his chest. He grunted weakly, one arm dragging across the ground to brush my hair off his face.

"Oh, Hawk!"

I threw my arms around him. He grunted pathetically again. Finally, I realised he couldn't breathe. Clumsily, I rolled off his chest.

He sucked in a huge lungful of air. I let him take two more before I grabbed his arm and urged him to get up. He did so, painfully slowly. As his face gradually lifted to meet my anxious gaze, I saw the deadness in his eyes.

"Why ... Kess?"

"Oh, Hawk," I said again, my voice breaking. "It's not your fault." The muscles in his face hardened, and I reached up to grab him. "Listen to me, Hawk. Your dad is *not dead*. He was still alive when the ambulance arrived. He was hurt bad, but I'm *sure* he's going to be okay. You hear me?"

For a moment, nothing changed in his face. Then, as it slowly sank in, the relief drained all the tension from his body. He staggered. I grabbed him, trying to keep him upright. We still had to get *out* of there.

He sucked in a jagged breath. "What ... happened?"

"The whole Flight was on your tail, trying to help with causing chaos and confusion so the Evos would get snarled up in all the mess and we could lose them, and find you. I was right on your tail as you ... when you hit the lorry, I ... I thought..." I couldn't breathe, tears slicing at my eyes.

"Hey, Kess, don't cry, I'm okay," he said awkwardly, and his arms moved around me.

I turned into him and reached up at the same moment as he leaned down. Our lips met, and suddenly we were kissing.

Intense, raw emotion overpowered everything else, all the pain and fear. I forgot to breathe, forgot to move. My whole body fizzed.

Then something exploded in the burning helicopter in the next street. We flinched, breaking apart.

"Um," I said, blushing.

Hawk pulled me back towards him, but I reluctantly lifted my hand to his mouth before he could kiss me.

"We can *definitely* do that again, but maybe *after* we've finished escaping from the Evolutionaries?" I suggested.

"Promise?" he asked, hope colouring his voice.

I smiled. "Promise." I tugged on his hand. "Come on, the helicopter's crashed. Let's go while we still can."

As he followed me through the bushes of the dark back yard, I emptied my pockets of the last few rocks. Hawk groaned.

"We have to get some better weapons."

I giggled a little hysterically. "Why? It's worked twice now."

Before he offered a comeback, more sirens and yells interrupted. Hawk moaned in pain and his hands covered his sensitive ears. His head was probably still ringing from the impact with the pickup truck.

Glancing up, I could just identify five silhouettes circling several hundred feet above, beyond the reach of the orange streetlights and invisible to the human eye.

"Hawk, can you fly?" I asked urgently. "Just one more time."

He sagged for a moment, but his brown wings twitched, and he pulled himself upright. "I'll make it."

Miraculously, or perhaps thanks to Owl's engineering, both of our tails were bent but not broken. They'd be enough for us to escape. With my constant encouragement, Hawk followed me up a tree, then onto the roof of the nearest house, hoping its dark windows meant it was one of the few homes still unoccupied at that time of the evening.

From our vantage point, Hawk and I surveyed the carnage in the next street. It appeared that everyone on board had survived and, with murderous faces, were extracting themselves and their tranquiliser guns. I didn't have to ask Hawk again.

We launched from the roof, Hawk's flapping rough and heavy, and mine not much better. The Evolutionaries saw us, but we were beyond the range of their tranquilisers, and soon we were beyond the range of the streetlights, and surrounded by the Flight.

"Hey guys, when did you get here?" Hawk said to Tui, Falcon, Owl and Raven.

"Oh, just before the outbreak on social media about your *insane* city stunts," Falcon said, grinning. "We couldn't let you have all the fun taking down a helicopter, could we? And my ass was fine once I actually got in the air, thanks for asking."

"Wasn't planning to, but all right." Hawk laughed, but the sound was broken with pain.

Miguel approached carefully as Hawk and I struggled into the rough formation. "Are you all right, Hawk?"

"Been better."

"You can do it," I said.

Miguel fell in beside him. "Not far, and then you can rest."

"Okay."

"Uh, where exactly *are* we going?" I asked Tui, who was on point.

She pointed towards the sprawling suburbs. "We stashed the gear before we came looking for you. Just a bit further."

Hawk's breath was as ragged as his flapping, and he was beginning to sag in the air. I glanced at Miguel and saw the same worry in his eyes, even through his goggles and in the gloom of the night sky around us.

"We might have to land earlier, Tu," I said. "I don't think Hawk will make it that far."

Even as he tried to protest, Hawk's wings faltered, and he slipped several metres below the formation. I swore, and tried to dive for him, but there was no way I could grab him while in mid-air.

"There, Hawk," I said, pointing. "Can you get to that field?"

Wearily, Hawk turned towards the large dark expanse of grass a few hundred metres away. As he struggled through the air and I glanced around, worried about who was waiting for us on the ground, I saw the nearby playground and attached dark buildings that suggested it was the playing field of a suburban school.

Hawk didn't land so much as collapse on the grass. The Flight quickly gathered around him protectively as he lay in a heap, breathing heavily.

I dropped to my knees next to him, my tail bands cutting into my calves through my flight boots. "Hawk, talk to me. What's going on? Where are you hurting?"

His eyes met mine, and I was relieved to see they were mostly clear. He tried to smile, and his left hand gripped mine, while his right was cradled on his chest. "Sorry, Kess. I just need one minute."

"Don't be silly, you just crashed into a *truck*. Take at least three."

Hawk's lip twisted into the ghost of a smile. I held his hand tightly. He was going to be okay. I just knew it.

He had to be.

27

MIGUEL

As Hawk lay on the ground, Tui pushed everyone aside and began checking him over, the rest of us hovering like anxious mothers. Hawk hissed as she gently manipulated his right arm, and my hand instinctively clutched the cross around my neck.

"Fractured wrist," Tui said tightly. "Probably cracked ribs too. How's the head?"

"Sore," Hawk grunted.

Tui opened one of the new pockets on her flight harness and pulled out a tiny flashlight. Hawk winced as she checked the dilation of his eyes, the tiny beam almost too much for our sensitive retinas in the darkness.

Kestrel stuck close to Hawk, watching everything Tui was doing. My heart ached to see how much pain she was in on Hawk's behalf.

"Where did you get that, Tu?" she asked.

Tui sniffed and continued checking the impressive collection of bruises that were developing on Hawk's light brown skin. "One of the few extras I picked up today. Thought a proper kit would be useful. Lucky for you, bro. I didn't expect to use it so soon." Putting it away, she picked through her supplies for something else. "I don't think you've got concussion, Hawk, but under *any* other circumstances I'd be taking you straight to the emergency room."

"No hospitals," Hawk said forcefully, his breath wheezing.

I winced as it reminded me of Abuelita's final breaths. I was so tired, physically and emotionally. I couldn't even sit or kneel like the others because of the healing wound in my butt. The constant stabbing reminder of the evilness that was stalking us across the Earth.

But it was worse knowing there was almost nothing I could do to help Hawk, to help the Flight.

How long will this go on, Lord? Are we meant to keep running forever? Or are the Evolutionaries meant to get us?

A sharp movement made me glance sideways. Raven stepped back, her hand tight over her mouth and her eyes wet. Owl followed her, whispering words even the rest of us couldn't catch. Raven's face was that of someone remembering something horrific, but her shocked stare into the distance began to ease as she listened to Owl's murmur. I wondered again what pain they had lived through. I knew I couldn't change the past, but I felt paralyzed every time I tried to think of a way to make the future better. For all of us.

A sign, Lord. Please. Anything. Some guidance is all I'm asking. What do we do now?

"So," Falcon was saying, easing himself to the ground with his wounded leg held straight, "exactly *how* the hell did the big bad guys track you down in the first place?"

Hawk groaned as Tui strapped up his wrist. "They must have bugged Mom and Dad's house, or something. I didn't see or hear *anyone* taking any notice of us the whole way across town."

"Was it worth it, though? Did you get any information?"

"Yeah. The Evos took all the evidence weeks ago, but I got the name of the doctor and the clinic in Beijing." With his less-damaged hand, Hawk extracted a piece of paper from his pocket and passed it to Kestrel.

She stood up and showed the rest of us. "Doctor Kris Schmidt. Golden Goose Fertility Clinic."

Tui frowned, her dark wings two rustling shadows in the night. "So, not Goldberg."

"No, but if you were a normal person trying to hide from the Evos, the first thing you'd do is change your name," Kestrel pointed out, brushing her messy blonde hair off her face and giving the paper back to Hawk.

"And the *Gold*en Goose. *Gold*berg," Falcon said, brightly. "Huh? Anyone?"

"Could be a coincidence," Tui said, slowly.

"Unlikely, though!"

Aware that we didn't have time for a full discussion, I gently interrupted. "Did you get the other supplies we needed?"

Falcon nodded. "Hiking packs. One each. Full of camping gear, food, et cetera. We can wear them on our fronts and use the waist belts as extra support while we're flying."

"But Hawk is badly injured. I'm not letting him fly again until after I've had a *proper* look at his wings, in daylight," said Tui, sternly.

Kess bit her lip and my heart flipped. "Then what will we do *now?*" she asked, her accent thickening.

"We *have* to retrieve the new gear first. We can't leave everything behind again, not if we're going to last out there ... wherever 'there' is," Tui said.

"But how? Can Hawk even walk?"

Hawk grunted and forced himself to his feet. "I'm not completely busted."

"But, if we're grounded," Falcon said from the grass, "we won't see the Evos coming."

Anything, please Lord. I'm begging you.

Kess sighed and pulled out her phone. "Let's check online, see if there are any reports of pissed-off Evos rampaging through LA. Might give us an idea of where *not* to go."

After a quick search, the phone began projecting a babble of voices.

"I've found a live feed," Kess said over the tinny noise, turning the screen to show us.

"You have *got* to be joking," Falcon said disgustedly. Tui helped him stand up so he could watch along with the rest of us.

The camera was following a flock of people in white robes marching along an LA street, waving signs and looking determined.

As the rest of the Flight broke into murmurs, I couldn't take my eyes from the little screen. The Angelists were rushing up to people on the sidewalk. As the camera panned to take in the scene, I could hear snatches of their pleas.

"*Angels are in the sky! We have to protect them from the evil Evolutionary Corporation...*"

"*...would YOU dissect a messenger of God? Would YOU allow it to happen?*"

"What if it was your children they were after?"

"Protect the Angels!"

"Help us!"

Then some Angelists ran right up to the camera.

"Join us! Join the Angelists of the Lord!"

"Have YOU seen the Angels?"

"If you truly believe, call us!" The woman held up a piece of paper with a phone number and a website, thrusting it forward until it filled the screen. *"Join us!"*

My heart trembled and my thoughts raced. *Is this the sign? Is this what You want us to do?*

"We should call them," I said, almost to myself. I pulled out my phone and tapped in the Angelists' number.

Falcon grabbed my wrist and squeezed hard. "Whoa, dude! What the hell?"

"They want to help us!" I said. "We can't keep doing this on our own."

Falcon's scowl filled my vision. "They want to use us as much as the Evolutionaries do, Miguel. Don't fall for it."

My feathers bristled. "Just because they're religious? You think they're the bad guys too, just because they believe in God?"

"How do you know that's what they *really* believe? What if they're trying to trick us?"

"I have faith that God will protect us. I believe that the Angelists are here for a reason!"

Falcon threw up his hands and turned away, starting to pace, although he was limping. "And what if that reason is to catch us and use us, just like the Evos?"

I hesitated, and gazed around at my friends. The big eyes that stared back at me held a mixture of emotions. Fear, contempt, anxiety, hope. Even Owl and Raven watched and waited.

"Look," I said, quietly. "I know most of you don't feel the same way I do about God, and about my faith. And that means you're suspicious of the Angelists. I get it, I do. But you haven't even given them a chance. They actually *helped* me and Kestrel and Hawk save the rest of you! Which is the complete opposite of everything the Evolutionaries have ever done. And most regular people!"

"You're forgetting my dad took a *bullet* for us," Hawk said, his voice low and shaking. "He might be dead now."

Kestrel clutched his upper arm. "He was alive when—"

"That was *then*. We don't know if he even made it to hospital!" Hawk gently shook her off and stepped closer to me. "Where were the Angelists when my sister was screaming? Where were they when my dad was shot? Where were they when I was wiped out of the sky? Where was God then?"

My throat tightened. I couldn't answer him when I only had the same questions.

"I'll tell you who *was* there, though," Hawk said, his voice softening. "You were. Kestrel was too. In fact, the whole Flight was there."

Falcon turned back and met my gaze steadily. "Look at us, *Miguel*. It's me, Falcon. And Tui, Hawk, Kestrel, Owl, and Raven. Your friends. The only ones who've been on your side from the beginning. It's time to decide, *Miguel*. Are you with us, or are you with *them*?"

"This isn't a game, Fal—"

"No, it's a war, Miguel." Falcon glared, and I saw the others were agreeing with him, even Owl and Raven. "And if you go to the Angelists, we won't wait for you to come back."

I stared at him, not giving an inch, but my mind went into freefall. I hadn't considered *leaving* the Flight. I was just searching for guidance. If the Angelists could offer that...

With the terrors and exhaustion of the night, joining the Angelists and their promise of protection and support and spiritual fellowship was tempting.

But the Flight saw them as one of our enemies. It was now clear that if I went to the Angelists, I'd lose the Flight. And right now, with three couples staring at me with varying degrees of fear and anxiety, I felt they were already pushing me away.

If I left, would they even miss me?

The Flight had been there for me from the moment I'd met each of them. Falcon had always dragged me into his games, and Tui had been tough but kind. Owl was like the big brother and Raven was the little sister I'd never had. Hawk had always had my back.

But what had I offered them in return?

As I glanced at Kestrel, she pushed forward between Falcon and Hawk. She reached out and took my hands. "Miguel, don't leave us. We need you."

A tear slipped from her gray eye, and my heart stuttered. I hated to see her so upset. She was so strong and caring, beautiful and smart, but she was vulnerable. I wished I could protect her, protect all of them. But I had no idea how I could do so.

"What do you need me for?" I whispered, my voice breaking.

She smiled through her tears. "You're our conscience, Miguel. You're our friend. You're part of our *family*. We *all* need each other, Miguel."

I knew then I couldn't leave. Not yet.

Maybe not ever.

Maybe the answers were with the Angelists, maybe they weren't. But I was no longer prepared to lose my family over a 'maybe'.

I just had to have faith that the answers would find me, wherever I was, as long as I kept my heart open.

As I turned off the live video of the pleading Angelists and deleted the number from my phone's screen, acceptance settled in my mind and heart like a blessing from heaven.

"Condor," I heard myself say, quietly.

"What?"

"Condor," I said again, more strongly. "Call me Condor."

After a moment, Falcon's dark face split into a blinding grin. "All right!" He held up his hand and I automatically slapped a high five. Kestrel's expression melted into relief, and even Owl and Raven had a slight smile. Hawk just nodded.

"About bloody time, bro," Tui said cheerfully. "Now, how the hell are we getting out of here?!"

"Can't we just 'borrow' a car?" Falcon said. "We could hotwire it or something."

Everyone looked at him.

He stared back. "It was just a suggestion! Why does everyone assume that I actually know *how* to?"

"Well, do you?" Hawk asked.

"No!" Falcon snapped. "When I was normal, I played basketball and read comic books! I didn't steal cars."

In the back of my mind, memories I had tried hard to repress began to stir, awakening from a time that I regretted with my entire soul.

Hawk groaned. "Does *anyone* know how to acquire a car without the owner's permission? Kestrel?"

She shook her head. "Security systems and basic computer programs I can break into, sure. And I've been known to pick locks. But hotwiring a car? I've never done that."

"We can't fly out, we can't catch public transport if there's seven of us, we don't have enough money to get a new car, and none of us know how to steal one."

Oh, Lord. Please forgive me. If there was ANY other way…

"I do," I said, reluctantly.

Now it was my turn to be in the crosshairs of the Flight's stare. Again.

"What?"

"I know how to steal a car."

"Are you serious, Mig — Condor?" Hawk demanded, astonished. "*Really?*"

Tui crossed her arms. "This isn't the time for kidding around, bro!"

I sighed. "I'll explain later. For now, please just trust me."

"All right!" Falcon said enthusiastically. "I *like* this new Condor!"

I grinned weakly, wincing inside. *This is NOT what I was intending to happen…*

But I will do what I have to.

For the Flight.

28

HAWK

As Miguel/Condor reluctantly began the process of 'acquiring' an old cargo van that the Flight found parked on a nearby street, I leaned my folded wings against a brick wall, shut my eyes, and concentrated on breathing.

But it didn't stop the vivid rerun of the evening's highlights.

My mom's face. My parents' arms around me. My sister crying in terror as the Evolutionaries broke into the house. Dad's face as the bullet smashed into his back. Helicopters on my tail. Being swatted from the air by a speeding big rig. Desperately trying to fly, but my wing feeling like it was swirling through mud, my skull crushing my brain. The helicopter hovering above me, the downdraft pounding at me, trying to squash me like a bug. Kestrel knocking me out of the sky and smashing me through a tree.

My back and wings still ached where I'd hit the ground so hard it had thumped every atom of air from my lungs.

But all that pain had been nothing compared to the thought that my dad was dead. Because of me.

Then Kestrel had said the impossible. Dad was still alive.

At least, he had been.

And I just ran away. When he needed me most…

A deep, dull, burning sensation began to smolder in my gut.

Shame.

Suddenly, there was pressure on my sore ribs. I opened my eyes to find Kestrel slipping underneath my arm to hold me up.

"You were starting to slide off the wall," she said, her smile uncertain. "You okay?"

"Don't know," I said honestly, my eyes falling from hers. "If my dad…"

Her other arm slid around my waist, and her head gently rested on my shoulder. "Why don't we call your mum and find out?"

The feeling of her warm body against mine made my lips tingle with the memory of her kiss. The pleasure mixed uncomfortably with the guilt, turning into nausea. I let my head droop forward and my cheek leaned on her hair. I breathed in her smell and closed my eyes. "Would it be safe to call Mom's phone?"

"The Evos might have bugged it too, you mean? Hm." Kestrel nestled her head closer to my neck as she thought.

Behind her, Falcon and Tui were muttering and swearing under their breath as Miguel/Condor struggled to get the engine running. Owl and Raven fidgeted as they stood watch nearby, but, being close to midnight, the suburban street was empty.

At last, Kess said, "I'm sure there must be apps that let you send encrypted messages, or hidden numbers, like burner phones. I'll see if I can download one of those, and then you can contact your mum."

My arm tightened around her, but before I could find the words, the engine finally fired in the van.

"All aboard," Fal called, quietly. "Hurry up!"

One by one, the rest of the Flight climbed into the vehicle. It was old and dented, rusty and dusty, and ghosts of chemicals past were haunting the air inside. But it was otherwise empty. The windows were painted over, although the signwriting had long ago faded or peeled off. It was perfect for hiding and transporting an exhausted pack of birdkids.

No, not birdkids. Icari.

As Kestrel stepped up into the van in front of me, a glint caught my eye.

"Is that my hunting knife?" I asked, blinking stupidly. My long primary feathers bumped against the step as I clumsily climbed in after her.

She glanced down at her boot. "Oh, yeah. I thought you might want it back." Sliding it out of her tail straps, she offered it to me handle-first. "Couldn't bring the bomber jacket, though, sorry."

"This is probably more useful," I said, smiling weakly, as I removed its sheath from my belt, and tried to secure the blade inside. But, with my strapped wrist, I didn't have the fine motor control and nearly sliced my own hand trying to put it away.

"On second thoughts, how about I hold onto that a bit longer for you?" Kestrel suggested, gently, taking the knife back, along with its sheath.

My cheeks warm from embarrassment, I slid down onto the floor of the van and leaned back against the wall, resting my head against the cold steel, and closed my eyes. Kestrel sat close to me, keeping me semi-upright.

Despite the pain, and the cold, uncomfortable flooring in the back of the cargo van, I must have fallen asleep during the trip through the backstreets to the Flight's cache, because suddenly we'd stopped, the door was open, and Falcon was threatening to drop his pack on me if I didn't move out of the way.

After a suggestion from Tui, the Flight unzipped and layered all the new sleeping bags to form a passable mattress. But before I could stretch out and lose consciousness properly, Kestrel was pushing her phone into my hand.

"I'm assuming you know your mum's number," she said, grinning.

I smiled weakly back. "Yes, as long as she hasn't gotten a new one in the last few months."

Before I could begin composing my message, Falcon said, "So, now we have a van and supplies, but we still don't have a destination."

"Where were the sightings of White Wings concentrated?" Miguel/Condor asked.

"East somewhere?"

"Let's go north then east, *around* the desert, and see if we can track them down."

"Unless it's a wild goose chase."

Falcon snorted. "Or a golden goose chase." There were a few chuckles.

"Put it this way," Kestrel said, as reasonably as always. "We haven't got anything else to aim for, so this direction is as good as any. We can always change our minds later."

There were various noises of agreement, and I dropped my eyes back to the phone, hesitantly tapping out a message with my non-strapped hand.

In the driver's seat, Owl pressed gently on the accelerator, and the van pulled away into the night. Even the slightest turn made me sway, the shifting pressure on my injured ribs making me hiss and wince.

Tui and Falcon were rummaging around in one of the packs, and as I finally pressed 'send', Tui passed me a water bottle and a couple of pills.

"We also picked up some pharmaceutical supplies, seeing as you buggers keep hurting yourselves," she said. "That should help you sleep, too."

"Thanks, Doc," I said, gratefully.

She snorted and arranged her wings so she could lean comfortably on Falcon, who was propped up in the corner on a pile of packs.

As I swallowed the painkillers, the phone buzzed in my hand. With shaking fingers, I opened the message from my mom.

Honey, I'm so glad you're okay. Dad is still in ICU but he's stable, and he's survived worse in the AF. Cherie and I are going to stay with Nanna and Poppa for a while. You just be safe out there. This is NOT your fault. You didn't fire the bullet. If anyone apart from those bastard Evolutionaries are to blame, then it's that damn clinic. They had NO RIGHT to mess with my son like this!!! We'll get that Schmidt/Goldberg, I promise you that. But no matter what, I love you. XX Mom.

At first, I nearly passed out from the surge of relief. Dad *was* going to be okay.

And, strictly speaking, I knew that it wasn't my fault that armed intruders had rampaged through my house.

But I was the one who had run away afterwards. That was completely, totally, undeniably on me.

I was weak. I was a coward.

I was a total failure.

The shame settled deep into my soul, not fierce, but solid and immovable. I tried to turn away, pretend it wasn't there, but I could feel it underneath me.

It was going to be a very long time before I might be able to exorcise it, if I even deserved to.

Feeling someone's gaze on me, I glanced up. Raven was peeping at me over the front seat. Although most of her face was hidden, I could feel the sadness in her eyes. I wished that she could talk to me.

But instead, Owl murmured something to her, and she turned away to look out the front window.

At the rear of the van, Miguel/Condor stretched out, holding his cross and whispering a prayer to himself. Falcon was already snoring, and Tui wasn't far behind him.

Beside me, Kess leaned over and took the phone from my unresisting hand.

"Your dad is going to be okay, Hawk," she whispered, her voice tickling my ear. "Just give it time."

I didn't answer, picking at the pocket on my thigh with my non-splinted hand. Something crackled inside, and I rediscovered the piece of paper my mom had scribbled the precious clues on. Despite the pain that came with the thoughts of my family, it was a reminder that all wasn't as hopeless as it felt.

One day I'll find you, Dr. Schmidt-Goldberg of the Golden Goose. But right now, the Flight is more important. After we find the other Icari, we'll hunt you down together and get some answers.

But not tonight.

"Come on, Hawk, you need to rest," Kess said.

"So do you," I protested feebly.

Using the light from her phone, she surveyed the narrow space left on the floor. "Rock Paper Scissors, then."

On the silent count of three, we both held out paper. Then we doubled up on rock, and then paper again, and then scissors.

"That settles it," Kess said, chuckling quietly. "We'll have to share."

She carefully inched down in the small space and sighed as she let her wings and head rest. After a moment, she said, "Well, come on, then."

"It's okay," I said, awkwardly, although I *did* really want to lie down next to her. The idea was appealing enough to override all other thoughts, and even some of the dulling pain.

"There's plenty of room," she said, shuffling closer to the packs to make her point. "I'm not that fat."

Miguel chuckled from beyond her feet. "You can't win when a girl uses that argument."

"That's the idea," Kess said, yawning. "Get your feathery arse on the floor, Hawk. You need to sleep."

I eased myself down as casually as I could, one aching limb at a time. I lay on my side, leaning back slightly on my folded wings, facing her. There was less than two inches of space between us, and as the van turned a corner, her body shifted to press against me. She didn't meet my gaze, but her hand slipped into mine, and her head rested against my shoulder. Warmth seeped into my body, easing the last few aches that the painkillers hadn't reached, and my heart quietly hummed with a returning hint of happiness.

The muted purr of the engine was soothing. I shut my eyes and breathed in the warm smell of Kestrel's hair and feathers, letting everything else go. Just focusing on the knowledge that, once again, whether I deserved it or not, I was safe in the Flight.

Owl drove carefully and quietly out of the city, and together the Flight let the road carry us toward whatever our future held for us next.

Want to know more about the Flight's back stories? How did Kestrel pull off her Gremlin stunts? What is Falcon's real name? How did Tui cross the ocean? Find out in the *Icarus Origins* novellas! Coming soon!

In the meantime, read on for a sneak preview of *Generation Icarus Book 2: Take Flight...*

TAKE FLIGHT
CHAPTER 1: TUI

The cool morning air flowed through my feathers as I hummed along to the music blasting in my earbuds, my wings moving in time with the bass line. I touched the warm green stone of the *pounamu* tied around my neck and remembered the day my *koro* had placed it there, so it would always tie me to my people and my land. The forest below was majestic and slowly becoming familiar, but it still looked and smelled foreign. Except, of course, I was the foreigner. Aotearoa, my home, was very far away.

The music seemed to bring it a little closer though, as I soared across the mountain valley like an eagle. Only, this eagle had a four-metre wingspan, a strap-on tail, and a phone that was almost permanently on flight mode. One of my new family's favourite in-jokes.

The ridge ahead marked the limit of how far I was supposed to stray from camp, but I didn't want to go back just yet. I'd been in desperate need of this physical and mental space. As much as I loved the Flight, being together 24/7 sometimes drove me crazy. But the combination of fresh air, dawn light and music was *te rongoa* – and I could feel it working.

I rolled a few degrees, my right wing dipping and the left lifting high, as I approached the mountain summit.

Then the shock of adrenaline pulled me back up.

"What the *f*–"

A huge black helicopter rose in front of me. The pilot's surprise instantly spread into a triumphant grin.

My wings snapped into a tight fold. I dived sideways, treetops whipping past me as I accelerated. Now that the chopper wasn't hiding behind the mountain, I could hear the hammering of its rotors over the music.

Ripping my earbuds out, I shoved them into the chest pocket of my flight jacket, and dodged around a skyscraper tree towering above the forest canopy.

Why can't these arseholes just leave us alone!

Three weeks. We'd had just three weeks of peace and quiet. Enough time for most of our injuries to heal. Enough time to feel safe. Safe enough to sleep through the night instead of taking watches. To go for a gentle cruise through the valleys while listening to our favourite music and not keeping alert for *goddamn flapping helicopt*–

Screaming curses in Māori, I flinched and sheared sideways. A couple of red-fletched syringe darts disappeared into the trees below. Tucking in my wings, I whipped through an aileron roll, spinning on my long axis. As the rotation slowed, I flicked out my right wing and sliced a steep curve through the air.

Let's see how well you can fly in your expensive toy, eh?

My own shadow fled ahead of me as the helicopter chased me away from the morning sun. Away from the Flight.

And then another shadow appeared before me.

There were *two* helicopters.

Desperately, I swept my wings forward and back, faster and faster until my muscles were soaked in lactic acid.

Come on, you flockers, chase the birdy. Take me, not the Flight!

But if the Evos had hunted us down in the back of nowhere, with multiple helicopters, they already knew where we were. And they wouldn't go home with just one of us.

Have to warn–

As I swung around a huge tree at high speed, the skeleton of another loomed directly in my path. My arms and wings wrapped around my head as I crashed through the clawing branches. Twigs stabbed my exposed skin, then a massive bough whacked me in the stomach. I deflated around it with a heavy *oof.*

The first helicopter sped past before pausing, turning tightly, and sauntering back towards where I hung in the tree like a dead animal. The second hovered a little further away. I was trapped in the centre where the violent air collided and pummelled me from all sides.

Grunting to refill my lungs, I pulled myself up. Blood dripped from my hands, and I could taste it in my mouth where I'd bitten my tongue. My head throbbed. At least my flight glasses had protected my face, and my jacket had shielded my arms.

The first helicopter moved closer and turned side-on. Through pain-blurred eyes I saw men with seriously scary weapons.

Gripping the branch, I felt for the next one down with my boots. Luckily, the air turbulence was also causing problems for the helicopter. It was bobbing around as much as I was, and I could see the gunmen waving and shouting at the pilot. The other helicopter's downdraft was interfering with their aim.

I just have to get out while they–

As the second chopper banked away, the blast of air threw me sideways through the dead tree. A sharp branch speared through the feathers of my wing, missing the wing-arm but stabbing my huge primary feathers. I was snared prey. And the chopper was coming around for the best angle of attack.

Roaring with effort, I pulled. Several flight feathers ripped from their follicles, but I was free.

Dropping onto the closest big branch, I ran. It swayed, creaked, and as I launched off, cracked beneath my boots. Tilting my wings high, I flew hard on an upward angle.

I have to warn the Flight! If only–

Snatching my phone from my jacket pocket, I swiped it off flight mode.

"Text the group 'Flight'," I shouted into the microphone. As I wiped my bleeding mouth, my own slipstream flicked spots of blood onto my glasses.

The phone's automated reply was lost under the roar of the chasing helicopter. Slinging myself sideways, I glanced at the screen. No reception.

Cursing and spitting blood, I knew I had to make altitude before the helicopter ploughed me into the forest.

I flew up the wall of trees and reached air that would have seemed clear to human eyes. But I could see enough muddling in the light to realise the wind force from the helicopter was crashing into the updraft from the other side of the ridge. As I flapped, my wings were battered by surf-like currents. Strands of hair came loose from the knot on my head and whipped around my face.

A massive gust pushed me off balance, so suddenly that I instinctively threw out my arms to steady myself. And as I did, the phone slipped from my bloody hand and vanished into the trees.

Swearing, I dived over the ridge and aimed for the lake in the next valley. My target was a waterfall that I knew created vicious, dangerous updrafts. If I could just lure the helicopter close enough...

Something huge flashed past overhead. It seemed to fall back and claw at my tail, bouncing heavily off my boots as I shot out from underneath it.

WHAT THE–

I quickly spun through a single aileron roll to see what it was. A net. And they were winching it up, ready to fire again.

Now the sun was directly ahead. I swerved through the air, side to side, then pushed high before diving again, evading the helicopter as it pounded after me. Trees gave way to grass, and I shot out over the lake.

Just keep moving–

The other helicopter appeared ahead of me. I dodged the oncoming dark blur, and a second net clipped the end of my wing. Shrieking, I fought to correct the spin, falling towards the water.

As the tips of my feathers brushed the surface, I pulled hard and levelled out above the pure glacier-melt. My reflection paced me only metres below, fleeing her own upside-down helicopters through the once-serene mountains. Ripples shattered the picture as the choppers came in from each side.

BANG-WHOOSH

A net closed around my body. I fought them all the way. More than four square metres of resistance thrashed through the air, wrecking the chopper's finely-tuned balance. But I was upside down and exhausted. As my legs were drawn in, I threw out my wings and jammed myself against the fuselage of the chopper.

I screamed as my shoulder muscles battled the winch, the net cutting into my face. Finally, I was hauled into the darkness of the helicopter.

The door slid shut. I was their prisoner.

And now, they would go after the Flight.

GENERATION ICARUS
A SHORT HISTORY

In 2011, aged 21, J L Pawley completed the first draft of the first book in the *Generation Icarus* series. After receiving a rejection letter from a major publisher that indicated manuscripts were not accepted for consideration unless they had been reviewed by a professional manuscript assessor, she set about finding one.

The assessor she contacted happened to be an author in her own right, who was in the process of setting up her own publishing company. After the assessment was complete, she offered to publish the books herself.

Unfortunately, just as the first tiny print run of the first book, *First Flight*, rolled off the press in December 2012, the company closed down. No other publisher would touch a half-published book, so J L Pawley decided to re-publish herself under her own label, Nineteenth House Publishing.

After another round of professional editing and book design, *First Flight* was released in 2013, earning an award from Readers Favorite. *Second Chance*, *Third Time Lucky*, and *Final Stand*, along with the *Icarus Origins* companion novellas, followed over the next two years. The final book came out in December 2015.

Along the way, J L Pawley also posted the series on the ebook streaming site Wattpad. The first two books reached #2 and #3 globally in Science Fiction, and the series earned over a million reads between 2014-2015. A small but devoted fandom, calling themselves the Flight Fam, was born.

Then, in early 2016, the series was noticed by the Eunoia Publishing Group. The director offered J L Pawley a publishing contract under the Steam Press imprint. As part of the deal, the original version of the series was withdrawn from Amazon and Wattpad, ready for redevelopment.

After a year of rewriting, the books were given new titles. *Air Born* was launched by Steam Press in Auckland in September 2017, followed by *Take Flight* in November 2018. Russian translations of *Air Born* and *Take Flight* were released soon after, as well as a traditional Mandarin Chinese translation of *Air Born*. *Take Flight* earned a Notable Book Award in 2019, putting it in the top 10 YA books published in New Zealand that year.

Then came 2020…

Partly due to the challenges caused by the COVID pandemic, the third book was delayed. Later, after an agreement to condense the 3rd and 4th book into a final single volume, *Sun Strike* had a limited release online in December 2020.

In March 2023, the English language rights to *Generation Icarus* were re-acquired by J L Pawley and Nineteenth House Publishing, leading to the revamped edition you have just finished reading.

If you enjoyed the story, and you think the crazy journey to get here was worth it, please let Jess and the Flight know by rating and reviewing online.

Thank you!

AUTHOR'S NOTE

Icarus-eyed readers may have noticed some apparent spelling inconsistencies throughout the book. Over the last 12 years, after many, *many* rewrites, and several shifts back and forth between American and British English systems, I finally made an Executive Decision for this definitive edition.

American characters, which in this book are Hawk and Condor, write with American spelling.

British and Commonwealth characters, in this case being Kestrel and Tui, write with British spelling.

Any inconsistencies or spelling errors beyond this are entirely my own responsibility.

However, it is incredibly difficult to get 80,000 words 100% correct (just think about how hard it is to text a 20-word message with complete accuracy!). Even books released by publishing industry giants, which have been professionally proofread by multiple editors, still occasionally have errors and typos. So, your understanding and forbearance for any errors in this book is greatly appreciated.

ACKNOWLEDGEMENTS

I would not have been able to try this again (again, again – by my count, this is the 5th release?) if it hadn't been for a small but incredibly devoted fanbase, who found me and my books on Wattpad in 2014-2016 and have been virtually by my side ever since. This elite Flight Fam, as I think of them, I am now lucky enough to consider friends. It has been a privilege to watch you grow into strong, empathetic, and passionate young adults. Thank you for your love and support over this roller-coaster of a career.

I am grateful to everyone who has ever read a copy of one of my books, in any format, in any edition. I am especially grateful to those who have patiently accepted multiple versions and re-releases, with unwavering understanding and enthusiasm. Most notably, this includes my family, Richard, Elissa, and Fletcher, and my bestie Carlina. Thank you.

Thanks also to those readers who sent me messages over the last few years, asking when the Flight would return. If you hadn't made the effort to send me those brief notes, letting me know that the Flight was still wanted and missed, I might not have had the energy to try this again. So, if you've ever thought about messaging someone whose work you appreciate, please do so. Especially in these strange and unsettling times. It might make all the difference.

As this is book is a lightly edited and tightened update, I have included below the (also lightly edited) acknowledgements from the first edition of *Air Born*. It is a reminder of how far my books and I have come, and how many people have been cheering for us along the way.

2017 ACKNOWLEDGEMENTS

Thanks to Sue Copsey, Suzanne Main, Shelley Iñón, and Cheryl Smith, without whom I would never have successfully self-published and might never have been found by Eunoia Publishing Group.

Thanks to Steam Press for your valuable input into the redevelopment of the story, and for opening doors for the Flight they would never have otherwise had a chance to peek through.

High fives and hugs to all of my Wattpad fans. We made it! I couldn't have lasted this long if it weren't for your support, loyalty, and sometimes-bordering-on-crazy fanaticism. I learned so much from you. I couldn't have invented a better cheerleading team.

Special shoutouts to Lily, who wrote the first ever *Generation Icarus* fanfic; to Amy, who made the first ever fanart (and sent it to me by snail mail, no less!); and to Abigail and Amaya, who started the first *Generation Icarus* fan accounts on social media outside of Wattpad. Also to Kristin, Moana and Rebecca, and Jaimi and Jordan, who coordinated fan birthday cards for me in 2015 and 2016. You guys are beyond amazing.

Massive appreciation to my parents, who invested so much in me and gave me a solid foundation in life, even paying for extra creative writing courses when I was a teenager and money was tight. You've always believed in me, and that let me believe in myself, even when my dreams were victims of arson.

And, to the Captain, who read almost every single one of the several million words it took to get to this point (sometimes more than once), patiently enabling my mad obsession and supporting me every millimetre of the way in every way possible, thank you. I love you.

The Official List of Awesome People of 2015

The following people went above and beyond the call of duty in showing their support for *Generation Icarus* online. The list is alphabetised by first name or username, and was originally included in the self-published edition of the fourth *Generation Icarus* book:

Abigail Boyer & Maddie Gallagher, Adrianna, Aleksei Sisco/@Flashwing, Ali Lane, Amaya French, Amy Curtis, Alex Boyer/@Athenschild, Diana Nielsen, Emily Schellhammer/@_Emi_G_, Heather McIntosh, Jaimi & Jordan, Janée Polino, Joel "Dragoel" Arthur, Kristin, Moana & Rebecca, Laurence Mifsud, Lily McLean, Macady Watson, Nelanka Halgamuge, Peter Pulisic, Ricky Pine, Ruthie W. Irungu, Samantha Bantugan, Sophie Lin/@gagaga149

The Icarus Fan Army of 2016

The following is the list of Wattpad users who earned a dedication in the original edition of *Generation Icarus 1: First Flight*, before it was signed by its first real publisher and metamorphosed into

Air Born. These fans actively participated in a *Generation Icarus* promotion on social media in an effort to show publishers and agents how much the series meant to them, and in doing so earned an eternal place of gratitude in the author's heart. Listed in chapter order and with the username that was current at the time of the campaign:

RickyPine, Neverstopwriting101, ShelleyIn, HiFunctioningFangirl, fantasyfan38, Of-Mice-And-Misfits, Hawthorngold1932, cherripiie888, TheSilentSleeper, UnnoticedSilence, -FrozenFire-, TheFirstShaymin, martiarianna, Corabellina, HalfbloodSlytherin12, arctxcskies, AC-Claire, wordsholdthepower, We_Are_Icari, oh_snap_its_carmen, Winged-Sin, jeffxitiseragon, AlphaGirlRules, Stewart352, orangetops, MissMystery0423, Jackie2805, jalexapenos, lilarose123, madeline_oneill_, doctorwhorox, MissCaptainA1, im_katwoman

The Most Dedicated and Loyal Fans of 2017

Abigail Boyer, Amaya French, Brigid J., Cierra Adney, Darby Fingerman, Ilse, Jaimi Lutes, Jordan Lutes, Makenna May, McKenna Maher, Merlin, and Michaella.
The Flight might never have been published without you, and I will never forget it.

www.ingramcontent.com/pod-product-compliance
Lightning Source LLC
Chambersburg PA
CBHW021307250626
47155CB00002B/411